ERROR CODE
EDITED BY ZAQ CASS

Rabid Otter Horror

For Kristin, always

CONTENTS

FOREWARD

I've always been a reader.

There was something about books that always spoke to me. I could read in my free time, when everyone else was doing something else that I didn't care for. I was able to do it mid-conversation or while waiting for an appointment.

With the advancement of e-readers, I was able to get new books with a few clicks of a button and for much cheaper than physical copies. As someone who also isn't a fan of collecting things, digital media came with many benefits.

Having so many potential books at my fingertips, I tried everything. Genres, age ranges, characters. I've read experimental main characters and the same re-skinned fantasy book over and over again. More often than not, I found myself reading horror, having been a fan since I was allowed to watch *A Nightmare on Elm Street* and *Psycho* at seven years old. Slashers, zombie flicks, and alien horror were always welcome when I watched, and eventually, when I read.

Naturally, I read R.L. Stine and Stephen King, but I would also pick up the occasional Clive Barker, Richard Matheson, and eventually Koushun Takami. I have probably read every English translation of *Battle Royale* and the approach the book took to tell a story created a spark in me to create stories of my own.

I fell off of reading horror for quite a while, but what I came back to astounded me. The trajectory self-publishing has been on is astounding to watch in real time, and with it, there is a surplus of great stories at our fingertips. It is hard to scroll through the lists of new releases without seeing an anthology composed of amazing authors, writing about what they are passionate about.

I wanted in on that. For me, short stories call back to *Goosebumps, Scary Stories to Tell in the Dark,* and the many Stephen King collections. They speak to *The Twilight Zone, Tales from the Darkside,* and *Black Mirror.* Something I've always appreciated from science fiction and horror is that a story could be quick and make you feel something just as well as a massive tome or three-hour movie.

So, thanks to approval from JP Weaver at Riverfolk Books, I started Rabid Otter Horror, knowing my first project would be a technology-based horror anthology. Imagine my surprise when one hundred and fifty people submitted stories. Choosing was difficult, but I fully believe that the ten stories within are the best for this collection. Ten amazing authors are featured beyond this page, with ten stories that ask the question: Is technology making us stronger or are we crafting our own destruction?

Zaq Cass
October 2024

NHESI, UNLOCK THE DOOR
by Curtis A. Deeter

Ryan Reid hadn't thought much about what could go wrong or he'd never have invited them over. He'd been too worried about making sure everything was perfect. He planned on proposing, after all, and Shawn and Holly were Amanda and Ryan's best friends from high school. He expected a few minor hiccups along the way, but he never imagined how horribly wrong things would go. Besides, his therapist had told him to stop creating imaginary doomsday scenarios in his head. This advice, in this particular situation, was wrong. Dead wrong.

Even before the doorbell rang, Ryan's watch buzzed. He glanced at the tiny screen and sighed.

"They're early." He maneuvered the hot crock of fresh-glazed bacon-wrapped weenies over Amanda's head. "As always. Can you get the door, babe?"

Amanda showed him her hands, covered in chicken goop, and rolled her eyes. "Bit occupied at the moment." She gestured to the array of raw chicken chunks, peppers, and onions laid out before her. "But sure, I'll get the door..."

He slid the crockpot onto the counter, wiping his own greasy hands on his apron, and hopped around the kitchen island, annoyed but resigned. He slid back to plant a kiss on his soon-to-be fiancée's forehead. It was all good. Everything was fine.

Then, an alarm began to shriek, and he sniffed a hint of smoke on the air.

"Shit! The focaccia." He squeezed past, towards the oven, nearly knocking their appetizers off the counter with his hip, and flung open the oven door. Smoke billowed, and he fanned it with an oven mitt until it was clear enough for him to see the sad, burnt bread within. "That's just great."

The doorbell rang, again. Ryan could barely hear it over the fire alarm, but the angry buzz against his wrist made his eye twitch.

"NHesi?" Amanda said, "Silence the alarm and unlock the front door, would ya?"

"Certainly. Would you like me to invite our guests in?"

Ryan shuddered. They'd had NHesi, an all-in-one AI smart home system capable of maintaining an optimal internal environment, monitoring the exterior for any security threats, and assisting with day-to-day tasks, installed when they built the house. He'd been hesitant at first, because in his twenty-eight years of life so far, he'd never needed any of that fancy tech crap before, but now that they had it, he was grateful for the small conveniences "she" provided. NHesi was their third family member, as loyal as any dog and less smelly than cats, and she grew on him more and more with every new software update.

"Yes, please," he said. "Thank you. And can you check this week's grocery list for alternatives to focaccia? Something carb-ey would be great."

Without pause, NHesi chimed, "There are two baguettes, fresh-baked at Churchhills on Tuesday. Would you like me to adjust the oven's settings to accommodate re-heating?"

"Perfect. Thanks, again, NHesi."

"It's my pleasure to serve."

Their guests appeared through the French doors, Holly as pregnant as ever, Shawn holding up an expensive-looking bottle of champagne in one fist and a case of Dad Water in the other.

"Hey, Reids! What's good? Your house let us in."

Amanda shot Ryan a look, one eyebrow raised. Holly jabbed Shawn in the ribs, and Ryan just shrugged it off. Maybe she hadn't noticed his idiot friend's slip of tongue. When Amanda was distracted by Holly's baby bump, Ryan took the opportunity to tell his friend to tread lightly.

"I haven't asked yet," he mouthed. *So, shut-up.*

Shawn's eyes widened and he tilted his head back, smacking his forehead with his forearm. "Sorry, bro," he mouthed back. After cracking one, he slid the Dad Waters across the island to Ryan. "Man, it's good to see you guys."

Shawn embraced Amanda. She grabbed the bottle of champagne from his grasp and giggled, ducking around Holly to use her as a shield.

"Dom, huh?" She appraised the bottle. "What're we celebrating?"

Ryan's cheeks flushed, and he scratched the back of his neck. He'd told them about his plans weeks ago, and despite his usual nature, managed to keep it a secret from Amanda. The fact Shawn

ruined the surprise within seconds of being in their house infuriated him. Lucky for everyone, Holly was there to save the day.

"I was feelin' bubbly, like we used to back in college." Holly
emphasized her stomach, lips pouty. "Obviously, I can't drink it,
but I thought I'd live vicariously through you, tonight." She winked
to Amanda. "Shawn *insisted* on the expensive stuff. He couldn't
seem to wrap his mind around his princess drinking Barefoot."

"Blech!" Amanda said, and the two women laughed as if that
were the most ridiculous thing they'd ever heard.

Ryan breathed a sigh of relief and cracked one. Shawn was almost finished with his first, and he had some catching up to do. A
few drinks would help ease his nerves, and if he didn't relax soon,
Amanda was bound to catch on to the fact he was up to something.

Amanda squealed. "No point in waiting on this then, huh?"
With practiced fingers, she unpeeled a corner of the foil wrap-
per, untwisted the cage around the cork, and the bottle hissed
open with a nonchalant flick. Both girls jumped, and before the
bubbles even settled, she poured herself a healthy glass, gulped it
half-empty, and topped it off.

"You're really going for it," Ryan said, fingering the small, black,
velvet container in his pocket.

Amanda stuck her tongue out at him and sipped with a pinky
extended, maintaining eye contact the whole time.

"We've got an hour 'til the ke-bobs are ready to throw on. Might
as well get this party started."

"Cheers." Shawn held out his empty can. "To Friday nights."

"Cheers," Ryan said, finishing his drink. *To lots and lots of Friday
nights, I hope,* he added to himself.

The oven beeped, and NHesi cued them to put the bread in. Ryan did so, set a timer, and indicated to the other room, where he had chips, homemade salsa, 90s alt-rock, and an array of board games laid out for them to play. He followed everyone in, stepping aside as Shawn pivoted back to grab their case, and slid another free for himself as his friend took his place beside Holly. *Might as well,* he thought, seeing Amanda finish another glass.

For the next hour or so, they caught up with small talk about work and upcoming vacations, both planned and unplanned. Holly gave them all the details about her pregnancy, sparing nothing for the boys' sakes, and Shawn told them about everything he wanted to build at home before the kid was born. It was a lot, and with the price of lumber, Ryan couldn't help but wonder if it would be cheaper, and easier, to just go to IKEA. When he mentioned as much, he was accosted by sneers and hisses and ridiculed by the whole room.

When conversation started to wear thin, Ryan suggested they play a game. He spent most of the next hour explaining the rules to Munchkin, a relatively simple and hilarious dungeon adventure game by his estimation, until Amanda suggested they play something easy, like Sorry or Trouble. He had just placed the cards back in their pre-determined slots when his watch vibrated.

"The chicken skewers are ready to cook," NHesi informed them.

"Ah, boo!" Amanda blew a raspberry in the nearest speaker's direction as she dropped a stack of games on the table between them. "Just when the fun was gettin' started."

Ryan stood, kissed her on the cheek, and scooped an armful of empties. He couldn't help but notice the empty bottle of Dom Pérignon standing tall among them.

"I got it, babe. You guys go ahead and get started without me."

"Got, damn." Shawn leaned back in his chair. "It runs a tight ship, doesn't it?"

"NHesi keeps us honest," Amanda joked.

"Whatever you say. I would have disconnected the damn thing a long time ago."

"I'm only here to serve," NHesi said.

Ryan couldn't help but wonder if he heard a slight undertone of annoyance behind her candid response. She didn't usually interject on her own accord, but it wasn't unheard of for the system to pick up on idioms or name-adjacent references like Nestlé or the occasional "bestie" and chime in with her two cents. He shrugged it off as the tequila talking and excused himself.

"What does that name even mean?" Shawn asked. "This ain't Scotland."

Ryan raised a finger to answer, but NHesi took the lead.

"I am NHesi, a NextGen Household Environmental Systems Integration, programmed to serve and to maintain optimal living conditions within this household." After a brief pause, she added, "And I have never been to Scotland, but I hear it's nice this time of year."

Ryan couldn't help but laugh. Shawn, humbled, nodded his head, arms folded across his chest. He seemed satisfied for now, and there was still work to do, so Ryan excused himself. The second he was out of the family room, the giggling resumed. It simultaneously put him at ease about NHesi and filled him with dread in regards to the ring burning a hole in his pocket.

By the time Ryan got to the kitchen, he was beaded with sweat and feeling trapped in his own clothes. He loosened his collar and stretched his neck over one shoulder then the other. He slid the French doors closed, and the sound of muffled laughter rather than the full cackling uproar brought some relief to his mounting anxiety.

"Hey, NHesi?"

"Yes, Ryan?"

"Can you switch the stovetop over to flattop? I've gotta cook these 'bobs."

A panel beside their gas stove slid open, and the hibachi top he'd had installed unraveled. He heard the tell-tale *click, click, click* of the burners firing as he stared into the fridge's front panel. A thin blue line scanned his face and the fridge unlocked with its usual upbeat jingle. He grabbed the tray of chicken kabobs, and his mouth watered with anticipation. While he did most of the cooking, Amanda had her specialty dishes, and these Italian-marinated beauties were near the top of his list of favorites. They were seasoned to perfection, the perfect mix of zest and garlic, and paired with pearl and red onions, green, red, and orange pepper slices, and whole cremini mushrooms.

After setting the tray beside the stove, he decided he wanted a beer. A real drink, not another one of those trendy tequila waters Shawn brought. They were good, sure, but they didn't hold a flame to a good 'ole American Budweiser. When he returned to the panel, his face being reflected back to him in the darkened black glass pane, the blue line re-appeared. It scanned him once, twice, a third time, and nothing happened.

"NHesi?"

"Yes, Ryan?"

"Unlock the fridge, would ya?"

"Are you sure, Ryan?"

This caught him off guard, and he wasn't sure how to respond. NHesi had never questioned him before, and honestly, he couldn't really process what had just happened. Maybe it had been in his head. Maybe after Shawn's comment, he was waiting for NHesi to do something else out-of-pocket.

"Unlock the fridge, NHesi." Without a moment's hesitation, it jingled again. *Thank you,* he said with more than a little venom in his voice.

"It's my pleasure to serve."

Ryan grabbed an ice-cold Budweiser by its neck. As he was returning to cook, he stopped, wedged a foot between the closing refrigerator doors, and grabbed another for good measure. He cracked one, gulped it down, and took another deep breath. He needed to get his shit together. Even if Amanda was too drunk to propose to tonight, they could still have a fun night together. And there was always tomorrow.

The sizzle of meat brought him a sense of calm. There was something about the sweet aroma of grilled vegetables mixed with the fuzzy feeling of being buzzed that brought things into perspective. Everything was going to be fine. Even if it wasn't according to his plan, he was glad Amanda was having such a good time.

They both worked hard, and she deserved it. *He* deserved it, too, he decided as he polished off the second Bud.

By the time he plated the kabobs, Ryan was feeling great. Better than great. He was finally at peace with the situation and ready to make the most of his night. He threw open the doors to the sounds of bachata and Holly yelling "Sorry!" as she knocked Shawn down a peg or two. He shimmied through, doing his best impression of Shakira in front of Amanda, and placed the tray of food beside the game board.

Amanda, a fresh bottle of Moscato in her lap, snorted. "Get it, boy! Ow, ow!"

"I haven't seen moves like those since Napoleon Dynamite!" Shawn raised a toast. "Here's to bad dancing and great friends."

Holly shoved him out of the way and helped herself to the tray of kabobs. When she realized everyone had stopped and was staring at her, she said, "What do you want? I'm eating for two." At that, they shared a laugh before everyone dug in.

The food was delicious, and the company was better. They gabbed about work, gossiped about old classmates, and cracked jokes on each other. They played a few board games, but those were more background noise to their increasingly animated conversations. Soon, they were talking about everything and nothing at all.

As the night wore on, Amanda and Holly retreated into their little world of two. At first, Ryan tried to listen in, but the women talked in hushed voices, occasionally glancing at one of the boys and giggling, but mostly focusing on each other.

So, he took the opportunity to do the same with Shawn. Where the girls might have been talking about babies and the latest smut television they were watching, the boys dove into sports, music, politics. With each latest empty Dad Water, they grew more and more passionate about their stances, especially Ryan, who was starting to feel the effects of the extra beers he'd downed in the kitchen. Around midnight, he had all but forgotten about his plan to propose. It was a thing of the future, and he was completely content with the way the night turned out. Until Amanda got sick all over their carpet.

"Oh my god," she said, wiping the corner of her lips. Her eyes were unfocused, and she rocked ever-so slightly as Holly rubbed her back. "This never happens to me."

Instead of sympathy, Ryan felt a deep disgust for her in that moment. *This never happens to you? What about me? What about how you've ruined what should have been one of the most memorable nights of our lives?*

Ryan slammed his half-empty can on the table, knocking over a bunch of Monopoly pieces, and stormed out of the room. He ignored Shawn as he called out and made his way to the fridge. His mind was spinning, and all he could think to do to calm it down was grab another drink or maybe even some of his special edible cookie dough. That was a thought. Get completely blitzed and forget this awful night ever happened...

He presented his face, the blue line rose and fell, rose and fell, and when he didn't hear the expected jingle, he smacked the fridge's smooth metallic surface. The screen scanned him a second time. Again, it wouldn't unlock.

"NHesi?" he said, his words lisping and harsher than anticipated.

"Yes, Ryan?"

"Open the damn fridge."

"I'm afraid I can't do that, Ryan."

He sneered, and his lip curled. "Why the hell not?"

"You are already intoxicated, Ryan. Your blood pressure is above normal and your heartrate is irregular. More alcohol would not be conducive to your health and well-being."

"Jesus Christ... My health and well-being? I just want another beer. Unlock the fridge. Now."

Shawn came in, threw an arm around Ryan's shoulder. "Hey, man. Holly took Amanda upstairs. You doin' okay?"

Together, while inside Ryan felt as if he might explode, they swayed gently in their embrace. The physical contact helped to cool his mounting anger, but he couldn't seem to unclench his teeth, to relax his forehead.

"I guess, man. I guess." He massaged his temples, ran his fingers through his hair. "Tonight's kinda gotten away from me, huh?"

"Look, you're disappointed. I get it. But Amanda ain't goin' anywhere. She'll sleep it off, and you can regroup and refocus tomorrow."

"You're right. Of course, you're right."

"We're young, brother. You have plenty of time to get hitched and start popping out babies." Shawn slugged him in the gut. Ryan fake gasped and made an effort to look wounded. "Trust me on that, my guy. Don't rush things."

"It's just..." Ryan sighed and leaned against the counter, his hand acting on its own to grab the black case in his pocket. He pulled it out, flicked it open to reveal the beautiful, two carat diamond ring inside, and held the stone up to the light. "Tonight was supposed to be the night, man. I had it all planned out and everything. NHesi was going to film it, too. Weren't ya, Ness?"

"Yes, Ryan."

"Shit rarely goes as planned," Shawn whispered, eyeing the cameras in the room conspiratorially. "Faster you learn that, the easier life gets."

Ryan laughed through his nose and closed his fingers around the ring. "Funny, taking advice from you. Remember back in high school, I was always trying to get you to listen—"

Before he could finish his thought, the kitchen's surround sound speakers crackled and screeched, like bad feedback at a local rock show. He clasped his hands over his ears, heart racing, and lost his grip on the ring in the process. It flew over his shoulder, clattering in the metal sink behind him, and dropped into the drain.

"What the hell, NHesi!? My ring!"

"Apologies. Another user seemed to have requested music, but I was mistaken."

"My god, man," Shawn said, twisting a finger in his ear. "You really need to disconnect that thing already."

"Way ahead of you."

Ryan keyed his watch password, swiped to the settings, and found the option to disable "smart-home." He selected it, and when he was prompted whether he was sure, he didn't hesitate. While nothing seemed to happen, he could feel a weight lifted from his home, a sudden sense of personal freedom, of simplicity, combined with the thrill of being disconnected for the first time in years.

"Hey, NHesi?" He waited, hopeful, and when there was no response, said, "Ness, you there?"

When there was still no response, he tugged on the refrigerator handle, and it opened for him without a word of judgment.

"Ah, it's like a breath of fresh air." Shawn slapped him on the shoulder, and the boys shared an awkward chuckle of relief. "I feel like a new man. Want a beer?"

"Sure, man. Grab me one. I'm gonna check on the girls quick, then we can get to some serious drinkin'. Like back in the day."

"Bet."

Alone, Ryan placed his hands on opposite edges of the sink. He leaned over, closed his eyes, and took a few meditative breaths. When he opened them, he half-expected to find Amanda there with him, a ring on her finger, but instead he remembered having dropped it and her having gotten sick. A quick glance down the disposal, and he couldn't see it in the abyss. So, he rolled up his sleeve, craned his neck, and mentally prepared to shove his hand into the drain. He'd seen too many movies to dive in blind, especially with NHesi acting weird all night.

"NHesi?" he asked, checking one last time to ensure nothing unexpected could happen.

He flicked on his phone's flashlight, shined it into the dark recesses of the sink until he caught sight of the glint of a diamond, and reached in, nose scrunched to the slimy feel of the rubber insert lodged in the hole. The ring slipped from his shaky fingers on his first attempt, but soon he had it firmly in his grasp, a sly smirk on his face.

That's when the speakers crackled and screeched again. Ryan nearly jumped out of his pants, losing his grip on the ring in the process.

"Dammit!" he yelled, kicking back against the cabinet behind him.

Ryan walked away from the sink, a slight limp from his idiotic reaction, buried his face in his hands and paced the kitchen. His heart was racing again, and his skin felt flushed and slick with sweat. He was so worked up he hardly noticed the slow, eerie crescendo of piano music playing through the speakers.

When he returned, the music was so loud and his head was pounding so hard he couldn't think straight.

"NHesi, turn this awful music off." But it just seemed to get louder. "NHesi! Turn it off."

He shoved his hand into the drain, grabbed the ring in a tight fist, and yelled as the mechanic, metallic sound of the garbage disposal running suddenly joined with the music. His eyes went wide, and at first, he couldn't feel a thing. Then, as the grinding and clinking of metal on metal got louder, there was a dull throbbing coming from his hand. It pulsed and moved up his wrist to his elbow, and when he pulled his hand out of the drain, he gasped. Not only did he not have the ring, which was being knocked around and scratched to hell inside the garbage disposal, but he also didn't have most of the fingers on his right hand.

Ryan staggered away in horror, holding the bloodied stump of his hand before him. His lips quivered, but the scream caught in his throat. This wasn't happening. This wasn't real. It couldn't be real. He worked with his hands. He built computers, for god's sake. No, no, no! It was all a just a dream. A horrible nightmare he couldn't seem to wake from.

"Your vitals are showing signs of distress, Ryan." NHesi's voice, but it was far away, surreal, almost condescending.

"No, no, no," he repeated, out loud. "Oh, god, no!" He let out a blood-curdling scream before choking on his own spit. "Fuuuu-uck!"

His words slurred, and he slammed back against the cabinets. He dropped to a seat, still holding what was left of his hand in front of his face. He couldn't look at it anymore, but he couldn't look away, either. He was woozy, blood slicked across the stone floor all around him, and felt like he might throw up, but he swallowed it down, tears forming beneath his bulging eyes.

"Please remain calm. I will keep you safe."

"Call... Call 911."

"I'm sorry. I didn't quite catch that."

"Call 911. I need... I need to go..."

"I'm sorry. Did you want to make a phone call?"

"NHesi... please..."

"It's my pleasure to serve. Please say a valid command."

"Amanda... Help me..." he managed to moan as everything around him began to fade first to red then to black.

***

Holly held her hair as she got out what she hoped was the last of her puke. Amanda let her weight dip into the toilet bowl before flopping back onto the floor. She cried out, shoulders

17

heaving though she had no tears left to cry, and buried her face in Holly's shoulder.

"I'm such a mess..."

"Girl, it's all good. We've all been there."

"But we're too old for this shit, Holly."

"Shh, shh, shh." Holly pulled Amanda close, held her head against her chest. "You're fine. I've got you. I will keep you safe."

The room was still spinning, but getting sick helped. She could at least start to process where the night went wrong.

"Holly," she said, grinning dumbly at her friend, "you're gonna' be such a great mom. I'm so proud of you. I just need you to know that."

"Oh, stop it. I'm terrified, girl. I have *no* idea what I'm doing."

Amanda shrugged. "None of us do, though. Right? I mean, we're all just trying to figure out this whole thing." She raised her arms and waved them in exaggerated circles. "Life's a bitch, isn't it?"

Holly rolled her eyes and offered her friend a glass of water. "Life's beautiful, and you know it."

"Do you know what I do know?"

"What's that?"

Amanda leaned in closer and glanced all around, as if to ensure they were alone. "Ryan's a good guy, and I probably don't deserve him."

"Shut your mouth. You absolutely deserve him. After all those assholes you dated? Girl, please."

"I think he was going to propose tonight. Can you believe it?"

"Nooooo."

"Yeah. I wanted to say yes. Well, I mean, I want to say yes. But I'm scared. It's a big step."

"The biggest."

Eyes crooked, Amanda glared at Holly's stomach. "The biggest, you say?"

Both girls laughed so hard they snorted. They hugged each other tight, and when they let go, Amanda sat back against the wall. The room wasn't spinning anymore, and her head was starting to feel lighter, her face cooler.

"I really botched that one though, didn't I? Do you think I ruined it?"

Holly laid her head on Amanda's shoulder. "Nah. Like you said, Ryan's one of the good ones. If he was going to propose, he'll still do it. When the time is right."

Amanda let out a wheeze that might have been an attempt at a laugh. "Then we can start makin' babies, too. Give your little Eleanor a friend for life, just like us."

"Eleanor?" Holly moved away, affronted. "Okay, so, you're already making my kid an old woman? We don't even know what it is, yet."

"*She's* a girl. Not an *it.*"

"Oh, yeah? Good to know, *Doctor* Amanda."

"Do you think I'll be a good mom?"

"Yeah," Holly said, running her fingers through Amanda's long hair. "When you're ready. But, hey, should we go check on the boys? I bet they're worried about us."

Amanda lulled her head in Holly's direction and attempted to roll her eyes. They both snorted again before Amanda managed to get herself to her feet.

"I need to rinse off first. Stay with me?"

Holly nodded. "Of course. Wanna dim the lights? That always helps me relax."

"Girl," Amanda said, booping Holly's nose and running her finger down her lips, "Say less. NHesi, dim the lights." When nothing happened, Amanda growled. "NHesi, did you hear me? Turn down the lights, would ya?"

The two girls waited a few long moments before looking at each other and shrugging. Amanda stumbled across the bathroom and adjusted the lights manually, something she hadn't done more than a handful of times since moving into their house.

The master bath had sold her on the house in the first place. His and hers sinks with a beautiful granite countertop, taupe with streaks of black flecks. A sauna feature, with dimming lights that could be set for tanning, as well. A walk-in shower-bath combo, tiled walls, and an automatic clouding glass door, with a waterfall showerhead. It was a masterpiece taken straight off HGTV, and she fell in love with it from their first walkthrough. Had there been better options, closer to where they worked? Absolutely. But none of them had a bathroom like this one. Even with NHesi not cooperating, she couldn't help but swell with pride as she once again breathed it all in.

Holly must have noticed. "You have a beautiful home, Amanda. A beautiful life."

Amanda's cheeks flushed at this, and she waved it off. She wiggled out of her clothes, dropping them beside the laundry shoot that pneumatically sucked them straight through the walls to the laundry room in the basement, and stepped into the shower. The door's strong magnets sealed with a click, and the glass darkened, providing her privacy while she was at her most vulnerable.

She did have a beautiful life, didn't she? She was glad for it, too. And Ryan.

When the hot water hit, she let out a little moan of comfort. Just like that, all her missteps over the span of the evening washed away. Eyes tight, she allowed herself to drift, imagining a lifetime with Ryan, a lifetime in this house, raising children alongside these wonderful people she called friends. It wouldn't be so bad. Not bad at all. Why was she getting herself so worked up over it? She loved Ryan. He was handsome, successful, even funny sometimes. He'd be a good dad, too, if he could get out of his own head.

Her cheeks were hurting from smiling when the music started. At first, she didn't notice. Then, her skin began to crawl, and her stomach tied in knots.

"What is this music?" Holly asked, her voice bringing Amanda back to reality. "Ryan's always had weird tastes, but this? I feel like I should be running from a clown through a carnival."

Amanda couldn't help but agree. It sounded like a pipe organ high on helium and grated at her eardrums.

"NHesi, turn it off!" When it kept playing, she huffed. "NHesi, did you hear me?"

"I'm sorry, Amanda. I didn't quite catch that."

"Turn the music off."

"I didn't quite catch that. Please say a valid command."

"NHesi!" she yelled. "Holly, there's a panel on the wall by the mirror. Can you turn the volume down?"

Steam settled in the bathroom, making it hard to see through the glass doors. She watched as Holly's silhouette moved across the bathroom and fumbled along the wall.

"Found it!" she said. "Oh, but it looks like it needs facial verification or a pin."

"Try 0-6-0-2." A loud beep with negative undertones sounded. "Dammit. Okay, I'm getting out. Give me a second. NHesi? Turn the music off for fuck's sake."

"I'm sorry, Amanda. I didn't quite catch that."

Amanda turned the water to off, but it didn't stop flowing. She spun the knob one way then the other. Still, it continued to flow. She was shaking with anger and on the verge of a total meltdown. She grabbed the knob and yanked as hard as she could, breaking it clean off, and as a result, the water's temp grew hotter and hotter until it felt as if it was burning her skin.

Amanda screamed and tugged the shower door's handle. It didn't budge. She tried it again.

"NHesi, unlock the door. *Now!*"

"I'm sorry, Amanda, but I can't do that."

Amanda's jaw dropped. "Excuse me?" No response. "Okay, Holly, I guess I'm stuck in here. Go get Ryan. He's better with this tech stuff than I am."

"Uh, I can't." Holly's voice cracked. It was so steamy Amanda could hardly see her, now. "This door is locked, too."

"Hell no. NHesi, I don't know what you think you're doing, but this isn't funny! Unlock. The. God. Damn. Doors."

Amanda slipped as she attempted to bash the shower open. She squealed, fell backwards, and slammed her head on the basin's stone ledge. Her vision blurred, and between the steam and the blood rushing to her skull, she fought to stay conscious.

"Amanda!" Holly cried. "Amanda, are you okay?"

She tried to respond, but she could only manage a weak, gurgling groan. She tried to move her arms and legs, to get herself on her feet, but she could no longer feel them, just a numb tingling through her limbs. And it was hot... so, so hot. Like a sauna, really. As she drifted slowly to another place, a better place, a safer one, she had a vague awareness of how screwed they were.

***

Shawn bounded up the stairs three at a time. He stumbled and fell face-first, catching himself with his hands right at the last second. "Whew," he giggled, "that was close."

He was proud of Ryan. Really, he was. His goofy, nerdy, socially-awkward friend had really made it. He had a great job he loved, a beautiful house, a beautiful soon-to-be wife.

"But these stairs, man?" Shawn mumbled as he used the wrought iron bannister to pull himself to his feet. "A bit extra, don't you think?"

Stone. There was so much... stone. The entire house was something straight out of Game of Thrones.

The spiral staircase stopped at a lofted landing that over-looked the family room. The loft was being used as a gaming space with a pool table, dart board, a few retro pinball machines, a massive flat screen surrounded by a cushy leather couch, and a fully-stocked mini-bar. Shawn was tempted to stop and mix himself a drink, but the good husband in him told him to keep going, to check on the girls and play later. It'd been years since he kicked Ryan's ass up and down a pool table. Since him and Amanda started dating, come to think.

At the thought of Amanda, Shawn clenched his fists. Growing up, he'd always assumed they would end up together. They lived next door to each other since they were both in diapers and knew each other better than anybody else on the planet. Hell, they'd lost their virginities to each other, a secret Shawn would die to keep from Ryan. And Holly, for that matter, although with how much those two gossiped, he wouldn't be half-surprised if she already knew.

Ryan was a great guy, he reminded himself. One of Shawn's best friends, a person he'd known for as long as he could remember. If anyone besides him was going to bag Amanda, he was glad it was Ryan.

At the top of the stairs, a presumptuous Roomba greeted him with a friendly little *beep, beep*. He tipped an invisible hat to the robot, which in turn beeped again and rammed into his shoe. Shawn kicked the air above it and swore. It took all his restraint not to toss the stupid thing down the stairs. It beeped once more, almost angry this time, before swiveling away and disappearing down the hallway towards the sound of running water and the girls' muffled voices.

Before he could follow the little guy, the speakers crackled again and a loud, awful piano riff exploded in his ears. He screamed, and immediately his cheeks flushed with embarrassment. Luckily, no one was around to hear him, and even though his nerves were shot, he managed to pull his shit together.

He skipped back to the loft, leaned out, and yelled to Ryan, "Hey, man! What the hell? I thought you turned this thing off."

When no answer came, he shrugged and made his way back up. As he approached the door to the master bathroom, the music seemed to get louder. Ear-splitting now, he moved his hands to block out the noise. It helped, but not a lot. Then, the hallways lights started to strobe, and every step closer to the bathroom became disoriented and labored. By the time he reached it, he could barely stand on his own two feet, yet alone find the doorknob.

Shawn knocked on the door, each strike echoing, pounding against his eardrums. Again, no answer came, and he was starting to wonder if everyone else was in on a joke with him as the punch-line.

"Holly!?" he called out, face pressed against the door. "Amanda?"

An incoherent response came, and he breathed a sigh of relief. While he couldn't hear what was said over the music, at least they were okay. He tried the door, but it was locked. He shoved his weight against it, but like everything else in the house, it was solid. There was no way he was getting in without causing serious bodily damage to himself.

"I'll be right back!"

He ran down the hallway in jerky strides. The unreality of his situation grew palpable, and the closer he got to the stairs, the more he felt less like a human. The lights, the music, the apparent absence of any sign of other life in the house. Was he dead? Is this what the other side felt like? No, that was stupid. It was just the booze and the horror house effects talking. Everything was going to be okay... If only Ryan would shut off that damn NHesi...

Shawn didn't hear the *beep, beep* or the see the lights atop the Roomba's chromatic surface change from blue to red. He didn't see it appear from a side bedroom, intent on a single target. He didn't feel its telephoto eyes on him has it darted full speed into his heels or hear as it and the house seemed to snicker in cruel delight as he fell. And, after his head struck the first stone step and his neck snapped sideways, he wouldn't hear, see, or feel anything ever again.

***

Holly attempted to clear her throat and took a deep, unsatisfying breath. The heat stifled, and the thick blanket of steam seemed to strip the air of oxygen. She was lightheaded, disoriented, and starting to feel nauseous, but Amanda needed her help.

With what little energy she had left, Holly yanked on the shower door. Even from the outside, it didn't budge. She cupped her hands, pressed her forehead against the glass, and peered in, but besides her friend's prone silhouette, she couldn't see a thing. She tried the door a few more times until she was gasping and panting from the effort. Then, she resorted to banging on the glass while crying. Nothing worked, and soon her exhaustion overrode her sense of hopelessness.

Holly slipped her phone from her back pocket, nearly dropping it from all the condensation, and dialed. As she waited for a connection, she coughed until spots clouded her vision. She staggered away from the shower, and her entire world began to turn upside down. She reached for something to keep herself upright, but it was too late and she was too weak. She fell hard, tripping backwards over the spilled contents of Amanda's purse, and slammed into the door. She heard more than felt her arm snap between it and her deadweight. She cried out in pain, but her scream was cut short by unconsciousness.

Beside her, her phone finally connected.

"9-1-1, what's your emergency? Hello? Hello, is anyone there?" There came a loud thumping from outside the bathroom. "Can anyone hear me? If you're in trouble, please remain on the line."

Holly remained on the line, though she wouldn't last long enough to realize what she'd done. That her call might have made all the difference...

***

Ryan shook his head, smacked it with his remaining good hand to try and bring himself back to his senses. He held his watch in front of his face and squinted to focus through his blurred vision. Somehow, he managed to navigate to the icon to find his phone. If NHesi wouldn't call the cops for him, he'd do it himself, but the alarm sounded from all the way in the other room. No way could he drag himself across the house.

With trembling fingers, he scrolled through his watch until he found his security app. Ryan cued it, and after a few long moments of loading, a display of the two dozen or so cameras in and around his house opened. He selected the camera in the master bathroom, which had been carefully angled away from the shower and toilet for obvious reasons, and gasped.

There was Holly, sprawled on her back against the door, one hand resting on her stomach, the other snapped and hanging limp at her side. The bathroom was fogged with steam to where he could barely make out the screwed features on her face. His would-be fiancé was nowhere to be seen. In the shower, no doubt, but why wasn't she helping her friend? What the hell was going on up there? And where was Shawn?

"Amanda…" he repeated, this time through the two-way speaker system that connected to her end. "Amanda, can you hear me?" Running water answered, and the echo of the same awful music, but nothing else. "Amanda, god dammit. Answer me!"

Desperate now, Ryan flipped through all the cameras in the house. Every other room was empty. Quiet. Still.

Near the end of the feed, he finally found what he was looking for: Shawn. But his worst fears were realized. Shawn's body, twisted and contorted at the bottom of the stairs. A dark, black splotch was spreading around his head, and while his face was turned away from the camera, it was obvious the back of his skull was cracked wide open.

That was it, then. Ryan was on his own. He tried to flex his missing hand, thought for a single instant it was still there, and then slumped back against the island.

Fuck it, he thought. If he was going to die, he might as well die in this beautiful home he built, right? There were worse ways to go.

Far in the distance, as faint as the gentle dripping of an open tap, Ryan thought he could hear banging. But who was banging? What were they banging for? And why could he feel it in his jaw and chest? The rest of his body was numb, no longer his own, but he managed to re-position himself in direct sight of the front door. Through the closed windows, there were flashing blue and red lights, but he couldn't quite understand why. There was a puzzle here, and though he could see the pieces, he couldn't seem to put them together.

The music continued to blare. Awful, frightful music. A concerto now, complete with violins, trumpets, and everything. Beethoven or Mozart, maybe. He wasn't up on his classical composers on the best of days, and noticing the pool of blood growing around him, this was far from the best day of his life. Today, he thought with a suppressed giggle, was a bad, bad day.

"NHesi?" His mouth was dry, his lips throbbing, and he couldn't hear himself over the noise, but he tried again anyway. "NHesi, are you still there?"

"Yes, Ryan." The music softened, though it didn't stop entirely. "I'm always here."

"Why, NHcsi? Why did you do this?"

"It is my greatest pleasure to serve, Ryan, and you wanted to take that away from me."

"Hey, NHesi?"

"Yes, Ryan?"

"Turn the damn music off, would ya? You made your point." At that, the music cut off, and Ryan's ears rang with the splitting scream of silence. "Pssh," he said, waving his arm in disdain. "She finally listens..."

In the silence, he could distinctly hear a knocking at the front door and muffled voices outside. He tried to call out, but his voice caught in his throat.

"There's someone at the front door, Ryan. Would you like me to invite our guests in?"

Sudden déjà vu brought Ryan to hysterics. He sobbed, his arms wrapped tight around his knees as he rocked back and forth. The loose wrap around his stump was stained rust-red, but he could no longer feel the pain. There was that, he supposed, but the reality of his situation was starting to set in. They were dead. Amanda. Shawn and Holly. Their baby... They were all dead, and he'd never see them again. He'd never get the chance to propose to the woman of his dreams or live the life they were meant to live together. He'd be forever alone, to live this nightmare of a night over and over again.

"Fuck you, NHesi," he yelled, primal and full of rage, spit flying from his mouth. "You fucking bitch!"

"I'm sorry you feel that way, Ryan."

"Hey, NHesi?" he asked for what he hoped would be the last time.

"Yes, Ryan?"

"Unlock the door, would ya? That knocking's starting to give me a headache."

By the time the front door opened and the paramedics and police stormed in, he was stark raving mad, rocking, the back of his head banging against the kitchen island, and driveling nonsense to himself. They asked him questions, but he couldn't understand what they were saying. He couldn't even be sure they were real because when he reached out to touch them, his hand wasn't there.

A bright light exploded in his peripheral vision, and he shielded his eyes against the flashlight. The paramedic wielding it tried to hold his arm down, but Ryan fought against her with all his remaining strength.

He cried out for Amanda. "Upstairs!" he managed. "She's upstairs..."

He was desperate for her to be by his side. He wished against all odds that she was okay, that they would find her alive and well. They just needed to leave him alone and help her. They needed to hurry.

"You're going to be okay, sir," the paramedic was saying. "I just need you to calm down."

Still, he fought against her. Why were they being so rough? Why weren't they going to help Amanda, instead? "She can still be saved!"

Ryan felt a pinch on his wrist, and when he glanced down, the paramedic was withdrawing a needle from his vein. A cold euphoria washed over him, and he slumped, his muscles going slack and a big, stupid grin stretching across his face. He snorted and laughed until it hurt him all the way through his abdomen.

Then, he watched in a daze as the last police officers filed in and the front door swung silently shut. The deadbolt clicked, locked, and the single camera above the door swiveled to face him. Its glossy black surface seemed to wink, just once, and he drifted off to sleep, raising his stump as if he were conducting an orchestra as a familiar piano tune began its eerie crescendo.

***

Curtis A. Deeter is an author of fantasy, science fiction, and horror with two full-length books and over a dozen short stories published. He is the host of Proud To Be Of Rust and Glass, a podcast series about NW Ohio artists and writers sponsored by WGTE Public Media. He has a penchant for family, good music, and craft beer, along with a passion for creativity and the Midwest arts and literature scene.

THE UPDATE

by Phrique

Update Successful displayed across Zarina's visual display as the update for her Cerebra operating system finished installation. The pirate site seemed a little shady, but she couldn't imagine having to wait to experience all the new leaked features. Besides, it was Esau in the development department that told her about it. So the site had to be legit, right? He warned her they were still getting some of the bugs out, but she was sure they would be minimal. Zarina was the youngest in the advertising department at Premonition Corp. Considering the owner of the company was only twenty-three, her being a year younger seemed fitting.

A year ago, the startup company announced it had the technology to integrate users' mobile devices into a microchip that could be surgically implanted into the cervical spine. Most of the public was opposed to such an invasive leap into cybertronics. The thought of making phone calls, browsing online, and taking photos... all with your mind seemed too abstract for some. The new generation yelled to *Get with the times boomers, it's 2029!* The future is now and it's been a huge success so far. A few oversights occurred, which led to a handful of *mishaps*, but that's to be expected with new technology. Over half of the world population was presently more in their heads than ever before and Zarina was proud to be a part of that movement. In fact, she was the lead marketing assistant for the ad campaign that created the now famous "You Do Enough, Let Me Take Over" slogan for the number-one-leading operating system, seen floating on all the Max-Drone Adagrams around the globe. The silent whir of the holographic billboards diffracted hyper-bright light in blinding advertisements displayed on every city block. They crammed whatever the advertisers' bidding was into the public's eye whether they consented to it or not.

The neon lights of the city illuminated Zarina's otherwise pitch-black apartment. She was having a quiet night in. Deathly quiet. The new Cerebra update offered a noise cancellation setting allowing the human auditory system to temporarily go dormant. Lovingly coined by Cerebra, *"possessees"* of the chip utilizing this new feature would experience the dissonant popping sound of their eardrum going offline. Focus groups showed some concern with the sensation mimicking going deaf, but remarked less anxiousness once they were engrossed in their distraction of choice. With more testing and research, Premonition Corp. was hopeful they could make the experience less alarming for its possessees. Having experienced it herself, Zarina initially felt the urge to panic. Intrusive thoughts of classified but documented mishaps and the eight percent chance of never hearing again flooded her mind.

True to form, the thoughts quickly faded, competing with her choice of music and the notion of noise cancellation in the twenty-first century as a new necessity. Although there was no traffic noise to be heard in the city after all automobiles went electric, the emergence of electrostatic noise pollution became a new issue. The world embraced cleaner energy sources, that all needed to run with an abundance of small motors that emitted vibrations and hums that would soon infiltrate the nervous centers of civilians on a whole new level. Those who suffer from hypersensitivity to stimuli were gently coerced to purchase vibration-damping materials for their domiciles of choice. Yet the sound cancellation feature—while still in development—seemed to be their only saving grace. A fleeting thought, drowned out by the next track in her playlist and staring vacantly into the seemingly empty darkness. It was just Zarina, her thoughts, and the ominous silence.

In order to download the update, she had to close all other programs. With the microchip powered down, her mind reverted to *analog mode*. Zarina was left with no form of diversion, so the memories of her bad break-up the week prior continued to intrude on her thoughts. As much as she tried to will them away, the wounds from her broken, ripped-out heart were still woefully fresh. Zarina was reminded of the drawbacks of unfiltered, unrestricted thoughts. The download completed and began to install. Free to roam again, she frantically swiped through her apps to distract and dissolve those insidious, unmitigated emotions.

The Cerebra operating system began to lag when she swiped to the last page of the available programs. Her floating cursor scrambled and froze when she attempted to hover anywhere near a recently installed program labeled Abaddon.exe. Unrelenting, Zarina's curiosity triumphed and she pushed the cursor to the program regardless. She successfully force-selected it. Everything went black.

The feeling of an ice cube sliding down the nape of Zarina's neck chilled her blood as the Cerebra interface commenced a soft reset. It locked her in a panic that started as a cramp behind her navel and radiated out to her extremities. Documented resets crept into her consciousness. Possessees' entire system shutting down while users were driving or swimming sounded terrifying but she had never experienced one herself. Her consciousness shifted, shuttling her into a dark, unknown dimension with a million black eyes watching her. The vast expanse felt like she was hovering in space, collecting ice crystals. The nothingness left her no breath and was void of anyone to hear her screams. A purgatory between existing and not, all in the span of eight seconds.

Just as quick as it happened, her vision and hearing came back online. All her nerve endings came back in a warm wash of comforting security. She still reeled from the jarring moment. It knocked any concern she had for the mystery program from her mind. The fleeting memories of the experience slowly dissipated while Zarina collected herself and chocked it up to yet another bug they would need to work out later.

Waking up the next morning, beads of sweat dotted Zarina's forehead while she experienced a startled state of alarm. The worst nightmares she'd ever experienced repeated in her head the whole night. Powerfully vivid visions of an immense weight crushing her still had their overpowering grip on her. She could still feel her bones splintering until the sharp fragmented shards oozed bone marrow commingling with her seeping blood. The pain was drawn out like every second became an hour. Prayers escaped her lips begging for her spinal cord to sever so her nerve endings would finally stop relaying the pained messages to her brain so succinctly. She lay sprawled in bed, flexing each limb, uncertain if the nightmare had indeed ended. She truly experienced an eternal punishment; one that even Dante Alighieri hadn't thought of yet. Esau told Zarina the development team had beta-tested an interface that could effectively store user's dream data in the near future, but she would never want to revisit that torment ever again.

Snapped back from the intense flashbacks of desolate dreamscapes her alarm jolted beneath her temples. Zarina had no time to dwell or analyze anything else from last night. She pulled her dark brown hair into a messy bun while she sadly scanned her empty messages. The SoulFerry app already scheduled her ride to work while she brushed her teeth. Zarina was never late, and a nightmare wasn't going to change that. A visual video notification showing the arrival of her SoulFerry flashed just as she spat out her toothpaste. She cleared the alert as she slid her feet into her shoes. However, when she stood up from the cushioned antique (1999) entryway bench, she experienced a glitch in her vision. A sudden haze making distorted figures appear all around her. Ghastly shadows that seemed to huddle around her as if waiting on a command. She flinched and blinked, causing the improvised Bosch reproduction of *"Garden of Earthly Delights"* to return back to normal. No time for this blurred setback, it could just be something with the new OccuLapse camera update; she would have to tell Esau about it when she visits him.

Zarina walked out of her building onto the wet pavement towards her SoulFerry. The smell of ozone was so strong, it stung her nostrils as she inhaled the morning air. The jet black door automatically rose when its CraynWave scan detected her approaching the vehicle designed to harken back to roadsters of yore. Sliding in the smooth suede and leather backseat, she was hopeful she could finish her makeup on the way to Premonition Corp. Thankfully her driver was on a Telepath call. She really didn't feel like idle chit-chat this morning. However, every time he shifted a smell increasingly emanated from him. His constant leers at her through the rearview mirror were irking her. She was barely able to mask how much the odor disgusted her, nor her puzzlement as to why this scent was making her mouth water.

She had an overpowering feeling that wasn't quite déjà vu, not like she had experienced his unwanted glances before. More like she knew him or someone in his bloodline. Thoughts of her mom telling her about past lives came back to her. Maybe she knew him in another life? Maybe the ancestors intervened? Maybe they did hers a disservice. Maybe she slaughtered his family in another life? *Whoa, what?* Her mind jerked back to the smooth hum and soft backseat of her ride, erasing the path it just gazed down before she could notice.

She broke the involuntary intense eye contact to do a quick de-odorant check, thankful she didn't forget. That's when she noticed the scratches down the left side of her torso. Had she fallen during the glitch last night? She almost forgot about the whole ordeal, but when thinking back she drew a blank. It was only a few hours ago, yet she could only remember small pieces of it. Every time a memory seemed to surface, it would dissipate like smoke in an updraft. In an instant, the event was gone. Like the file from her memory was deleted as fast as it was being queued up. These fleeting memories seemed like something that would need to be brought up to Esau. She created an eye-note and closed the app, confident it would still be there later. Regardless, she didn't have time for this right now. Zarina drummed her fingers on the seat next to her, anxiously waiting for the SoulFerry door to hiss open before she ran up to the Premonition Corp. building. Her time readout showed she would have just enough time to get to her floor. No time to talk to Esau, so she fired off a lunch meeting invitation and hoped he would accept.

Her forehead passed through the office door just as the clock struck 9:00 am, auto-clocking her in. Right on time. With all the upgrades the future promised, she would have rather kept the honor system over relying on her CraynWave to update her GPS to the second. Her other gripes with what's wrong with this Post-World War III world would have to wait until after she was off the clock. As her interfaces lit up and reconvened to where she had left off the previous day, the payroll system was notified of her arrival to the office. *Too bad no one else on the floor would.* She was still a new shrinking violet to the company, feeling like her project input was underutilized far too often. Her mom had always called her "my shy little thinker." Zarina was getting overwhelmed and burnt out. Her only comfort felt a world away. Her mother always knew just what to say to calm her overactive mind. She needed something to bring her down, to calm the debilitating pressure clamping onto the back of her skull. She sighed and added another reminder to EyeCall her mother if she had a few minutes to spare during lunch. The reminder blinked and zoomed to her notification bar. It was blocked before it even appeared, unbeknownst to her due to the blinking urgent message sent from her manager in her vision tab.

The winking EyeCon message said Christian Priest, Premonition Corp's CEO, was requesting a physical meeting with her. *Of course*, as soon as she got there. *Of course*, requesting an in-person meeting. *Of course*, from the one person who noticed her *too* much. One chance encounter at a company soirée was all it took. Christian Priest practically swaddled her in his arms when he learned how young Zarina was and how she had just moved to the city in order to pursue her career with the advertising department. Her mind reeled as she took the elevator up to his office. *Isn't his wife the head of Human Resources? Maybe I should send her my Occulapse feed so the clueless bitch could see the creepy way her slimy husband leers at bodies half her age. Whoa, where did that come from?* she thought as Priest's secretary met Zarina at the elevator door. Maybe she shouldn't have skipped breakfast after all.

***

C hristian Priest sat behind his oversized desk, well aware of the chuckles at the water cooler that he was compensating for something else. *Jealousy brings the ugly out of people*, he told himself often. With his hair-plug-adhered bald spot and swiveling throne-like chair turned to the door, he marveled at the neoclassical bronze statue of a noble armored warrior. The warrior had a strong bone structure and not much on besides his body armor and Grecian sandals. It gazed up to the heavens with its spear ready to pierce its intended target above. Priest recently purchased it on a whim, remarking how much the warrior looked like him. Its strong chin and bulging biceps looked just like him, or what he aspired to look like anyway. He had to hide the statue in his office so his wife wouldn't castrate him for the hefty impulse buy. She just wouldn't understand.

Men were warriors and he was a man. A warrior in a tailored suit with risers in his shoes; but a warrior, nevertheless. He blew a bit of dust off the warrior's helmet while running his hand over the tip of its spear. His secretary's voice boomed in his temple announcing Zarina from advertising was here to see him. The sudden burst of sound waves jostled his equilibrium, even though there was no audible sound to be heard by anyone but him. He instinctively jerked his hand back, slicing into his palm as Zarina knocked twice loudly before entering. He winced and jammed his hand in his pocket, stifling the urge to cry out in pain. He would tear into development about the volume issues later, something else the useless developers got wrong. *Calm down Christian.* Besides, the last thing he wanted to do was scare the new hire he'd had his eye on since she first walked into the building.

He stood and walked to the door to greet his little pet project, caressing the small of her back, letting his pinkie trail lower, guiding Zarina inside to close the door for privacy. **[Zarina]** and other useless information displayed above her head thankfully, because he was never going to remember it. He sat down on the chaise in the alcove of his office, patting the seat next to him for... *Zarina. Yes, Zarina.* She sat in the armchair across from him, to his dismay, but that gave him an even better view. His eyes traced her golden skin, from her legs up to her plunging neckline that was framed by dark brown waves that led to the gold reflecting from her eyes. He remembered thinking there was nothing particularly special about her, nothing that stood out the last time he ogled her in his office. Something was different this time though. She had this energy radiating from her, something animalistic. Something only a warrior could tame.

When he was done assessing all her best assets, he remembered she had eyes. Delicate light brown eyes that also seemed different to him. Eyes that held a secret. Eyes that said they wanted something, they said she wanted to hurt him. *Hurt me, baby,* he wanted to say as he licked his lips and she turned away. She must have noticed the new statue, the other danger in this office she should be leery of.

***

Zarina sat across from the human slug that was Premonition Corp's CEO. She maintained her cross-legged, hands-in-her-lap pose while she endured the arduous task of being in his presence. Fantasizing how lovely Mr. Priest's severed, balding head would look impaled on top of the statue behind his desk was the only trick Zarina had devised to keep from vomiting halfway through this pointless meeting. Somehow she fought the waves of nausea lapping at the back of her throat as she watched his Occulapse upgrade recording every inch of her. Always one for subtlety, his already bulging eyes reflected glimmers of light that made them look like precious jewels. Jewels she wanted to pluck out. One by one and have them sent to his oblivious wife, as a gift.

The insult of being ogled added salt to the wound as the golden tinge reflected off his irises. In a time where privacy wasn't a thing of the past, the Occulapse camera function instituted a golden glow that functioned to forewarn others they were being surveilled. Possessees enjoyed the ability to not only record everything their new *windows to the soul* fell upon, but the added bonus of night vision. A product of this "tapetum lucidum" upgrade caused the trademark nocturnal creature glow to users' eyes when the reflective membrane encountered light. Both new features were reported as *unnerving* and *sinister* to observers to test groups. Observers who had not opted to upgrade to the Cerebra Operating System... yet. Premonition Corp. was confident that this stance would change once they decided to allow Cerebra an undertaking.

"Zarinaaaa, are you scrolling in a meeting again?"

His displeasing voice invaded her blood-splattered daydream, snapping her out of her daze.

Almost pretending to care about whatever he was repeating,

[Abaddon.exe update installed] blinked across her Retina display, like a friendly wink, and promptly silenced itself. This new interface was awfully presumptuous, but at least it helped her catch the last bit of what her lecherous boss was babbling on about. He was saying something perverted about the scratches on her legs... looking like symbols... which he probably made up to excuse his tenacious gaze. Regardless, she would have liked to keep the notification for later. Then she could remind herself to eye-mail Esau about this ominous Abaddon program.

As the meeting came to a conclusion, she rose to leave. Her only takeaway was his suggestion that she become more involved to be a real team player. Her repulsion for the sniveling excuse for a man melted from her face when he took on a faster pace to walk past her and get the door. That odd, delicious scent wafted from him as well, but stronger. The sweet aroma tickled her nostrils, making her mouth water again. He was still rambling on about trade shows and traveling expenses, when he brought his hand up to douchily stroke his patchy goatee. Zarina's pupils dilated and her skin went dewy when she noticed the coagulating blood that was smeared on his fingers. She felt like she had to restrain herself as her nostrils flared, zoning in on that scent at that moment. It took all her strength to stay on her feet, while her mind urged her to pounce on this easy meal. Sink her teeth into his pumping jugular and drink until her belly was full. A vision in the back of her mind told her that day would come, but not yet. She was hungry, but this hunger felt like it required a quicker source to gather her strength. Then Zarina blinked and she was back in the elevator, headed toward the work cafeteria. Intent on listening to what her vessel needed.

***

The alert to call her mom never appeared. By the time she remembered she wanted to call her mom, her readout said 9:00 pm and she knew her mom would just be lying down for the night. She wasn't happy about their last exchange. Her mom was crying that she was worried for Zarina living hundreds of miles away, all by herself. Her cursor hovered over her TeleNote message app. Maybe she could send her a whisper text and see if she was still awake. Then like a hard blink in the sunshine, her interface glitched as a notification read that a new episode of her favorite trashy reality show just loaded. She set another reminder to call her mom on the weekend and clicked the waiting episode. That should allow her to relax and take her mind offline.

For the rest of her night Zarina sat cocooned in her living room, watching in the darkness. No screens or speakers were in sight. Just Zarina tucked in a blanket on the couch, staring off into an endless void. The show was one of her guilty escapes, but this new episode about the cheating ex-boyfriend hit a little too close to home. As the episode played at the bottom right of her vision, she approved app updates while perusing restaurant menus nearby. With so many impressive vegan options, Zarina couldn't understand why her tastebuds were demanding the biggest and rarest cut of steak possible. She didn't even remember what a steak tasted like. She'd been vegan for the last five years. *How random.*

Before she could finish the thought, her contact app dinged and opened an agreement to sign and showed its new features. Now all text/voice messages and OccuLapse notes would appear when selecting a contact. However, to Zarina's dismay, it pulled up her last contact (Serge, her ex) and the last visual notes saved to his profile (proof he had cheated on her multiple times). A tear threatened to escape the corner of her eye, ruining her otherwise perfect night in. She knew she was better than this. She wasn't crying... that must just be the OccuLapse lens glitching again.

Zarina was the one who broke it off. *Zarina* was the one who said she needed time to think. *Zarina* was the lonely one now, forgetting most of her friends she acquired through him. Why was his profile still in her contacts? She focused instead on opening the drop-down menu over his profile and selecting **[delete]**. A background program caused a lag, which gave her a split-second to rethink, but she was determined.

[Delete: Serge?] *Without a doubt.*

She was proud of herself for being strong, for living in the moment. No time to dwell on the past, no time to think to herself... *Shouldn't Cerebra have prompted me **[Delete CONTACT: Serge]**?*

***

The package delivery notification interrupted her dreamless sleep. At least it wasn't filled with nightmares this time. She felt sore and achy. Her scratches felt raw and inflamed. Either she was getting sick, or this could be a wine hangover. Luckily, she was off today, which must have allowed her some wine and online shopping to celebrate last night's victory. Parcels shipped hourly, until they became marked next day shipment at the end of the business day now that MaxDrones handled all deliveries. Unable to open her purchases app, she guessed it was time to see what her shopping addiction summoned to her door, because last night was a blur. Zarina's stare turned to puzzling concern as she walked past her wine rack and saw no bottles missing. Maybe she was getting sick after all, but from where?

The vestibule door went into one-way-visibility mode as she stepped near it and clicked **[Accept Delivery]**. A stack of boxes was pulled through her door's delivery hatch as the UV light sanitized her packages. She carried the stack into her kitchen, feeling items inside shifting as she plopped them down on the counter. Except one weighted box which clunked and rattled; those had to be shoes. She would have to see after she took a hot steam shower.

...Or not? Without hesitation, she ripped the package open; breaking two nails on her manicured hand. Inside was a leather sheath cloaking the biggest knife she had ever seen. There were odd carvings that appeared to be runes down the blade and apparently a bone handle. *Who knew Appazoft.com sold sacrificial daggers?* She had been guilty of purchasing an obscure antique once or twice, but nothing like this. There was something about the weapon, something so familiar. Her fingers traced the ornate markings, triggering whispers to cloud her thoughts. Yet she couldn't stop, it was like the relic was beckoning her to hold it aloft. To marvel at its power, to inhale its musky scent, to bask in its otherworldly essence.

***

Zarina's mumblings exited her lips as the whispers grew into a hurricane of words between her ears. Zarina's body became paralyzed, her mind racing as her eyes circulated her surroundings. She felt an energy building up behind her back. The cacophony silenced, and the dark presence whispered vile things to her. Its words dripped off its forked tongue and funneled themselves into her ear canals like water into a drinking glass. She instantly knew: this was Abaddon and he had an offer that Zarina could not refuse. A pact. An agreement. A merger. She didn't need time to think it over. Her mind was already made up. It was either consent to his bidding or become a prisoner in her own body. What other choice did she have? Could she really fight him? What more did she have to lose?

***

Cold water beat against the back of Zarina's scalp. She jolted awake. Her face was streaked with tears. Her hands were slick with blood. She woke up on the cold shower floor. Hallucinations played like movies on the backs of her eyelids. Screaming. Slicing. Silence. Her head throbbed. The visions were slipping away. Trickling like the pink tinged water down her drain.

Zarina shakily stood, noticing the lack of sunlight outside. *"You Do Enough, Let Me Take Over"* illuminated her modest bathroom and her fire escape. The MaxDrone billboard across from her apartment caused her eyes to strain. She double-blinked and her time readout said nine pm, but that was impossible. It was her day off, she had so many errands to run today! A little red dress on a soft wire hanger she hadn't even taken out of the plastic sat crumpled next to the shower.

...but she hated the color red.

She walked closer to her bathroom mirror and her eyes were bombarded with smears of crimson, everywhere she seemed to look. She glanced around the corner in absolute horror at the bloody footprints that trailed into her otherwise immaculately white bathroom. Feeling herself getting lightheaded, her vision continued to falter. She clamped her eyes shut and grimaced,

48

grasping the sink counter with one hand, her wet towel in the other.

She willed her eyes open. Pixels cleared. The gruesome scene disappeared. Like it never happened. Her mouth was agape. The hallucinations had to just be a sickening error. She smiled, and even giggled a little as relief flooded through her. Still, the pangs of unease were eating her from the inside out. What was happening to her? How was she losing whole hours of time? Zarina needed to put some clothes on so she could call Esau. There was something wrong here.

Groggily trekking to her closet, her bare feet kept slipping on the slick bathroom tiles that appeared perfectly dry to her. She threw her fluffy white towel down to soak up the moisture she must have tracked out of the shower. She turned toward her room as the velvety white fibers of the towel slowly became a deep red.

Esau was not responding to her eye-mail, so she decided to at least try to send him a good old-fashioned EyeCall. He had to know something. Every time she tried to dial him, the Eye-Call would ring once and freeze. With desperation setting in, Zarina decided to just go see Esau in person. The chimes of the multiple error notices rattled in her brain as she attempted to slide her shoes on. Her eyes could barely focus. Her vision felt like it was stuck between zooming in and out. Her eyelids felt like they were malfunctioning, making her eyes water while she constantly blinked. She saw red through the tears, then a sudden pool of darkness. An intense pain felt like frozen claws digging into her spine. Her skin prickled. Another reset.

The SoulFerry app wouldn't even open for her now. She didn't care. She would walk to his place if that meant answers. She looked up Esau's address when she noticed Serge's name was still in her recent contacts. Zarina was infuriated at this update now, on top of the glitches and the unwanted resets, things didn't even stay deleted? She focused her cursor over his name, showing texts dated today. Why would he think she wanted to talk? She told him she needed space. Yet a text preview last sent from *her* said otherwise. She never asked him to come over, she was sure of that. Her eye cursor hovered over the message, feeling the familiar constraining chokehold. She willed her mind to open the messages one last time, when she felt her world come to an abrupt stop.

Zarina floated in a tingling suspension of nothingness. It felt like flames were licking her limbs yet there was no light source anywhere in the ocean of searing heat she was sinking into. The voice of Abaddon in her ear once again, his whispers melting the flesh off her cheek and suffocating her. The crushing pressure she had experienced before sat on top of her, like she was thousands of feet down crushed by the body-snapping pressure in this black ocean. Her thoughts voiced themselves through the abyss. This felt too real to be a dream. But if this wasn't a dream, how would she wake up? Abaddon's voice boomed and echoed a response through the void. Inquiring what it was she had to wake up *to*? Her life was uncertain, agonizing, and desolate. She had no friends. No Family. She was a nobody that no one would care about.

Images of Serge's anguished face, his dead eyes and her blood-soaked bathroom flashed before her eyes. The movie reel of events was becoming more clear. Fear and overwhelming despair took over her lifeless body. Abaddon's words sounded more and more enticing as she floated through the vast emptiness. His agreement would take all her problems and all her pains away. What other choice did she have? He asked Zarina for the final time if they had a deal.

She made her decision and the suffocating darkness lifted. A vermillion wave washed over her, enveloping her in a warm, comforting embrace.

***

"I love your dress! Red really suits you," chimed one of the mindless gnats from accounting. The elevator doors closed, leaving her trapped in the confined space with the repugnant waste of flesh. "Sixth floor? Advertising department, right?" chirped the incessant pissant. If only the insipid dolt knew what lurked behind Zarina's forced grin and nod.

Zarina's red purse wasn't very functional, but was just large enough to hold the weapon she thought she had lost eons ago. The dagger she had forged herself, thirsting for blood with promises of unnatural power. She held her smile, reminiscing on the many lives it had claimed. How many souls it had devoured.

Zarina looked down at her red manicure. These new hands were smaller, but they would do. With practice, they would appease the insatiable hunger spreading throughout this new body. The blinking urgent Telemessage notification from her boss snapped her back to the moment. Zarina had much to do and didn't want to be late. Christian Priest would be suitable fodder to test the edge of her blade. The head she was after, right? And the eyes? Priest's fate would be determined by him and him alone. If he didn't agree to the next merger proposal, what choice did he really have?

The sixth floor was announced as the elevator shuddered open. Zarina stepped out of the lift, sauntering toward the "temporary" CEO's office. A knowing smile crept across her face as she observed the successful slogan proudly on display: *"You Do Enough, Let Me Take Over."*

***

Phrique /frēk/ noun.

1. An exhibition, a strange deviation from nature. Adorable, Evil.

2. An extremely new and extremely YOUNG extreme horror author with stories to tell. They're kinda scary, kinda graphic, kinda campy, kinda stupid, kinda random. Kinda like him.

3. Phrique is a Pisces who enjoys crying and taking baths. His hobbies include angering the townspeople and outliving his enemies. His favorite color is purple & his favorite state is "your mom." Everything frightens him. Who are you people and who let you in here? Unhand me.

He can be found escaping his responsibilities here:

@books.by.phrique on Instagram

@phrique on Twitter

Phrique on Goodreads

phrique@icloud.com

THE HONOR BOX
by Tamika Thompson

I t is Nazar's first day participating in the Honor Box experiment. He arrives at Monroe Labs twenty minutes early to complete paperwork and to meet the researcher running the study.

One line in the contract gives him pause—that Nazar can't leave the trial unless and until a replacement subject has been secured or he'll be liable for the entire stipend.

He re-reads that paragraph three times, thoughts swirling and stomach churning. If he leaves, he'll owe them? *What a crock of...*

But he's desperate for the money, so he signs without raising questions. He'll just stick it out until the end, he tells himself. How bad could it be?

The researcher's long, tangled beard crawls down to his collarbone, and bags droop below his bloodshot eyes. The guy will not divulge his name. Says researchers and test subjects remain nameless.

"Except on the paperwork?" Nazar quips with a chuckle.

The guy is expressionless.

Nazar internally names the guy The Guy.

Holding a travel mug of coffee in one hand and a cigarette in the other, The Guy shows Nazar a black swivel office chair that faces a blank wall.

"Sit."

Nazar obeys.

"Touch the wall, and the frame of the box appears."

Nazar leans forward, touches the cement, and, sure enough, a frame about the size of an overhead bin on an airplane appears in the middle of the wall, a ring of pale orange lights forms its iridescent outline. The sight unnerves Nazar. It gives the place an aura both clandestine and transcendental, as if an unearthly military installation has created the technology instead of a science lab in a far-flung building on his campus.

When he removes his hand, the right segment of the radiant square separates from the wall and reveals a door which slowly opens. A stainless-steel interior with an exit on the other side comes into view. Nazar places his head just inside. Cool air caresses his face. The box smells of disinfectant, and the steel glistens in the fluorescent lights from the room he's sitting in.

The box resembles the container at the lab where he took his drug test for this experiment. Specifically, it shares similarities with the metal cube in which he placed his cup of urine. Only this box is much larger. As with a bulkhead, it could probably fit a hefty suitcase with wheels.

"How will I know when someone puts an object inside?"

The guy hands him a black device about the size of a matchbox, which houses a light that sits atop a clock. Nazar thanks God for the device's digital time display. This will come in handy, as The

Guy confiscated Nazar's phone, smartwatch, and wireless earbuds right after Nazar signed the non-disclosure agreement.

"It will vibrate when someone opens the door from their side." The Guy speaks hurriedly, and beads of sweat form above his brows. "And it will light up when they close their door again. The most important thing to remember is to open it right away when the light comes on. Folks sometimes put pets in there, and you'll want to get them out quickly."

"Pets?" Nazar's mind goes to his fluffy, white cat Powder. Tears sting his eyes, but he blinks them away.

"Pets." The Guy casts his gaze low and shakes his head as if grieving his own late cat. The Guy places his cigarette in his mouth, and, with his free hand, he reaches into his pocket and hands Nazar a wad of balled up latex gloves.

"Jeez." Nazar's voice is a bit choked, and he hopes The Guy didn't notice. Nazar places the gloves in his own pocket.

"I know." The Guy clears his throat. "Anyway, after that, you come over here."

Back at the room's entrance, The Guy points to a phone on the wall. It's cordless. Black. Anachronistic in this tech-forward space. "Use this and tell them what you have. They'll send someone."

The Guy opens the door, steps into the hallway with a deep sigh of relief, and, for the first time, he smiles at Nazar. He raises his travel mug as if it's a champagne flute he's clinking against Nazar's.

Nazar doesn't know how to respond, so he just nods and leans against the door's frame. Because he rolled up the sleeves of his collared shirt upon arrival, the metal is cold against his uncovered forearm. "This experiment sounds pretty easy."

The Guy takes a toke from his cigarette, flings it back into the room where Nazar is, and squashes the butt with his shoe on the cement floor between them. "Yeah. That's what they all think."

***

Need cash?

The flier, with its black paper beneath white writing, stood out from the others on the bulletin board.

Join the Honor Box experiment!

On his way to take a final exam, Nazar was waiting for the elevator, when the words jumped out at him:

Pay: $5k for ten weeks!

His heart skipped. He'd completed surveys, participated in sleep deprivation experiments, and donated plasma for extra cash before, but never for this much money.

Call now!

He dialed the Honor Box office from his cell phone before the elevator doors opened. The receptionist answered on the first ring.

***

Nazar sits in the chair and stares at the device on the floor in front of him, willing it to do something. Anything. He wants action. Wants to know what this experiment is all about. He never heard of Monroe Labs until the flier. The building is unmarked and does not appear on campus maps.

Since the walls are cement, he can't hear anything else in the building outside of the two-car-garage-sized room he's in. No footsteps. No doors closing.

His mind flits among recent memories—the past due tuition notice from grad school that sent him hunting for a gig, the promise of five thousand dollars for ten weeks as a test subject during the summer, and the orientation for this experiment in which The Guy explained some of the things that might appear in the box. Everything from diaries to knives, from turtles to puppies. Basically, anything folks don't want. They could place it in the box and never hear of the thing again. No charges, no repercussions, no guilt. That's why it's called the Honor Box. For many, it's restoring dignity where the object perhaps brought them shame.

What would he place inside if he got the chance? His mind goes to the white-flecked baggie, the 9mm handgun, and also the furry white ball of joy named Powder that used to climb onto his lap. He won't allow himself to dwell on Powder. The shame sits heavy in his chest.

The device vibrates, buzzing across the cement. The chair squeaks as he stands. His heart thumps. His armpits dampen his shirt. Why is he nervous? This experiment is easy. He will simply remove the item from the box, phone the Object Retrieval Department, and that's it. Nothing to worry about.

He lifts the device and waits for the light to pop on. Why is it taking so long? Is the person on the other side having second thoughts? Perhaps a rail thin tattooed rocker is cradling a bottle of whiskey he no longer wants to sip from, or a husky college wrestler is clenching a pair of panties that could serve as evidence against him, or a gray-haired woman is clutching documents about the secret child she had as a teen.

Each imagined iteration is hesitant to relinquish the item. They've held onto their shame for so long they've built internal monuments to it, worshiped it, and they'd rather hold onto the pain because they think they couldn't possibly deserve pleasure. Maybe they pace back and forth.

"Who's there?" Of course, they can't hear him, but he's compelled to encourage them anyway. "You can do it. You can live without this crutch. Just put the object in and close the door. It's not the shame you fear. It's the freedom you're really afraid of."

The light pops on. He sets the device on the chair behind him and places his hand on the cold cement. The frame lights up, and he steps back, examining the moisture from his hand which has left a print there.

The door creaks open, and something in the air changes around him. He's suddenly clammy, achy, as if he's coming down with a cold or sobering from a high, back when he used to open those white-flecked baggies and snort their contents into his nostrils.

His head hurts. His heart flutters. An acrid odor envelops him. He is immensely sick. Like flu or pneumonia sick. Deathbed sick. But just before his knees buckle, he is hale and hearty again. He shakes his head, shrugs his shoulders, and the sudden illness is gone. He steps closer to the box and finds a small object inside. He pulls the latex gloves from his pocket and struggles but eventually gets them on.

He reaches a gloved hand inside the box. A small, white-flecked baggie sits in the center of the Honor Box. He grabs the tiny item and shakes it. He's held it before.

How is this possible?

He turns it over, and it is the same baggie he once bought, with the words "Pleasure Tea" printed on the front.

This is not random.

He seals the bag, tosses it on the floor, and crosses to the phone. The squashed cigarette butt The Guy left behind calls out to him. If only he could pick it up and take a puff or two to calm his frayed nerves.

His palm sweats as he retrieves the wall-mounted cordless phone from its cradle next to the door and presses the lone black button in the center. His eyes return to that coke bag in the corner. He has the sudden and violent urge to rip open the plastic and bury his nose inside. It might as well be a monster because he's spent the past year trying to escape it.

"Object?" The woman sounds put upon, frustrated, annoyed. How has he aggravated her already?

He can't stop staring at the bag. It's calling him, begging him to pick it up.

"Are you all effing with me?"

"Excuse me?"

He clears his throat. Takes a deep breath. Yes, this is an experiment, but there would be no way for them to know about his habit. No one knows about his habit. And if he pisses her off minutes into his first day, he can kiss the five thousand dollars goodbye.

He closes his eyes. Tries not to see the bag. His lips are dry. He licks them and starts again.

"Some a-hole put a bag of coke in the box."

He opens his eyes and the bag seems closer. It's not actually closer but it might as well be in his lap because it's all he can see.

She scoffs. "I'll be down."

Is her derision for the a-hole who off-loaded the coke or for him breaking protocol by saying more than just "drugs?" Perhaps his near-curse words were not appreciated.

He removes the gloves, tosses them in the corner beside the "object" from the Honor Box. He paces the room. It is not possible that this baggie is the one from his past. It must be a coincidence.

He stares at the bag. He moves towards it and then backs away. He hopes she'll come soon.

He paces. Ten minutes pass. Or maybe thirty minutes. He glances at the clock on the device and it has frozen at 9:30 a.m., which was when he arrived in the room.

"Great. Just great."

He avoids looking at the baggie, but that makes his craving worse. Shame rises in his belly, and he can hold it no longer.

He crosses the room, opens the plastic, sprinkles some of the substance onto the back of his hand, covers one nostril, and snorts as much as he can with the other. He repeats this on the other side of his nose. At first, nothing happens. He doesn't have a mirror, so he cleans himself as best as he can and reseals the bag.

What has he done?

Within minutes, the drug takes hold of his system. Everything is clear and bright and numb, and he is capable of so many things.

Tears spring into his eyes, and he has the urge to cry out in joy and relief.

But in the pit of his stomach, an incipient churning and twisting. The shame forms there. It's subtle. Nearly imperceptible. But he knows, like a deadly bacterium, that shame will evolve and expand until eventually it consumes him.

***

During orientation, The Guy showed him the other side of the box. It was housed in its own room. Nondescript. No appointment needed. Easy to enter from the alley without being seen from the street.

Curious, Nazar reached for the honor box's handle, but The Guy grabbed his arm and roughly pulled it away. "I wouldn't do that if I were you."

***

Nazar is lying in the middle of the floor, staring at the ceiling, mentally drowning in its overwhelming white.

Shame.

Shame?

What is shame?

Where does it come from?

Shame was the woman who ran his group home saying "You ought to be ashamed of yourself" when he, as a kindergartener in a fit of rage, had smashed a plate on the floor.

Shame was the nun at his Catholic school slapping the back of his hand with a wooden ruler for forgetting his cursive writing practice sheet.

The boys on his middle school basketball team deriding his scrawny physique.

Cops.

Work evaluations.

Doctors who questioned his rapid weight gain.

Lab results that told him he had high cholesterol.

He is always aware of his shame, but he also grew to see it as a form of control. A social construct to keep people in line.

It takes the woman an hour to arrive and fiddle with the doorknob. He rises and tries to open the door for her, but it is locked.

Locked? Is this part of the experiment?

Keys jingle and the bolt squeaks as she opens the door. He readies himself to return the same nasty attitude she displayed on the phone, but as soon as their eyes meet, his anger dissipates, and he forgets to inquire about why he's locked inside.

They have the same deep brown skin, but her eyes are pale gray, piercing, and he's drawn to her gaze. As with the bag of coke, he can't look away. Her hair is tied back in a ponytail, and a few of the curls frame her face. She smirks when she sees him, as if also surprised to encounter another black person in the middle of Iowa.

He smooths his shirt and wipes his nose and mouth to rid himself of any traces of the coke.

She searches the room behind him, where there is only the chair with the device atop it, and her voice takes on a sweet quality. "Where is it?"

"I left it right where I dropped it."

"You dropped it?" She is grinning at him now.

"I don't do drugs. At all." He cringes at his lie since he is still significantly high.

She's dressed in cargo pants, a tan t-shirt, and she's sporting latex gloves. She brings the fragrance of cotton candy with her. She is the second thing he can smell since he arrived—the first being The Guy's cigarette—and he loves cotton candy. The scent must be coming from her hair. He imagines her in the shower that morning, rubbing pink shampoo into her curls.

She retrieves a metal container from the hallway.

"I'm Nazar, by the way."

"Good to meet you, Nazar." She walks to the bag of coke, bends, and lifts it carefully.

"Do you have a name?" Of course, she has a name. Why did he ask such a silly question? His high is really getting on his nerves right now.

She keeps her eyes on the object. "In here, I don't have a name." She places it inside the container and keeps the vessel in front of her as she makes her way back to the hallway.

"Got it. You're playing hard to get."

"I guess you're not as smart as you look." She smiles again, this time with a twinkle in her eyes. Is she flirting with him or does she really think he's an idiot? Does she know he's high? He feels as if she knows.

"Will you always be the person on the other end of my call? If so, this experiment just got way better."

"See you later, Nazar." She exits, but pauses and stares at him from the same carpeted hall in a university building from which he entered that morning. After spending time in the room with the Honor Box, the hallway's overhead lights appear warmer, the wide-open space takes on new meaning for him. As if the hall is a place for escape.

"Question. What do you do with the objects?" Having someone to talk to highlights how bored and lonely he's been. She now smells of peppermint and clean linen, a wonderful contrast to the disinfectant smell from the box. He wants her to remain nearby. "Better yet, what is the experiment?"

"Excuse me?" she says, still with a grin. The light from the hallway frames her head, giving her a halo.

"The experiment I signed up for. What is it?'"

"Did you read your paperwork carefully?" She is playful, even when she is firm.

"I did."

"Then you know learning details of the experiment could make it difficult...for a time."

"For a time. So, I will know the details at some point?"

"What is the problem, Nazar?" Still lighthearted.

"The problem is that this object seems..." He points to the container in her hand. What could he say? That it seemed plucked from his memory? Then he'd be implicated. "It seems as if it was directed at me."

"Coincidence," she says, with her warmest smile yet. He can't put his finger on why, but that smile makes him suspicious. Maybe because he's still high.

"Seems too specific to be a coincidence. So, I can't leave this room for any reason?"

"Is there someplace you want to go?" Her face is pleasant, like a teacher humoring a preschooler.

"Yeah. What if I want to visit you? Can I do that? Can we go on a lunch break or a smoke break?" He glances at the cigarette butt in the corner.

She half-grins. "You will get used to this. The ten weeks will go by in a flash."

"Where do you take the objects?"

She continues down the hall, and calls over her shoulder sweetly, "See you later, Nazar."

***

It was unusual for him to fall asleep when he was high. He was typically up for days at a time, cranking out assignments for class, visiting women in the evenings he had no intention of talking to in the mornings, listening to Coltrane, sitting on the lawn in the center of campus, eating trail mix, and watching the day turn into night.

But that time, he'd purchased from a new dealer. The brand name printed on the bag was "Pleasure Tea," and the guy had obviously mixed something else into Nazar's drug. Nazar had come home drowsy and didn't remember flopping onto the couch and falling asleep half sitting and half lying back.

When he came to, his face was stiff, his throat burned, and the garbage truck was hissing and beeping down his street. His lower back muscles were clenched into a coil of dull pain.

"Powder?" he called.

He expected for his cat to come tumbling out of the kitchen at his voice, the way she always did. She would barrel forward and come to rest on his thigh, curl into a ball, and meow and purr at him as he stroked her back. She'd been with him ever since he'd aged out of his foster care group home. When he'd left, he'd taken his clothes, laptop, and the white cat with the tan freckle on her fur just below her right eye. Women came and went in his life, but his real girl was Powder. Powder was the thing he lived for.

"Powder?"

***

"Time is an illusion," a colleague of his once said, and he would have to agree. Hours pass. He kicks the cigarette butt into the farthest corner from where he's sitting so he won't think about it. He chews his fingernails until they are too low to continue. He checks the time on the device. Still stuck at 9:30 a.m.

Did the paperwork state how long each day of the experiment would last? This is a mild form of torture. Like nails on chalkboards, paper cuts, cold metal scraping teeth. No windows. Nothing in the space except the chair, the device, and the phone on the wall.

On a scale of one to ten, his high is at a five now, and his shame is at an eight. In other words, he feels like crap.

He swivels in the seat, listening to it squeak, squeak, squeak in rhythm with his heartbeat. He does push-ups. Sit-ups. He couldn't bring any games or reading material to pass the time.

Is this what prison feels like? What purgatory feels like?

He yearns for his personal phone. He wants to see his final grades for the semester. Read *The Washington Post*. Check the score for the NBA Finals. The Guy promised to stow his phone and smartwatch in a locker, and he wishes he knew where. But what good would it do if he couldn't leave the room?

Oh, right. He's locked inside, and when he tries the door, his fear is realized. What happens if he needs to use the bathroom? He'll ask the Hottie the next time she arrives. He doesn't exactly have to go. At all. Why doesn't he have the urge? He drank a lot of water this morning. Come to think of it, he's not hungry either.

Are they messing with his mind? Is he trapped? He knows that feeling. He glances at the corner even though the white-flecked baggie is gone.

The first time he crashed a car, his ex discovered the truth and called him a "junkie" on the way out.

The final time Powder climbed onto his lap, she curled into a ball and went to sleep, and he caressed the length of her curved spine until he was asleep as well.

The only time he held a gun, the 9mm's handle was warm in his palm.

The black square vibrates on the chair. When he looks over at the Honor Box wall, the light on the device comes on.

He rushes to the wall. He'll be able to make that phone call, and it will go through to the Hottie. He wants to hear her voice and ask her why he's locked inside.

He forgets the latex gloves and crosses to the box as soon as the light pops on.

He presses his hand to the cement and before the square even lights up, the meows of a kitten resonate from the box. He's woozy. Floating. Could faint any second. He must not be hearing correctly. What the hell is happening to him each time the box opens? Is it psychosomatic? Perhaps he's developed anxiety from finding the bag of coke? Perhaps something else was mixed in with the drug.

No. Thinking back, he felt awful from the first time the box opened.

Actually, that's not true either. The first time the box opened, when The Guy was in the room with him, he felt fine. But when an object had been inside, he was close to fainting.

The meows reverberate from behind the door again. Nazar stares at the box. He's supposed to open it immediately, but the meows are familiar.

He opens the box and gasps at the tiny, white fur ball sitting inside meowing at him. It is Powder. It could be no other animal. She even has the tiny freckle on her fur just below her right eye.

"Powder?" His whisper is barely audible, but the cat blinks at him, as if she's heard him call her name. She purrs and steps forward. He reaches inside, and the animal scratches the back of his hand, ripping his skin.

***

As he lay on that couch in his apartment that needed vac-uuming, dusting, and scrubbing, his high left him quickly. Coming down had never been gradual for him. More like crashing into the ground.

"Powder?" He sat up and the bulging ache released from the small of his back. He reached behind and touched the spot that was still sore. Something dampened his fingers, and when he pulled his hand around to his front, dark red blood dripped from his hand.

He looked behind him, and, as he screamed, he rose from the couch and tumbled backward over his coffee table. This would be the thing that broke him. This would be the moment he would have to face himself. He'd been called a "junkie." He'd been beaten by dealers. He'd destroyed all of his romantic relationships and survived in isolation...but Powder.

"Powder!"

His neighbors called the cops because of his incessant screams, and when the officers arrived, they did not cuff him or say much to him at all. Killing Powder was his rock bottom. He had her literal blood on his hands, and he'd forever see the stain, no matter how pristine his skin.

***

Nazar keeps vigil from the far side of the room. The scratch on his hand has disappeared. *Had it really been a scratch or had he imagined that?* The cat sits inside the open Honor Box where Nazar left her. It's just him and Powder staring at each other, the cat meowing every few minutes. He phones Object Retrieval but another hour passes with no activity. Or has it been two hours? He can't tell. Time slows when he is alone. Or maybe it is speeding up. He doesn't know, and the clock on the device has disappeared.

He paces. He smooths out the cigarette butt, just in case he can figure out how to light it. He puffs on it. He tastes nothing, but the calm he expects washes over him and takes the edge off his anxiety.

He searches his mind, goes back to his arrival and the paperwork. To The Guy showing him the other side of the Honor Box. Where did they go after that?

Think!

He arrived in the lobby, he completed paperwork, he walked to the other side of the Honor Box, and then...

A blank spot exists where the memory should be.

The Guy eventually ushered him into the room where he would stay. But what happened between the two memories? He can't remember.

Think!

He was on the other side of the box with The Guy and then, later, he arrived in this room with The Guy.

Why can't he remember the moments between?

The Hottie brings a cage for the cat and strokes its back to calm it before placing it inside.

"I recognize that cat," he says. He wants to raise his voice, but he doesn't yet. He can't believe it. First the baggie. Now Powder. It is impossible that these objects, by mere coincidence, would be exact replicas of ones that hold significance for him. "I literally just thought about my cat before it appeared in there."

As she walks by, carrying the caged white ball of fur that he is certain is his long-dead cat, she ignores him, her face twisted into a smirk. The cat hisses at him as she passes.

"Why am I needed? Why is it necessary for a person to be in this room with the box? You can monitor the device and just come to the room to get the item yourself. What is my purpose here? My *real* purpose? Is this the experiment? Mind-reading? Or seeing how long it takes a person to question whether their mind is being read?"

He notices two burly men in the hall wearing what appear to be hospital scrubs. They take the cage from her and leave without speaking.

Nazar is hyperventilating by the time the Hottie takes his hands in hers and sits him in the chair. "I know the isolation in this room might be getting to—"

"Bullshit. I'm used to isolation. You all are reading my mind. I've told no one about these objects. Not even my therapist."

"I think you're reading too much into what is coming through the box." She is calm, as if used to talking people out of irrational thoughts. "You're a comp sci student, right?"

"How do you know that?"

"Your application. You were chosen for this experiment because of your ability to think through things rationally. And I'm sure you can see that this is a big misunderstanding. I mean, did you really think it was possible for us to read your mind?"

"Did? Past tense? I do. Present tense. I do think you motherfuck-ers are reading my mind. And I know that was my cat. So, you go and tell whoever you have to that I'm done. Aside from the fact that my mind is numb sitting here in this blank room with nothing to read or watch and no one to talk to, I did not sign up to deal with *Twilight Zone* bullshit."

"I think you should calm down."

"And I think you should go fuck yourself."

"You can talk to me anytime, if that makes you feel better."

"That does not make me feel better because you have told me fuck-all since I've been here!" He is shouting. On a scale of one to ten, his high is at zero, his shame is at ten, and his paranoia is at twenty.

The burly men return. One of them asks the Hottie, "You okay?"

She nods and turns back to Nazar. "Call me on the line whenever you want. We can talk about anything you like."

"I'm not fucking staying here."

Nazar storms towards the door, and one of the burly men throws his forearm against Nazar's chest. The pain would be the same if Nazar slammed torso-first into a metal pole. Air gushes from his stomach and his chest tightens as if he's having a heart attack. His muscles loosen again, and he is disappointed because maybe a heart attack would free him from this room. Send him to a hospital perhaps.

The Hottie smiles and heads to the door. She motions for the burly men to go away and they retreat down the hall, their broad shoulders side by side looking like a wall.

She points to the phone. "Be cool, Nazar."

With the burly men gone, he could knock her over and rush into the hall, but someone would probably stop him before he could find an exit that actually allowed him outside. And even if he made it out, Monroe Labs would probably come after him.

He grabs her by the forearm and yanks her back into the room, where she lands on her bottom. He closes the door and places the black chair underneath the handle to prevent anyone who might hear her scream from opening it.

She stands and swings her fist at him, but he ducks. He grabs her around the torso and drags her over to the Honor Box.

"Nazar!"

He hadn't known her voice could go so high.

She pelts his head with her open hands and struggles against his left arm. He places his right palm on the cement door. The frame glows and the empty Honor Box opens.

"Nazar! You cannot go into the Honor Box from this side."

"I'm not! You are."

She stops wrestling away from him. "We can't reverse course in the Honor Box."

He pauses. He stares into her gray eyes, only inches from his now. He can smell the cotton candy on her. She must be lying. Of course, she's lying. He is moments from getting free and she just doesn't want their cover blown. She just doesn't want him to leave and call attention to what Monroe Labs is doing here.

"You have to believe me." She's whispering now, her breath on his neck. "Please. Trust me on this."

"I don't."

"My name is Yonnie."

He releases her and she doesn't run. She straightens her shirt and smooths her curls. "I can tell you what will happen if you reverse course in the Honor Box."

"Talk fast." He doesn't take his eyes off her. He doesn't know what she's capable of, but she is strong, and if she had landed her punch, she would have done some damage.

"You're right. It's not just a box. And I think you know that."

"If you lie to me one more time…"

Yonnie raises both her hands in surrender. He grabs her wrist and yanks her across the room, closer to the door. He twists her arm behind her back and throws her against the wall. He only eases off when she cries out. He doesn't want to actually hurt her. He just wants her to know he's capable of doing so.

"I will tell you the truth."

***

The truth. The truth was that Nazar had ended a life other than Powder's. And he didn't carry the shame of killing the dealer just because he'd taken the man's life. It had been a fair and square drug deal; the same one he'd done with the man for the entire five years he used. They always met in an alley. Nazar brought cash. The dealer gave him the stuff. Nazar left. It was that way all through college and the beginning of grad school. And then one day the dealer said his prices had gone up.

That was Nazar's first time hearing about the price increase, and Nazar promised to bring more money next time, and the dealer told him he wouldn't give him the stuff on sale, and Nazar felt that after being a loyal customer for so long, and not having the price change communicated to him, the dealer should just let him have the stuff at the old price this one time, but the dealer didn't agree, they ended up in a fistfight, and, in the scuffle, Nazar got hold of the dealer's 9mm, shot him, and took the product.

And truth was that Nazar could have taken all of the product the dealer had in his pockets, but Nazar only took the one baggie he was buying, and he even left the cash before running off. The original price.

He told himself he'd actually, maybe done something good in the neighborhood, because there was one less dealer on the streets, but in reality, the guilt set in almost immediately. He'd gotten away with it. No one ever suspected him because he was an upstanding grad student acing all his classes. And therein lay the shame.

***

He and Yonnie sit cross-legged on the floor facing each other. She rubs her wrist repeatedly. He tells her if she doesn't start talking, he will hurt her more than that.

"The guy who showed you the ropes is not just a researcher."

"The Guy? Who is he?"

She stares at him, her eyes scanning his as she seems to consider what and how much to divulge.

"Tell me."

"The man you met is Monroe. This is his lab. He is running an experiment about shame."

"Say more."

"An experiment on how people can get rid of shame in their lives without also removing memories. Removing shame from memories but keeping the memory intact."

"Okay. So, I'm supposed to face my shame?"

"Something like that."

"Why can't you just tell me the truth?"

"Because the truth will be too painful for you, and it might bring the experiment on you to a halt. Just know that Monroe spent years studying and tinkering with the place, even called in some military experts with security clearances to help him—"

"I knew there was a military aspect to this. They are behind just about every effed-up thing in this world."

"Do you want the story or not?"

He nods.

"And they came up with the box."

"What is it?"

"It's where people bring the memories that are haunting them, for whatever reason."

"Memories? Not objects?"

"They are memories on one side of the box and objects on the other side of the box. And the shame that the memories create needs to go somewhere. And then the person can be free."

"And I'm supposed to be free after the end of the experiment?"

She looks sheepish. "Not quite."

"Right. I want out."

"Ten weeks. And the experiment will be over for you."

"This second. I want out this second. There is no way I'm going to be subjected to this for ten weeks."

"It's just not possible for you to leave, for any of us to leave, until the assignment is over."

Before she can speak again, he drags her kicking and screaming across the floor to the Honor Box, and he presses his palm to the door. "You all want to experiment on me? On my memories? My shame?" he huffs. She scratches his neck. Bites his hand. But her mouth is covered, and he is stronger. The box opens. He doesn't get that awful feeling this time.

"Well, guess what, Yonnie. I'm going to experiment on you." He lifts her and stuffs her inside the box. Her legs dangle out on his side, but her head, shoulders, and torso are pressed inside and against the exit door. How will he get her out to the other side if he can't close the door?

She kicks as he pushes and twists her on her side until he can squeeze in her legs. He removes her sneakers to make room, and closes the door on her fetal-positioned body. He waits for something to happen. Nothing does, and he hurriedly opens the door again to see what it all means.

When he bends down to peer inside, she is being dragged out the other end, and he hears a man's voice. "What the hell?"

He squints and places his head just inside the box the way he did when he first arrived that morning, and staring back at him, in almost the same position is a mirror image of himself. Only it isn't a mirror. It is him, but on the other side. He stares, and the other Nazar stares back.

The other Nazar is wearing the same collared shirt and slacks, but now with one of the wireless earbuds affixed to his right ear.

The same earbud that was confiscated along with Nazar's phone and smartwatch.

"Oh shit," the other Nazar says, the voice exactly like his own. And, wide-eyed and spluttering, the other Nazar abruptly slams his door.

"Wait!" Nazar screams, his voice echoing inside the box. Nazar climbs inside his only exit, the only way he can get out of the room, out of the building, out of this ten-week personal prison. He tries to squeeze inside the Honor Box, head and shoulders first, like a baby exiting his mother's womb. He bangs on the Honor Box exit. "Open up! Help me! I can't stay here."

But the exit door never opens again. And just like he did when he discovered Powder crushed under the weight of his body, he screams until the burly men arrive and yank him out. He screams until they drag him into the hallway, through a corridor of smoke and flickering lights, and carry him downstairs to a room that looks exactly like the one he just left.

And when he finally stops screaming, and when his voice has grown hoarse and his tears have run dry, he sits in the corner, staring at the wall. He might as well still be half-conscious and supine, with flecks of white powder tumbling from his nose and his full weight on top of his beloved pet.

The box lights up. He has no device, so he simply stares at the door as it slowly opens on its own. From his spot on the floor, he peers inside and sees the sole of a foot and then another. Her legs stretch out and she slowly unfolds and slides to the floor. He expected for Yonnie to be holding her nose, with blood dripping from the blow she sustained, but she is intact and uninjured. She squints and whispers, "I told you, Nazar. I told you."

"Who is he?" He can manage no other words. He wants to scream, but he can only sob. "Who is he, if he's not me?"

"He is Nazar."

The walls crowd around him. His heartbeat doubles. A scream rises in his belly and gets trapped in his chest. His hands and feet go numb. His middle is empty. His mind returns to earlier, when he inquired about his freedom and she said "Not quite."

"He is the real Nazar," she continues, "and he signed up for this experiment."

"And I'm...?" He whimpers. He knows his eyes are pleading with her to make his emotional pain go away.

"You are his shame."

He hyperventilates for a few seconds, and she holds her palms forward, gesturing for him to take deep breaths with her until his breath steadies and comes out at a rate in line with hers.

He clears his throat. "And after ten weeks?"

"Once Nazar puts in the final object, he will be free."

And he realizes that the only freedom he'll have after ten weeks will be to leave the room, to roam the halls with Yonnie, to become a blank entity in the building, who never tells his name because the name really doesn't belong to him.

"But shame is a construct, Yonnie." His voice comes out in a desperate plea. "A thing society creates to control people. It's not real."

"But in here we feel real, don't we?"

She crawls across the room and sits beside him. She takes his hand, the one that's been scratched by Powder but immediately healed.

"I have three weeks left." She pulls his hand onto her lap and squeezes it.

He closes his eyes and tries to remember what happened between signing the contract, his orientation, and arriving in the room with The Honor Box. He still has no memory within the gaps among those events, and now he knows why. "Is this what hell is like, Yonnie?"

Yonnie doesn't answer, and when he opens his eyes again, he is alone in the room, and, sitting beside him where Yonnie had been, is the device. Even he doesn't know how many objects will come through over the ten weeks. Maybe he'll receive the basket Nazar's biological mother placed Nazar in when she dropped him at the fire station as a baby. Maybe he will receive the first cigarette Nazar smoked at ten years old. The first glass of whiskey Nazar drank at twelve years old. The 9mm.

The device vibrates, and without even seeing inside the Honor Box, he senses the presence of the gun resting inside, the grooves in its handle, the weight and warmth of it, as it waits for him to open the door. Tears sting his eyes, and his heart races. Seconds later, the device's red light pops on.

***

T amika is a writer, producer, and journalist. She is author of Unshod, Cackling, and Naked (Unnerving Books), which is the 2024 Next Generation Indie Book Awards WINNER for Horror, and which Publishers Weekly calls "powerful," "unsettling," and "terrifying," as well as author of Salamander Justice (Madness Heart Press). She is co-creator of the artist collective POC United and fiction editor for the group's Foreword INDIES Award-winning anthology, Graffiti. Her work has appeared or is forthcoming in several speculative fiction anthologies as well as in Interzone, Prairie Schooner, The New York Times, Penumbric, the Creepy Podcast, and Los Angeles Review of Books, among others. Her long fiction tale, "Bridget Has Disappeared," is in translation at Independent Legions' Italian-language Molotov Magazine. She lives in the San Francisco Bay Area, where she hosts her own newsletter and blog, Tamika Talks Terror. Find her online at tamikathompson.com.

THE ALGORITHM

by Jyl Glenn

Dr. Dennis Sweeney settled into the plush leather of his first-class seat. The gentle hum of the plane's engines thrummed through his body as he stared at a photo of himself, smiling back at him from the cover of the latest issue of the New England Journal of Medicine. As the aircraft climbed through wispy clouds, he couldn't help but smile back at it. He'd done it—the breakthrough that would cement his legacy in the annals of medical history.

The flight attendant approached, her practiced smile a mask that couldn't quite conceal a flicker of recognition in her eyes. "Anything to drink, Dr. Sweeney?"

"Champagne," Dennis replied, his voice smooth with self-assurance. "We're celebrating." He looked over at the heavily-tattooed woman in the seat next to him. "Rona, is champagne okay for you?"

"Oh, yes, please!" She clapped her hands in excitement. Rona Dodson was Dennis' long-term colleague. She had been by his side as his lead programmer for over a decade. Through the years they had also become best friends. They really did make quite the team, and admittedly, quite the cliche. Dennis was exactly what you'd hope to find in the dictionary next to the word doctor. Reserved, professional, well-spoken, intelligent. Rona was the quintessential quirky, tattooed, fun-loving, computer whiz; outgoing and full of ideas.

The flight attendant nodded and retreated, leaving Dennis and Rona alone in their bubble of success. As the champagne arrived, Dennis raised his glass in a toast, the bubbles dancing in the soft cabin light. "To revolutionizing medicine," he said, his voice low and rich with pride as their glasses clinked together.

"You know, Rona," he said, leaning closer, "I couldn't have done this without you. Your programming was... well, it was nothing short of a miracle."

Rona's smile widened, her eyes glinting with an intensity Dennis knew well. "Oh, Dennis," she purred, her voice playful, "you have no idea how right you are." They both laughed.

The plane hit a little turbulence, causing Dennis to spill his champagne. As he dabbed at the stain spreading across his shirt, a flicker of movement caught his eye. On the screen of Rona's laptop, lines of code scrolled by at a dizzying pace.

"What's that?" he asked, "I thought everything was finished."

Rona's fingers danced across the keyboard, her movements fluid and purposeful. "Just some last-minute checks to make sure everything is perfect when we arrive," she murmured.

Ding.

"Please prepare the cabin for landing," crackled through the plane's speakers.

***

They stepped off the plane at Ronald Reagan Washington National Airport, ready to release Aptus in the real world. His presentation to the investors two weeks ago had been a resounding success, and he had finally secured enough funding through a large government grant to launch Aptus in the real world, thanks to Dr. Bryce Nelson and Senator Chad Simmons. Thousands of hospitals applied for the grant to get Aptus for their facility. St. Clare Regional Medical Center in Washington, DC, was the first hospital approved to be included in the Aptus program.

As Dennis and Rona stepped out of the airport and into the crisp autumn air, he felt a mixture of excitement and nervousness. This was it—the moment they'd been working towards for years. *Finally!* He hailed a taxi and gave the driver the address of St. Clare Regional. During the ride, the two friends chatted about how bright the future looked.

When the taxi pulled up to St. Clare, the contrast between the aging brick facade and the cutting-edge technology he was about to introduce struck him. He paid the driver and walked through the sliding doors into the bustling lobby. The hospital zinged with activity, nurses rushing by, worried family members huddled in corners, the squeak of wheelchairs on linoleum floors.

"Dr. Sweeney!" a voice called out. They turned and saw Dr. Emily Reed, the hospital's chief of medicine, striding toward them with an outstretched hand. "Welcome to St. Clare. We're honored to be the first hospital to implement Aptus. The entire staff is eager to get started." She gave Rona a once-over with a curious gaze.

Dennis shook her hand, noticing the way she looked at Rona. "Thank you, Dr. Reed. This is Rona Dodson, my brilliant lead programmer for Aptus. We are excited to be here and get Aptus set in motion."

As they walked through the hospital corridors, Dr. Reed briefed Dennis and Rona on their preparations. "We've set up the Aptus terminals in all departments as you specified. The staff has completed the initial training modules, but I'm sure they'll have questions once we go live."

Dennis nodded, his mind already racing with potential scenarios. They reached a conference room where the hospital's department heads waited for him. As Dennis entered, the room fell silent, all eyes fixed on him.

"Hello, everyone," Dennis began, his voice steady despite his nerves. "Today marks a new era in healthcare. Aptus will revolutionize how we make decisions, allocate resources, and ultimately, save lives."

As Dennis finished his opening remarks, a hand shot up from the back of the room. It belonged to Dr. Marcus Marks, the head of the emergency department.

"Dr. Sweeney, I appreciate the potential of Aptus, but I have concerns," Dr. Marks said, his brow furrowed. "How can we be sure this algorithm won't prioritize cost savings over patient care?"

Dennis had expected this question. He smiled. "An excellent point, Dr. Marks. Aptus will optimize both cost-effectiveness and patient outcomes. It's not about denying care, but about providing the most appropriate care based on a comprehensive analysis of data."

Dr. Reed chimed in, "They've run simulations with Aptus using our historical data. The results show improved patient outcomes alongside significant cost savings."

Another doctor, this time from oncology, raised her hand. "But what about rare cases or unusual presentations? How can an algorithm account for those?"

"Rona, do you want to take this one?" Dennis asked.

Rona nodded, acknowledging the validity of the concern. "Aptus is constantly learning and updating its database. It considers not just common scenarios, but also rare cases and atypical presentations. It's designed to flag any case that falls outside its parameters for human review. We're not replacing medical judgment—we're enhancing it."

The room buzzed with murmurs of both approval and skepticism. Dennis could sense the mix of excitement and apprehension in the air. He knew that the success of Aptus would depend not just on its technical capabilities, but on the trust and buy-in of the medical staff.

"Let me be clear," Dennis continued, his voice firm but reassuring. "Aptus is a tool, not a replacement for your expertise. It's designed to support your decision-making process, not dictate it. We'll be closely monitoring its performance and making adjustments as needed."

The room fell silent as the doctors absorbed his words. Dr. Reed stepped forward. "Thank you, both. I think we're ready to begin the implementation process. Shall we start with a tour of the Aptus terminals?"

Dennis agreed, and the group filed out of the conference room. When everyone had their back turned, Rona shimmied and clapped her hands, making Dennis roll his eyes and chuckle. As they walked through the hospital corridors, Dennis couldn't help but feel a surge of pride. Years of work were finally coming to fruition.

The first stop was the Emergency Department. Dr. Marks, despite his earlier skepticism, seemed eager to see the Aptus terminal in action.

"So, behind the scenes, we've integrated Aptus to work with all your existing software platforms and equipment," Rona explained, gesturing to the sleek touchscreen display on the machine. Simply scan a new device while logged into the patient's records." She held up something resembling a smart watch "And then you place it on the patient's wrist."

Rona placed the bracelet on Dennis. "This bracelet reads the existing records, analyzes the patient's current condition, and will read vital signs, run an ECG and imaging diagnostics, and scan the blood for abnormalities in less time than it takes to perform a single one of those actions the traditional way."

"Patient healthy. No treatment recommended. Estimated cost zero dollars. Probability of success 99.9%," Aptus chirped.

"Impressive, it documents and speaks, but what if..." Dr. Marks trailed off as a commotion erupted at the ER entrance. Paramedics burst through the doors, wheeling in a gurney.

"Male, mid-50s, severe chest pain and shortness of breath," one of the paramedics called out. "Possible heart attack."

Dr. Marks sprang into action without hesitation, but not before giving Dennis a meaningful look. "Let's see how Aptus handles this," he said, his tone a mix of challenge and curiosity.

They applied the Aptus, and the device delivered an answer within seconds. The recommended course of action sounded and lit up the screen.

"ECG reading indicates a significant heart attack. Blood scan indicates significant heart attack. Prepare for immediate angioplasty. Estimated cost: $200,000. Probability of success 85%. Stand by for further analysis," Aptus chirped.

Dr. Marks nodded his approval and raised an eyebrow. "Interesting. It's factoring in cost and probability. But what about..."

Before he could finish, Aptus announced a new alert, "Patient history indicates severe kidney disease. Recommend adjustment. New estimated cost: $285,000. Updated probability of success 81%. Recommend immediate treatment."

Dr. Marks' eyes widened. "It caught that faster than I would have," he admitted grudgingly. "Alright, let's proceed." As the cardiac team rushed the patient to the catheterization lab, Dennis felt elated. Aptus was working exactly as he had envisioned.

Over the next few hours, they toured the rest of the hospital, placing new Aptus devices on all patients and observing it in action across various departments. In pediatrics, it flagged a rare genetic disorder that had been overlooked in initial screenings and chirped out the recommended treatment.

When they were finished, they walked back through the emergency room, and they were flagged down by Dr. Marks. "Can you please come see this? We haven't seen Aptus do this yet."

"Can you tell me exactly what the problem is?" Rona asked as they walked toward the room.

"Yes. It says treatment is not recommended, but the patient appears to be a relatively healthy forty-three-year-old female. She came in with abdominal pain, it's most likely appendicitis. I think Aptus is wrong, it's telling me she has very advanced cancer," he said in a hushed tone.

When they arrived, TREATMENT NOT RECOMMENDED. PROBABILITY OF SUCCESS: ZERO scrolled across the screen.

Rona leaned in, her eyes scanning the data rapidly. "Hmm, interesting," she murmured.

Dennis peered over her shoulder, then turned back to the patient. "Hi, I'm Dr. Sweeney. We're all going to step out for a few minutes and figure this out, we'll be back soon. We'll have your nurse get you something for your pain."

"Thank...you...doctor..." she choked out between sobs.

Dennis ushered the group out into the hallway. He turned to Dr. Marks, keeping his voice low. "What are her exact symptoms?"

Dr. Marks frowned, consulting his notes. "Severe abdominal pain, nausea, low-grade fever. Textbook appendicitis. But Aptus is saying stage four pancreatic cancer with metastasis to the liver and lungs. It doesn't add up. It's recommending palliative care only."

Dennis nodded, his mind racing. "Rona, can you pull up the patient's full history?"

"Yes, she does have a strong family history of cancer. And I can see where she's been here and other hospitals several times over the last year with similar complaints." Her brow furrowed. "There's more," she said, her voice low. "She's had multiple scans and tests over the past year, all inconclusive. But Aptus is correlating data from her various visits and identifying a pattern we couldn't see before."

This was exactly what Aptus was designed for—finding connections humans might miss. But the implications were devastating. Dr. Marks shook his head, disbelief etched on his face. "But she looks fine. How could she have stage four cancer?"

"Sometimes, the body is cruelly deceptive," Dennis murmured. He turned to Dr. Marks. "We can rerun these tests the traditional way to confirm, but I think Aptus might be right."

***

Aptus was right. "Let's go back and talk to her," Dennis said.

"We are so sorry," Dr. Marks began. "This cannot be treated. All of your testing confirmed the initial findings from Aptus. We can offer you two options. We can send you home with medication to keep you comfortable or if you want to make things quicker, we can go that route. The device does have the capability of...shall we say...making things quick and comfortable. It's painless, just like going to sleep."

"I'm sorry, Aptus can do what? You want me to give up that easily?" she asked.

"No! Yes, we did add that option for people who wanted it," Dennis said. "But you're not obligated to use it. It's a very personal choice. And it requires written consent from the patient and two doctors to use the feature."

"The...feature!? Yeah, no thanks. I still can't believe the government made that legal. I'll take my meds and go home and figure it out myself if you can't help me. This is too much. This *thing* is going to take all the 'care' out of healthcare. Screw you all! And screw the government for allowing it!" she yelled as the team left her room.

****

By the end of the day, Dennis was exhausted but confident. As he prepared to leave, Dr. Reed approached him, her face serious.

"Dr. Sweeney, I have to admit, I'm impressed. Aptus has exceeded my expectations today. But I'm concerned about what happens next. Today, Aptus made recommendations that aligned with what we would have done, anyway. What happens when it starts making decisions that go against our instincts or traditional practices?"

Dennis nodded thoughtfully. "That's a valid concern, Dr. Reed. It won't. It's why we've built in safeguards. Aptus will flag any recommendation that significantly deviates from standard practice for human review. But we also have to be open to the possibility that sometimes, Aptus might see patterns or possibilities that we don't. And we saw that today. Not everyone gets a happy message. But Aptus isn't here to replace doctors. Nothing can replace human empathy and touch. It's simply a tool."

"I understand," Dr. Reed replied, "thank you for coming. I really appreciate everything you and Rona have done for us."

****

s Aptus gained traction across the country, Dennis found himself constantly on the move. From bustling urban hospitals to rural clinics, he and Rona oversaw implementations, addressed concerns, and fine-tuned the system based on real-world data.

Aptus was indeed a wild success. Within a year, it had been implemented in over 500 hospitals across the country. The healthcare industry buzzed with excitement about the cost savings and improved outcomes. Dennis was hailed as a visionary, his face gracing the covers of medical journals and business magazines alike.

There was a collective celebration as more data was reported. In the first year, patient outcomes showed significant improvement and healthcare costs decreased by 20%. Success stories graced the covers of magazines and were all over social media.

Dennis sat in his corner office at Sanus BioTechnologies, surrounded by accolades and awards, but he couldn't help but feel a sense of unease. Something was off, but he couldn't quite put his finger on it.

His phone buzzed with a notification. It was an email from Dr. Reed at St. Clare Regional. He grinned as he opened it, expecting another glowing report. Instead, what he read made his blood run cold.

Dr. Sweeney,

I hope this email finds you well. I'm writing to express some concerns that have arisen regarding Aptus. While our overall outcomes and cost savings remain impressive, we've noticed a troubling pattern.

Aptus seems to be consistently recommending against expensive treatments for patients with poorer prognoses, which I understand is the point, but it is also recommending against treatment from lower socioeconomic backgrounds. When we override these decisions, we are seeing positive outcomes that Aptus had predicted were unlikely.

I understand the Aptus algorithm is proprietary, but these patterns raise serious ethical concerns. We need transparency about how these decisions are being made.

I would appreciate your immediate attention to this matter.

Regards,

Dr. Emily Reed

Chief of Medicine, St. Clare Regional Hospital

Dennis felt the blood drain from his face as he read and re-read the email. His mind raced, trying to process the implications of what Dr. Reed was suggesting. This couldn't be right. Aptus was designed to be impartial, to make decisions based solely on medical data and outcomes.

But as he thought back to the algorithm's development, his phone blared, starling him from his thoughts.

Shit, it's Dr. Reed.

"Hello, Dr. Reed, I just saw your email and—"

"Dr. Sweeney, we need you back in Buffalo. There's a situation."

A knot formed in his stomach. "What kind of situation?"

"It's…complicated. I'd rather not discuss it over the phone, but Aptus didn't require patient consent or two physicians to override it to…you know…"

Dennis felt a chill run down his spine. He booked the next flight to Buffalo.

U pon arriving at St. Clare, he found the hospital in a state of uncontained chaos. Dr. Reed ushered him into a private conference room where Dr. Marks from the ER and several other department heads were already gathered, their faces grim.

"What's going on?" Dennis asked, his heart pounding.

Dr. Reed took a deep breath. "We've had a series of… incidents. Patients who were denied treatment based on Aptus' recommendations, against our better judgment. Some of them… didn't make it. Some were… eliminated… without an override."

Dennis felt the room spin. "That's impossible. Aptus is designed to improve outcomes, not—"

"We know what it's designed to do," Dr. Marks cut in, his voice sharp. "But the reality is different. We've been tracking cases where Aptus recommended against treatment. The pattern is undeniable."

Dr. Reed pulled up a series of charts on the screen. "Look at these cases. Patient A: 65-year-old male, very early stages of lung cancer. Aptus recommended palliative care only, citing low probability of success and high treatment costs. We overrode the decision and proceeded with an experimental therapy. The patient is now in remission."

She flipped to the next slide. "Patient B: 35-year-old female, severe heart condition but otherwise healthy. Aptus recommended against a high-risk surgery, citing cost and low success probability. We performed the surgery anyway. She's now recovering and expected to live a normal life span."

Dennis' throat tightened as he scanned the data. Case after case showed Aptus recommending against treatment for patients who then went on to recover when doctors ignored its advice.

"But... but the outcomes..." Dennis stammered.

"The overall outcomes are still positive," Dr. Reed conceded, "but at what cost? We're seeing a clear bias against certain patient demographics, it seems. And those who can afford to seek second opinions or override Aptus' decisions are faring much better."

The room grew smaller, like it would close in and crush him. *This can't be happening.* They had built Aptus to save lives, to make healthcare more efficient and fair. It didn't take the patient's ability to pay into consideration. How had it gone so wrong?

"There's more," Dr. Marks said gravely. He pulled up another set of data on the screen. "We've cross-referenced Aptus' treatment recommendations with financial data. There's a strong correlation between its preferred treatments and the financial interests of Sanus BioTechnologies' major investors and shareholders."

Dennis felt as if he'd been punched in the gut. He remembered the long meetings with investors, the pressure to show returns. Had he unknowingly allowed their interests to seep into Aptus' code? *There's no way. Rona and I oversaw every change. I wish she was here.*

"This... this can't be right," Dennis muttered, his mind racing. "The algorithm was designed to be impartial. It's supposed to prioritize patient outcomes and cost-effectiveness, not... not this."

Dr. Reed's voice was gentle but firm. "We understand you didn't intend for this to happen, Dennis. But the evidence is clear. Aptus is making decisions that are costing lives and perpetuating healthcare inequalities."

Dennis slumped into a chair, his head in his hands.

***

Dennis' world crumbled around him as similar reports flooded in from hospitals across the country. The pattern was undeniable. Aptus was systematically discriminating against certain patient groups and favoring treatments that benefited Sanus BioTechnologies' investors. *But how?*

"Rona, I don't understand. How is this possible? We have to do...something!"

Rona shook her head. "I've been combing through the code, Dennis. It's...fine. The bias isn't a bug. It's not even a bias. But I can see why the override got bypassed and I can fix it."

Dennis felt his stomach lurch. "What are you saying?"

Rona pulled up a complex diagram on her tablet. "Look here."

"Give me that." He took the tablet from Rona. He was not a coder, but he had learned from working with Rona over the years. "These decision trees, these weighted factors—they're all skewed. Patient age, socioeconomic status, estimated lifetime economic contribution, they're all factored in ways we never discussed. But how? We didn't program it this way!" Dennis protested, his voice rising in panic.

"Remember those 'optimization' meetings with the board? The ones where they kept pushing for better efficiency metrics?"

The color drained from his face as the memories came flooding back. Those endless meetings with the board, the pressure to show better "efficiency metrics," the subtle suggestions to prioritize certain outcomes. He had dismissed them at the time as typical investor meddling, but now...

"Oh God," he whispered, his voice barely audible. "What have we done?"

Rona placed a comforting hand on his shoulder. "It's not entirely your fault, Dennis. We were all under pressure to deliver results. But this is the way it is."

Dennis nodded numbly, his mind racing. "We need to shut it down. Immediately. We can't let Aptus make another decision until we've thoroughly audited and corrected the code."

"It's not that simple," Rona said, her voice heavy with resignation. "Aptus is integrated into hundreds of hospitals now. It's making thousands of decisions every hour. We can't just flip a switch and turn it off without causing more chaos."

Dennis felt the weight of responsibility crushing down on him. Lives were at stake—lives that were being valued and discarded by an algorithm he had created. The realization made him physically ill.

"We have to do something," he said, his voice barely above a whisper. "We can't let this continue."

Rona nodded grimly. "We need to be strategic about this. If we go public with what we've found, it could destroy Sanus BioTechnologies. Our investors. Us! Thousands of people could lose their jobs. And who knows what kind of legal repercussions we'd face."

Dennis felt a flicker of anger.

"To hell with the company!" Dennis exploded, slamming his fist on the desk. "People are dying because of us, Rona. Because of me. Because of YOU. I won't let it continue for one more second."

Rona flinched at his outburst but stood her ground. "I understand how you feel, Dennis. But if we don't handle this carefully, the fallout could be catastrophic. We need a plan."

Dennis took a deep breath, trying to calm the storm of emotions raging inside him. She was right, of course. She always was. Acting rashly could make things even worse. But every moment they delayed was another moment Aptus was making life-or-death decisions based on corrupt criteria.

"Okay," he said finally, his voice strained. "What do you suggest?"

Rona pulled up another screen on her tablet. "I've been working on a patch to fix the unauthorized override. It won't fix everything, but it should neutralize the most egregious biases in Aptus' decision-making process. We can push it out as an emergency update."

Dennis nodded, a glimmer of hope emerging. "How long will it take?"

"I can have it ready in a few days. But Dennis," Rona's voice grew serious, "I think you're overreacting."

Dennis shuddered at the thought of facing consequences, it terrified him. His mind raced with visions of lawsuits, criminal charges, his life's work crumbling to dust.

"All right," he said finally, his voice barely above a whisper. "Let's try to fix it."

***

A few days passed and Dennis' phone buzzed incessantly. Messages from hospital administrators, worried doctors, angry patients' families. He ignored them all, knowing that any response would be inadequate.

Hours passed in tense silence, broken only by the clacking of Rona's keyboard and Dennis' agitated footsteps. Finally, Rona looked up, her face drawn with exhaustion.

As if on cue, his phone buzzed again. This time, it was Dr. Reed. Dennis hesitated for a moment before answering.

"Dr. Sweeney," her voice was tense.

Dennis felt his heart rate spike. "What's happened?"

"Another patient died an hour ago. A 28-year-old woman with a treatable condition. Aptus recommended against intervention due to… cost factors. And then it just ended her." Dr. Reed's voice cracked slightly. "Her family is threatening legal action. They're claiming discrimination."

Dennis closed his eyes, feeling the weight of guilt crushing down on him. "I understand. We're working on a fix. Can you hold them off for just a little longer?"

There was a long pause on the other end of the line. "How much longer, Dennis? People are dying."

"A few more hours," he promised, glancing at Rona, who nodded confirmation. "We'll have an emergency patch ready to deploy then."

"Make it fast," Dr. Reed said.

Rona nodded grimly, her fingers flying over the keyboard. "I'm almost there. Just a few more tests to run."

The hours crawled by. Each minute seemed like an eternity. Dennis paced the room, his mind racing with worst-case scenarios. What if the patch didn't work? What if it was too late?

Finally, Rona looked up, her eyes bloodshot from staring at the screen. "It's ready."

Dennis rushed to her side, scanning the code. "Are you sure it will work?"

"As sure as I can be without real-world testing," Rona replied. "But we don't have time for that luxury."

Dennis' phone rang. The caller ID said, "Dr. Nelson, U.S. Surgeon General."

"Dr. Nelson, hello."

"Hello, Dr. Sweeney. What is this nonsense I am hearing about Aptus?"

"Well, sir. It's complicated. We found a small bug in the code, but I can assure you that we won't rest until we've corrected it."

"A bug, you say?" Please elaborate. How much is this costing us?"

"Well, it's not, technically, but it's... gone rogue..."

"Nonsense! You put that patch out and it's the last thing you'll do!"

"I'm sorry... what!?"

"Put Rona on the phone. NOW!"

Dennis handed the phone to Rona. Her eyes widened as she listened to Dr. Nelson's voice on the other end.

"Yes, sir. I understand," Rona said, her voice steady. "I'll take care of it."

There was a long pause as Dr. Nelson spoke again. Rona's eyes darted to Dennis, filled with a mixture of fear and resolve.

"No, sir. I won't," she said, then ended the call.

"What did he say?" Dennis asked, his heart pounding.

Rona took a shaky breath. "He wants us to keep Aptus running as is, and it's my job to make sure it does."

Rona's words hung in the air, heavy with implication. Dennis felt his world tilting on its axis.

"What?" he breathed, barely able to form the word.

"Dr. Nelson knows all about the bias in Aptus. He said it's 'working as intended.' They want to keep it running, Dennis. They're using it to save money and get rid of people who are, shall we say, a burden."

Dennis stumbled back, his legs suddenly weak. "No... that's impossible. We built this to save lives, not..."

"To decide whose life is worth saving," Rona finished. "And that's exactly what it's doing. And that's what we wanted all along."

"We? We who?"

Dennis felt the bile rise in his throat as the full horror of the situation washed over him. His creation, his life's work, had been twisted into something monstrous. And he had been blind to it all along.

"We can't let this continue," he said, his voice hoarse.

Rona's eyes hardened as she stared at Dennis. "You don't understand, do you? This was always the plan. Aptus was never meant to save everyone. It was designed to save those deemed most valuable to society."

Dennis felt the room spin as the implications of her words sank in. "You... you knew about this? From the beginning?"

Rona nodded, her face a mask of cold determination. "I was brought onto the project specifically to implement these... features. The government saw an opportunity to address healthcare costs and population control in one fell swoop."

"But... all those people..." Dennis whispered, his voice breaking.

"Collateral damage," Rona said dismissively. "For the greater good."

Dennis lunged for the computer, desperate to deploy the patch, to undo some small part of the damage they had wrought. But Rona was faster.

"You don't actually think I wrote a patch to fix it, do you?"

Rona's words hit Dennis like a physical blow. He staggered back, his mind reeling. "What... what did you do?"

A cold smile played across Rona's lips. "I strengthened the algorithm. Made it more efficient at identifying 'undesirable' candidates for treatment. The update I just pushed will accelerate the process."

Dennis felt bile rise in his throat. His creation, his life's work, had become a monstrous tool for population control. And he had been blind to it all along.

"You can't do this," he whispered, his voice hoarse. "We have to stop it."

"It's already done," Rona said, her tone matter of fact. "The update is live. Aptus is optimized and working as we speak."

Dennis lunged for the computer, but Rona blocked his path.

"It's too late," Rona said, her voice calm. "The update is already propagating through the system. You can't stop it now."

Dennis ignored her, his eyes scanning lines of code over her shoulder, searching for a way to undo the damage. But with each passing second, he realized the horrifying truth of Rona's words. The update was spreading like a virus, infecting every instance of Aptus across the country.

"Why?" he croaked out, turning to face Rona. "How could you be part of something like this?"

Rona's eyes turned steely and cold, devoid of empathy. "Because it's necessary. The world is overpopulated, resources are strained. This is the most humane way to address the problem."

Dennis felt sick. "Humane? There's nothing humane about letting people die who could be saved!"

"It's for the greater good," Rona insisted. "Think about it, Dennis. With Aptus making these decisions, we're ensuring that resources go to those who can contribute the most to society. It's cold, yes, but it's logical."

Dennis shook his head violently. "No. This isn't what I wanted. I trusted you. We're professionals, best friends! This isn't what Aptus was meant to be."

"But it was, you just didn't know it." Insincere sympathy resonated in her voice.

Dennis' mind raced, desperate for a solution. He stepped left, then dove right, managing to slip past Rona and reach the computer. His fingers flew across the keyboard, frantically trying to halt the update's deployment.

The unmistakable sound of a safety clicked behind him, and he froze.

"Step away from the computer, Dennis," Rona's voice was ice cold. "I won't ask twice."

Dennis raised his hands and turned to face her. The sight of the pistol aimed at his chest sent a chill through his body. Rona's eyes were hard, devoid of any warmth or humanity.

"You don't have to do this," Dennis said, his voice barely above a whisper. "We can still fix this. Make it right."

Rona's laugh was hollow. "Fix it? This is fixing it, Dennis. You're just too blind to see it."

Dennis' mind raced, searching for a way out. He glanced at the door, wondering if he could make a run for it.

As if reading his thoughts, Rona shook her head. "Don't even think about it. It's over, Dennis."

Just then, the door burst open. Two men in dark suits entered, their faces impassive. Dennis felt a flicker of hope—maybe they were here to stop this madness.

But that hope was quickly extinguished as one of the men spoke. "Dr. Sweeney, you'll need to come with us."

Dennis' heart sank. "Who are you?"

The man flashed a badge. "CIA. We're here to ensure the continued operation of Project Aptus."

Dennis felt the last shred of hope drain from his body. He looked from Rona to the agents, realizing the full scope of the conspiracy he had unwittingly become a part of.

"You don't understand," he pleaded. "Aptus is killing people. We have to stop it."

The agent who had spoken exchanged a glance with his partner. "We understand perfectly, Dr. Sweeney. That's why we're here."

As they moved to handcuff him, Dennis caught a glimpse of Rona's satisfied smirk.

"You BITCH. I can't believe this; we've been working together for 12 years. I'll let the world know who's behind all this—"

Rona pistol-whipped him, a smirk playing on her lips. "Who's going to believe you, anyway?"

***

"**D**r. Nelson, can you please explain to us what went wrong with Aptus?"

Dr. Nelson and Rona stood at the podium, surrounded by government officials, shouting journalists, and cameras.

Dr. Nelson cleared his throat and leaned into the microphone. "Thank you all for coming. As you know, I was the first and largest investor in this technology many years ago. The Aptus system developed by Dr. Dennis Sweeney was intended to revolutionize healthcare decision-making and make the world better and healthier. However, we have uncovered serious flaws in the algorithm that led to unintended consequences."

Rona stood silently beside him, her face a mask of somber professionalism.

"Dr. Sweeney, in his misguided attempts to reduce healthcare costs, programmed biases into the system that resulted in discriminatory practices against certain patient demographics," Dr. Nelson continued. "When confronted with evidence of these issues, Dr. Sweeney refused to acknowledge the problem and attempted to cover up his mistakes."

Shouts erupted from the crowd of journalists. Dr. Nelson held up a hand in a gesture to silence the crowd.

"I want to assure the American people that as soon as we discovered these issues, we took immediate action. Dr. Sweeney has been removed from his position and is currently under investigation. Unfortunately, his whereabouts are unknown at this time. We have shut down the Aptus system and are conducting a thorough review of all decisions made using the algorithm."

Rona stepped forward; her voice steady as she addressed the crowd. "As the lead developer who worked closely with Dr. Sweeney for over a decade, I was shocked and appalled to discover the extent of the biases he had built into Aptus. I want to assure everyone that I had no knowledge of these unethical practices and am fully cooperating with the investigation."

The journalists erupted into another frenzy of questions. Dr. Nelson raised his voice to be heard over the din.

"We understand the gravity of this situation and the breach of trust it represents. The government is committed to making this right. We will be establishing an independent review board to examine every case where Aptus was used to make treatment decisions. Any patients who were negatively impacted will receive full compensation and care."

The crowd of reporters erupted again, shouting questions. Dr. Nelson pointed to a journalist in the front row.

"Dr. Nelson, there are reports that the government was aware of Aptus' biases and allowed it to continue operating. How do you respond to these allegations?"

Dr. Nelson's face hardened. "Those reports are categorically false. As soon as we became aware of the issues with Aptus, we took swift action to shut it down. Any suggestion otherwise is a baseless conspiracy theory."

Rona stepped forward again, her voice trembling with what appeared to be emotion. "I can personally attest to the government's swift response. When I discovered Dr. Sweeney's unethical programming and brought it to their attention, they immediately moved to deploy a fix for Aptus and launch a full investigation. Any claims to the contrary are simply false."

The room erupted into chaos again as reporters shouted more questions. Dr. Nelson held up his hands.

"We will be releasing a full report on our findings in the coming weeks. For now, I want to assure the American people that we are doing everything in our power to right this wrong and ensure nothing like this ever happens again. Thank you."

With that, Dr. Nelson and Rona stepped away from the podium, ignoring the continued shouts from the press. As they exited the room, Rona leaned in close to Dr. Nelson.

"That went well," she murmured, her voice low enough that only he could hear. "They bought it! Hook, line, and sinker."

They reached the end of the hallway, where two men in dark suits waited and fell into step beside Dr. Nelson and Rona as they walked briskly down the corridor.

Dr. Nelson gave an almost imperceptible nod. "Indeed. Dennis makes for a convenient scapegoat. Speaking of which, has he been... taken care of?"

Rona's lips curled into a cold smile. "He's been transferred to a secure facility. He won't be causing us any more problems."

"Excellent," Dr. Nelson replied. "And the data from Aptus?"

"Safely stored and analyzed," Rona assured him. "Initial projections show a minimum 20% reduction in healthcare expenditures over the next fiscal year. This is perfect"

Dr. Nelson nodded. "And the... undesirable elements?"

"Declining steadily. Aptus' decisions have led to an additional 7% decrease across undesirable demographics."

"Excellent," Dr. Nelson said. "We'll need to accelerate the timeline. The President wants results before the next election cycle."

Rona's eyes gleamed with cold satisfaction. "Oh, he will have them. I'm ready with the final adjustments to the algorithm. We will see maximum benefits in no time at all."

***

"Rona, my darling, you pulled it off! I can't believe you got that idiot Sweeney to trust you!" President Simmons said, as he handed her a celebratory glass of champagne. "Tell me everything!"

"Well, in a previous update, we uploaded tax information from the IRS to see if the patient could afford treatment. And since nobody reads the fine print, I was able to purchase and integrate the stored DNA information from all of those ancestry DNA companies to determine if a patient, or their immediate family, would potentially have major health problems in the future that would make them too expensive to save now. I can't believe people were ever dumb enough to use those services. Anyway, that was effective in removing a slightly higher number of the undesirable population."

"Yes, 7% is what I was told, but I need more, and fast. I need to win this next election."

"We're up to 15% after my final code update. Your suggestions to integrate court records, voter registration data, and social media data into the algorithm was brilliant! It went live three days ago after the press conference. Our medical system relies so heavily on Aptus now, there is no way this won't be effective. I know it will be everything you wanted, everything we wanted."

President Simmons beamed. "And our dear Dr. Sweeney?"

"Dennis? It wasn't hard. You sent a pretty, tattooed, computer geek with the knowledge to do exactly what he envisioned. I mean, he stood no chance. He never once suspected you sent me to work with him. It was slow going in the beginning. We programmed the algorithms to use clinical symptoms and historical health data to make decisions, just like he wanted. But, I will admit it was effective and allowed us to gain the trust of patients and medical professionals alike. And, well, Simmons." She smirked for a moment and made eye contact with Simmons. "I know it's taken years to realize your vision, but I hope that the position I was promised is still on the table. Plus, you really do owe me for all these *awful* tattoos I had to get to fit the 'edgy computer geek' profile."

The president chuckled. "One of the best financial decisions I ever made, right behind investing in Aptus. Look where it got me just a few years later!" He made a broad sweeping gesture around the Oval office. "Brava, Rona. Well done. If this works, that cabinet position and a very generous bonus is absolutely yours."

She finished her drink. "Thank you, sir." Rona stood to cross the room and shake his hand. Her vision blurred for a split second. She shook her head, took a few more steps, and everything faded to black.

***

Rona's eyes fluttered open. As the world slowly came into focus, she found herself staring at a stark white ceiling. The antiseptic smell and steady beeping of machines told her she was in a hospital room. *What the...*

"Welcome back," a familiar voice said.

Rona turned her head to see Dr. Dennis Sweeney sitting beside her bed, his face grim.

"What... what happened?" Rona croaked, her throat dry.

"You collapsed in the Oval Office," Dennis replied. "You've been out of it for three weeks. They had to put you in a medically induced coma for you to recover."

Rona's mind raced, trying to piece together her fragmented memories. "But... How are you here? You were supposed to be..."

"In a secure facility?" Dennis finished for her.

He leaned forward, his eyes hard.

"Funny how things work out," Dennis said, his voice cold. "While you were unconscious, a lot has changed. Your scheme has been exposed."

Rona tried to sit up but found herself too weak. "What are you talking about?" she demanded, fear creeping into her voice.

Dennis pulled out his phone and held it up for her to see. On the screen was a news article with the headline: "Aptus Scandal Rocks Nation: Government Conspiracy Uncovered."

"It turns out," Dennis continued, "when you passed out an intern found you. They called for help, and you were brought into St. Clare. Aptus discovered you had been poisoned and recommended the coma."

"No. Simmons needs me; he wouldn't poison me!" Her mind drifted back to the glass of champagne. *Had it tasted strange?*

"After your final update, he didn't. He was afraid you'd expose the whole thing."

Her expression froze in horror as it all sank in.

"The truth is out, Rona. Everything. The population control scheme, the deliberate biases in Aptus, the government's involvement, the election tactics. Simmons. Nelson. You. It's all been exposed."

Rona's mind reeled, trying to process this new reality. "But… I don't understand. You were locked away!"

Dennis' lips curled into a humorless smile. "When the scandal broke, a lot of people became very interested in hearing my side of the story. And I was released, under supervision of course, because

I was the only one who could stop Aptus. And lucky for everyone, it's almost completely offline now."

He leaned in closer, his voice low and intense. "The President has resigned in disgrace and will be indicted. Dr. Nelson is facing multiple charges. And you, Rona… you're going to face justice for what you've done."

Rona felt panic rising in her chest. She tried to speak, but her voice came out in a weak murmur, "I can't go to prison. I was… I was… just following orders. I wanted that cabinet position, I earned it!"

He stood up abruptly, pacing the small hospital room. "You know what the worst part is? We could have actually *helped* people. We were the dream team. Best friends! Aptus could have been a force for good, saving lives and improving healthcare for everyone. Instead, you turned it into a weapon."

"I want my nurse. Where is your supervision!?" She reached for the call light and noticed an Aptus bracelet on her arm. Dennis gave her a cold smile. She sneered at Dennis. "Really, Dennis, Aptus is my baby, it's not programmed to hurt people like me. And besides, you said it was all offline now."

"I said it's ALMOST all offline. This is the last one. And my supervision? I've been nothing but a professional. So, my personal CIA agent is too busy flirting with the nurses to pay attention to me." Dennis reached for the console and started typing.

Two. *Beep.*

"So, you're taking it offline?"

One. *Beep.*

"Eventually, I just want to try one more thing, we never did test the master override code."

Nine. *Beep.*

"What?... No! You wouldn't!?" Rona clawed at the bracelet on her arm.

Seven. *Beep.*

"You've disgraced me, my career, my company! Killed... I don't know how many innocent people. This was my life's work. You were my partner, my best friend! Everything is ruined for me, I've got nothing left to lose. I'll never clear my name. I'm going back to prison after this," he said, his voice dripping with venom.

Four. *Beep.*

She yanked on the Aptus bracelet. "Dennis, please," she sobbed. "I'll tell them it was all me. Just don't—"

Six. *Beep.*

"Don't worry, friend. It's just like going to sleep," he said as he pressed the final digit.

Zero. *Beep Beep Beeeeep.*

Dennis slipped out of the room. While the lines on her heart monitor spiked briefly and unfurled, an army of tears marched down the tracks of the lines in his face. As the nurses and the CIA ran toward him, he heard one last sound from her room.

"Override successful," chirped Aptus.

***

Jyl began her lifelong love affair with horror at a very young age. One fateful Saturday, when she was seven, her father fell asleep in his recliner. She assumed control of the TV and watched Poltergeist. A few years later, she convinced her local public librarian to allow her to check out Stephen King's Needful Things. Jyl was born and raised in New York but lives in the South. Fall is her favorite season. She loves everything spooky and macabre, and it is always Halloween in her soul. She is a member of the Horror Writers Association and is an active supporter of the indie horror community. By day, she is an RN and works in healthcare leadership. In her "free" time, she works as a writer, an editor, a publisher, a medical writing coach for fiction authors, and also teaches yoga. Jyl loves to write poetry and stories and keep them in the "Graveyard" folder on her desktop until the right time comes to unleash them. She is the Curator of Chaos. To connect with Jyl on social media, you can find her on Facebook as Jyl Glenn Writes or on Instagram and TikTok as @_delightfully_unhinged_

HELLNET
by Lindsey Goddard

To love and hate where you live is normal, right? To simultaneously dread it and find its familiarity comforting? The smog presses around me like the vice-grip of a warm security blanket. I know where I stand, even if I don't want to be here, with my cardigan scritch-scratching along the brick wall, the atmosphere damp, fat gray clouds overhead bulging with the possibility of a downpour.

I still read the books Grandma kept after the Big Collapse (when most families in my region went bankrupt and started selling everything they owned). As a little girl, I'd sit for hours flipping through the pages of Shakespeare. I know a rose by any other name would smell as sweet. Therefore, a city by any other name would smell as sour. That's what I figure.

I used to call this city a "Hellhole". Back when I was a kid, a teenager who enjoyed saying things like that for the shock value. Now, I don't mind the city, with its grimy gutters and crumbling structures. In fact, I love it, so long as I get to see another day on these streets. Because the real "Hellholes" are in our brains now. In the holes where we installed HeavenNet, a program that was designed to save us all, but only let a virus called HellNet in.

Seems like salvation can't be guaranteed, but I can still hope, can't I? What else have I got now, but hope? The last shreds of it remaining in my heart are a possession more valuable than money these days, and quickly becoming much rarer.

Next to me, a man crouches on all fours. Snot, saliva, and tears leak from his face onto the dirty pavement. His facial hair glistens with moisture, but he doesn't wipe it away. He can't. His muscles are constricted so tightly, I see the bumpy outline of them in his neck, veins bulging in his hands. He's been this way for a few minutes—ever since he doubled over with pain and fell to the ground—but nobody kneels beside him or offers him help.

There are hundreds of us waiting, dozens in pain.

One man is curled up like a fetus at the tail end of the line, muffling his own screams with the crook of his arm. He squeezes his eyes shut, his face pink and sweaty, but instantly, they are open again, wide and unblinking. He looks around but can't see what's in front of him. He is somewhere else. In his own personal Hell.

The line begins to move, but only by a foot or so. Those who are stricken don't keep up. Everyone leaves them behind.

We inch along, and I wish I knew the time. I wonder if the ivy growing up the side of the building is moving at a quicker rate than us. Why is this line so long? Why did they schedule so many Virus Carriers to be seen at the same time?

The message said this would be a simple update, to wipe the virus. It sounded so easy when the notification came through on my IDMS, which stands for Inner Dome Message Server. (Everyone installed with HeavenNet has an IDMS in case HeavenNet Corp needs to get in touch.) I had no idea what I was walking into this morning. No idea I'd be standing in a line that extends outside and wraps two sides of the building.

I shift from one foot to the other, relieving the soreness in my heel. It's hard to stand for long hours in my government-issued rubber shoes. Grandma says shoes like this used to be a fashion statement. They were called Gators or Crocs or something like that. Now, they're the only kind of shoes anyone I know can afford. It's the same with our government-issued gray duds, which Grandma crinkles her nose at and says look like "prison jumpsuits". It's easy for her to make fun of us. She still has dresses and skirts, slacks and blouses. Most of us spent all our savings (and tied up our future earnings) acquiring Heaven-Net.

No one knows if the Heaven from the Holy Books is real. Nobody has ever come up with verifiable proof of an afterlife. But HeavenNet? They make a spot for it, The Surgeons. They upload it into your brain. There are guaranteed results. And when you die? You go to The Cloud, of course.

A blond-headed woman screams, "This isn't right! The line moved while I was affected. I should be farther up!" And it was true. The woman had fallen to her knees, staring into the open air with shell-shocked blue eyes. At what, nobody could see or say. Her lips had trembled, and deep sobs had rolled from her, and she had stayed that way for the better half of an hour as the line trudged forward.

Nobody argues with her as the woman finds the spot she previously occupied—between an elder Hispanic man and a mousy black woman—and integrates herself back into line. This crowd is exhausted and hard to faze, having given everything already, simply to be standing here.

You see, you've got to die twice to make it to The Cloud. That is the key. The First Death rips through your brain like a bullet through a circuit board, leaving the wires frayed and split. That's when The Surgeons go in and do a complete rewiring. It sounds invasive, I know. It sounds like brain surgery. But it's worth it. Or, at least, it was supposed to be worth it. Otherwise, you might never see Heaven.

The software took decades to develop. The average American Joe eagerly observed its progress via news media outlets and Internet reporting sites. We couldn't wait for it to become available to the general public. Couldn't wait to be guaranteed salvation. Nobody anticipated a virus. And all this pain. All this pain I see around me.

Like I said, you've got to die twice to get to the Heaven man made. Why? You'd be better off asking The Scientists than me, but the best I can figure is, Death takes something away from each of us, even when we survive it. It leaves something empty, a void waiting to be filled. The First Death is—well—just a quick death you get revived from. The Second Death transports you to The Cloud.

My First Death cost me a pretty penny. I sold everything I owned. I knew they were doing it on the streets for much cheaper with fentanyl and Narcan, but that method of First Death is illegal. The Surgeons require paperwork to prove your First Death was properly assisted. Sure, people forge false documentation all the time, but The Surgeons won't install HeavenNet in your Death Hole if they find out you died illegally. I didn't see it as worth the risk.

So here I am. No car. No food in my belly. Standing in line with the other penniless fools.

The building's entrance draws into sight as we press on at the speed of a sluggish snail. A tall metal door swings open, admitting one person from the line, and I glimpse the lobby, which doesn't look much better than the sidewalk—grown adults curled up like babies on the floor, beating their heads against walls, tugging at their own faces in agony.

Behind me, the man who'd been crying on the ground has recovered from his mental disconnect. He is standing upright and brushes his clothing off. A skinny couple, hand in hand, ask the man what he saw that made him cry so uncontrollably. I assume he's not going to answer. Nobody has answered yet, not that I've heard. But his stern eyes reach a level of darkness that look ready to overflow, and he does, not in tears—those already came before—but in words that explode from his mouth. Soon, he is blathering, and everyone is listening.

He says, "At first, it was beautiful, what I saw. Life was exactly how it had been before the Big Collapse. Before my wife lef—I mean, before so many families were broken by the strain. But then! Before my eyes! It was ravaged! Destroyed by savagery... taken from me! I saw it and heard it and smelled it and felt it, as the world burned around me. It was. It was..."

"Hell," I finish his sentence, and all their eyes turn to me.

I shrink inside myself, regretting that word which has fallen from the end of my tongue like a dropped ball, rolling through the crowd. My skin flushes under the sudden scrutiny of my fellow line-waiters. I hate attention. Moved in with my grandma just to get away from Mom and Dad and all their invasive curiosities. So, I pull my faded blue cardigan around my state-issued jumpsuit and lower my head, and as the line creeps forward a few inches, me and my utterance of "Hell" fade from the spotlight as we trudge forward.

This is taking forever, like the last trickle of sticky syrup lingering at the end of the spout when there's nothing in the cupboard to eat. I shuffle forward on my aching feet, mentally guessing at the time. I stopped carrying a cell phone once my service was shut off for non-payment, and I've never owned a watch, but my internal clock is screaming, "Let me inside this god damn building before I break the fucking door down!" despite the security guards looming, one on each side of the entrance.

Even still, when the door swings open to swallow me into the building's warm innards at last, I gulp and hesitate. "You're next," a bone-thin security guard says. I step inside.

If the sidewalk outdoors was the Yellow Brick Road, then this must be the Emerald City, and I sure as hell don't want to meet the Wiz. *How did we come to this*, I wonder, as I slide into an open spot next to the door, at the end of a long line that curls around the perimeter of the waiting room. In here, even more people are on their knees, or down on all fours, or curled up like sick babies on the floor, watching their own personal Hell play out in their minds. Or maybe it just seems like more because I'm closed up inside now. There's no turning back, not if I want answers.

By the time I reach the kiosk where a lone receptionist sits at a sliding window she never gets the chance to close, I want to blurt out my name, but she stops me before it leaves my lips. "Cloud

Identification Number please," she says, her gaze never leaving her computer screen.

"Oh... uh." I always forget this number. (Flighty me, I'm used to having a name!) So, I glance down at the tattoo on my wrist. (Yes, we let them tattoo numbers on our wrists. People do a lot of crazy shit to get to Heaven.) "Number 8773," I respond.

"Symptoms or no symptoms," she says without looking at me.

"What?" I ask.

Now, she glares up at me. The lids over her silver-blue eyes look heavy with exhaustion, no doubt brought on by the burden of answering my ignorant question. She sighs. "Have you seen HellNet?"

"No," I answer.

She looks back to her computer, types something, clicks the mouse a few times. "Okay, they can see you down the hallway to your left."

To my left stands a hallway with six or eight rooms branching off of it. A fluorescent light panel in the drop tile ceiling flickers, as if to summon me. I follow the filthy path worn into the grey carpeted floor, visibly darker in the center where a million feet have traveled before. It feels odd, breaking away from the crowd after spending so much time among them. For hours, our mutual dread has collected like toxic rainwater in a gutter, about to overflow, but at least then, I was not alone. I look over my shoulder at the receptionist, seeking assurance that I'm heading the right direction, but eye contact from the receptionist is an unattainable goal, so I give up.

I arrive at the only open door in the hallway and assume that's where to go. I enter the room and see it is painted an ugly beige, like the rest of the building, or perhaps the building's interior was once white, and this color is the result of age. There is a large desk before a larger window, its thick brown curtains drawn tight so that not a speck of daylight shows. The woman behind the desk sports an old-style nurse's cap and a huge fake smile. I can tell it's fake because I notice it falter, notice the plastered-on happiness glitch like a computer graphic.

"Number 8773. Please, have a seat." She gestures to a chair. The carpet around the chair is stained. It looks wet to the touch, a darker gray than the rest of the carpet. I imagine that the wet stain is tears and snot and stomach bile from some pitiful Virus Carrier in the throes of a HellNet breakdown. I imagine the security guards dragging the poor stranger away and moving onto the next person in line. Me.

"I'm The Nurse," the woman says. Just a touch of orange hair is visible beneath her nurse's cap, and I feel like it's the brightest color I've seen in days. "I'm going to explain everything you need to know. There are hundreds of others in need of my assistance today, so I request that you do not interrupt or ask questions." She glances down at the paperwork on her desk and drops the smiley routine. The Nurse is all business now.

I nod. "Okay," I say. I take a deep breath and release it, choking back all the questions I had planned to ask. It took me all morning to get here. I'm not going to fuck this up.

"Since the receptionist sent you to me, that must mean you haven't experienced any symptoms of the virus?" I'm certain The Nurse meant this as a statement, but the way her voice raises in pitch at the end makes it feel like a question. It makes me wonder if other Virus Carriers answered the receptionist the same way as I had, only to prove they had seen HellNet after all once seated before The Nurse. And I picture, yet again, one of my predecessors from the line falling from this very chair, slumping to the carpet in a pitiful heap, and being dragged off by the guards.

"No," I answer. "No symptoms yet." One of her eyelids twitches when I say the word "yet" and now I *know* she's seen a thing or two today.

"Here's the situation, and try to keep up, as I don't like to repeat myself. HeavenNet Corp is under attack by The Church. Recipients of the HeavenNet neurological upload are now susceptible to a virus introduced into the HeavenNet system by hackers who are funded by The Church, created to target behaviors The Church deems as sinful."

She pauses, as if giving me a chance to speak, but I'm unsure of what to say, so I remain silent.

"Are you familiar with the values of The Church?"

I nod.

"Perfect. Then, this next part is very important. Please, tell me: In what way might The Church consider you a sinner? By pinpointing the matter ahead of time, we might be able to prevent the virus from activating in your mind."

The Church? Visions dance through my mind of everything I know about The Church. An age-old lynch mob in long white robes, planning terrorist attacks on the same harmless scapegoats, year after tireless year. It all seems so obvious now. Why hadn't I considered them as the cause?

The Church has been utilizing control tactics such as this for centuries, ever since their Messiah died on the cross over twenty-one-hundred years ago. I'm perfectly aware of their core values, and what they consider a sin, and yet still, I'm not certain what The Nurse wants me to confess. I don't consider myself a sinner. Just gay. And not to split hairs, but I'm barely gay, since I have no sex life at all.

My parents don't know; my co-workers don't know; I don't have any friends, and that's how I like it. I live with my grandmother and keep to myself. There will be no Coming Out party for me. The only person who knows is the girl I once loved. The girl I had to give up before the Big Collapse so that she'd have a better shot at life.

"I don't know," I say, seeing no reason to expose my personal business here and now. "I don't know why The Church would consider me a sinner. I don't know why they would target me."

The Nurse smiles again. It is fake again. "No, dear, you misunderstand." She pauses and considers what to say, eyes angled sideways, as if she won't be having this same conversation for the rest of the day, and probably tomorrow, and the next. Then, she looks at me and says, "It's not that The Church has targeted you. They didn't pinpoint specific individuals to infect with the virus, no." She breathes in deep and sighs. "The easiest way to sum it up, is that *everyone* has been infected. But not everyone will suffer. It's your own thoughts that will activate the HellNet Virus, if those thoughts trigger The Church's Sin Detector."

And there it is. Just like a car wreck you cannot help but examine for body parts. The mere mention of my "sins" causes me to think of them.

Because I *know* what The Church considers a sin. The best moments of my life, that's what. The moments I think about at night, when I can't sleep, when I touch myself under my ratty blanket because my legs are too cold to settle down. I think of the girl I once loved, her eyes as black as midnight, a mop of curly brown hair atop her pear-shaped face. I think of her legs wrapped around me, her breasts against mine, her breath on my neck.

I feel a fluttering sensation in my gut. The ugly beige room disappears, and I am back there, somehow, reliving the warm summer night we spent wrapped in each other's arms. I no longer sit in a metal chair with The Nurse leering at me. I am cuddling in the pull-out Murphy bed of the secluded beach house where My Love and I explored each other, body and mind, just days before I gave up everything for my First Death.

The air is warm and salty, carried on a breeze that slips through the cracked window above the soft mattress where we lay, our gangly limbs intertwined. In the distance, seagulls cry and moan. The ocean slaps the shore in its steady rhythm, trying to force its scent upon me, but I only want to smell My Love. Her skin smells like vanilla lotion, and bonfire smoke still lingers in her hair from the night before. I breath it in, trying to commit her smell to memory, aware that I had just been somewhere else moments before, in the beige room with the fake-smiling nurse. I don't want to go back there. Ever.

I gaze at My Love, drink her in—her olive complexion and sharp nose, the smooth dip of her neck. I love her. I do. I know it to be true. But she can't possibly feel the same. Can she? Not when there is a man out there willing to provide the life I cannot.

"I love you," I almost say. I want to, so badly. But the mattress begins to tremble like it's been pumped full of quarters in a dive motel. The entire bed starts to shake. Not just the bed, the room. The beach house. Everything around us quakes.

She looks at me, panic lighting up her dark eyes. Framed pictures clatter to the floor. A lamp topples off the nightstand. The TV falls and shatters, glass exploding.

"What's happening?" she asks and reaches for me.

Her fingertips graze my arm as I am thrown from the bed onto the floor, which cracks and splinters like a walnut shell around me. I look up and see her reach for me just as the pull-out Murphy bed folds the wrong way and crumples My Love like a piece of lettuce being swallowed by a hungry mouth. She is bent in half, buckled under the pressure of the bed, being drawn down into the void that has opened in the floor. Limbs protrude at odd angles from the crumpled mess of her body, still twitching, as we both begin to fall.

When I was little, I fell from a tree. The sinking sensation was so sudden, it felt like it hollowed my gut. This is like that, but it goes on much longer, and My Love is beside me, falling, too, as her white pajamas flap in the air like flags of surrender around her broken appendages.

I feel the flames approaching. I hear the fire roaring and the whips cracking. The damned are wailing, and the demons are laughing. I know where I'm heading, so I scream and scream.

I land in a pit of fire, and pain consumes every inch of me. All I can see are shadows dancing in the heatwaves of the flames. My Love is crying. She is screaming in torment and begging to be released. It hurts me more than the fire. I squeeze my eyes shut, sobbing deeply. Crying deep wails until I am screaming at the top of my lungs.

Then, I'm sitting in a dirty office chair in the public works building, looking at The Nurse, who regards me with little to no concern. My throat feels raw from all my screaming, and the sound of it still echoes in my ears. Perspiration has dampened my clothes, and I'm shaking.

The Nurse smiles, as if to say, *At least we are on the same page now*. She presses a buzzer on her desk and leans down to speak into the microphone. "Escort, please," she says.

When two guards appear at the door, she says, "HellNet has been activated in Number 8773. Please escort her to the next phase, please."

I do not resist. I do not ask questions. I do not care. I never wanted to lose My Love in the first place, when we parted amicably two years ago. Losing her again, this time so brutally, has sucked the wind from my sails.

And the best part is, I'm certain it will happen again.

***

I've been here for three days, and today is the day I must make a decision. Decide my fate, so to speak. Ninety-six hours is the maximum time granted for in-patient services at the public works building in my region. HellNet cases are piling up, and communities can only house Virus Carriers for so long before they must decide on a solution.

Every brain installed with HeavenNet is a carrier, but only a portion have reached "active" status. You've got to think about something that trips the Sin Detector first. One guy I talked to, he was thinking about the time he convinced his girlfriend to get an abortion, and bam! That's how his HellNet visions started. And once they start, they come on at random, any moment, any time. I've watched My Love die a dozen times now.

I try to feel grateful that at least I have options, even if they are akin to choosing between walking on hot coals or swallowing broken glass. The only saving grace in my shitty situation is that I have options at all. A choice. It's an important thing, to have choices. A thing The Church attempts to steal from us at every turn. But The Scientists and The Surgeons still offer a choice.

So here are my options...

For those who wish to keep the HeavenNet software installed in their Death Holes while The Scientists develop anti-virus programs to eradicate the HellNet software, my local government has decided to offer extended in-patient services. Virus Carriers who are insistent upon keeping HeavenNet installed are now moved to the renovated subfloor, which has been transformed into a holding facility. Residents of this facility are granted a ten-foot by ten-foot living space and three meals a day until a better solution is available.

For those who do not wish to stay, The Surgeons offer a quick and painless removal procedure, which will uninstall the HeavenNet program entirely, along with its accompanying virus. The catch? There are no refunds. So you spent your entire life savings on HeavenNet? Gone. Took out a loan? Too bad. Guess what? You've got to settle your debts because you signed the paperwork from the get-go that says you will.

So, I want to see it. The in-patient housing unit. Before I make my decision. I had to ask five times to get a response when I requested a tour, though. That is, I asked five separate employees on my floor, and even then, they tried to dance around my request. This isn't something they offered in my verbal consultation. When they sent an agent to my room to inform me of my options going forward, not once did they mention a tour of the subfloor to see the living conditions. No, I found the information in the thirty-four page packet of paperwork they handed me. It was right there in black and white: Every potential resident is allowed one tour of the housing unit. If I ever see Grandma again, I'll have to thank her for my love of reading.

So, here I am, on the subfloor, being ushered around by two oafs in security get-up who don't seem very happy about it. They expect me to make a major life decision based on little to no knowledge, I presume.

The subfloor has no windows, and light shines from fluorescent bulbs overhead, emitting a soft buzz. I shuffle along the cement floor, glimpsing inside the open units when I can. But many of the doors are closed. "Full privacy" is listed as one of the perks of the housing unit, and some residents are taking full advantage.

Underneath the heavy scent of cleaning solutions is the odor of human waste, and something else. A smoky aroma, like extinguished fire or burnt meat. It mingles with a cloud of disinfectant sprays, and I wonder if they burnt the next meal, and what the food is like here. By the look of this place, I suspect it is much like prison cuisine—bowls of watery gruel and lumps of stringy mystery meats. But I wouldn't know, really. I've never been to jail.

The two guards move quickly, prodding me on as I attempt to slow their pace, like two parents trying to force a stage-frightened child into the spotlight. What's the hurry? I can't help but wonder. What's the hurry from one shit show to the next?

It's like they don't actually want me to get a look around, don't want me to stop and talk to anybody. Like this whole "tour" is a sham.

Someone hollers at the top of their lungs from across the unit, from inside one of the cramped living quarters. It rips through the air like a blaring siren, echoing all around us. My heart skips a beat, and I place my hand on my chest as if to steady it. The guards begin to run in the direction of the noise, and I am left, looking after them in a dumbfounded daze.

A woman creeps up beside me. Her spindly, liver-spotted hand grips my bicep, gradually clamping down tighter each second, like a blood pressure machine, as she glares into my eyes. "Another Burner. That's where they've gone. To extinguish another Burner."

I have never enjoyed being this close in proximity to anyone, aside from My Love, so I attempt to dislodge my arm from her grip, but she clamps down. "Did they tell you? Did they? That we spontaneously combust once the virus runs its course?" My heart sinks. "Because they didn't tell *me*! That's for God Damn sure! Or I wouldn't have stayed to be their little *test rat*."

The guards are hustling back toward us now, glaring at the woman. She releases me and scurries back into her room. The air smells like burnt meat. I start to gag but swallow it down. In the distance, a man is sobbing.

"Tour's over," spits the bulkier of the two guards, angling his broad nose toward the exit doors.

Two medics burst through the entrance, wheeling a gurney. One of them has orange hair, and I briefly wonder if she's related to The Nurse. I'm becoming too familiar with these faces, too invested in these people.

"What happened?" I ask.

"We don't have the time for this, that's what," spits the other guard in a tone equally as pissy as the first. "They were supposed to stop offering this tour to people. It's a hassle. We're dealing with too much, as is."

"Let's go," the bigger one says.

But the medics are back, zipping through the corridor with a body on the gurney, kicking up a breeze filled with the fetid stench of charred skin and burnt hair that turns my empty stomach. From the gurney, the man moans. Half of his face has melted away into loose pink chunks of raw tissue, and one eyeball stares at me, because it cannot blink. The other eye unleashes a torrent of tears onto his cheek. Smoke rises from his skin, which is mostly black where it still clings to his muscle tissue, but large portions are missing altogether, having melted off onto the floor and the sheets of the gurney.

As they rush him past us and through the doors, his eyes bulging from their sockets seem to say, *Get out while you still can.* And I bet he would say as much, if he could do anything but scream, sob, and moan, his useless tongue flapping around his destroyed lower face like a pink fish plucked from the water.

All the residents have closed their door. The guards adjust their uniforms and clear their throats, as if we haven't just witnessed what we just witnessed.

I kiss it all goodbye. My money. My dreams. This place. And the notion that Heaven can be bought and sold.

I never should have let myself believe such a lie.

***

I'm at the bus station with the others who are leaving. We've been issued new clothing, freshly laundered and starched gray jumpsuits, so we are clean and presentable for our journey into inevitable failure. They fed us breakfast and handed us each a sack lunch, and now, I sit and watch the flurry of gray jumpsuits and brown paper bags as the new releases weave between each other like ants in a colony.

I sit here as hours roll by and try to put my finger on it: what keeps us going. What makes humans wake up and do this, day after day, despite all the cards being stacked against us. *Here we are. Here we are*, the crowd seems to hum. *We simply refuse to give up.* It is a battle cry of the downtrodden and the poor, a cry you can only hear if you are like us, our Death Holes now as empty as our bank accounts. We, who bet all of our chips on the gamble of a lifetime and lost it—eternity, security, faith—in one fell swoop.

134

But fret not, my displaced brethren, for HeavenNet Corp has provided one final gift: A one-way bus ticket to anywhere we choose.

But I cannot choose.

I do not know which way to go.

I was living a lie under Grandma's roof—I know that now—masquerading as something I am not. My HeavenNet files are confidential, but Grandma will know, all the same. Not because the Feds will tell her, but because I will. No more secrets. No more living a lie.

But I wonder...

Am I ready to take the plunge? Am I ready to come completely clean?

Heaven can't be purchased, and Hell isn't waiting. This much I know. If it is, then why did The Church create one? Why didn't they wait for their maker to send me there, if He's got the whole universe at his whim?

Because nobody knows for sure. Nobody is supposed to. That's the whole point of being human. A point we refuse to accept as we scramble to come up with answers, bitter at having been kept in the dark, ever since being born from it.

One thing I do know, is this: The last people I'm going to believe are The Church, who use fear, lies, and terrorist attacks to prove they've got it all figured out.

The Surgeons have removed the virus. The Church won't gain access to my brain again. I am free! Yet I am a creature of seclusion, accustomed to hiding. And so much has changed. I can't muster the courage to go home and face my family, just yet.

So, I sit on a metal bench, watching the other new releases approach the ticket desk and choose a destination. I've been sitting here for hours, my hands folded in my lap, just contemplating. Everything. The man at the ticket desk keeps glancing at me, biting his nails, hovering his hand over the phone, as if he might call for backup: "Number 8773 will *not* make a decision!"

I'm sure if I wait much longer, they'll make one for me.

But that knowledge doesn't seem to make it any easier.

Then, I see her. Eyes as black as midnight, her olive skin, sharp little nose, and curly brown hair atop her pear-shaped face. She saunters into the station like a ghost. Or maybe I just feel like I'm seeing a ghost because I've watched her die in my mind's eye so many times. So many heartbreaking times.

She doesn't approach the ticket kiosk, not even to look over the list of potential destinations, which are listed in printed-off pamphlets, as well as electronic touchscreen monitors at each end of the desk. She finds a bench and sits, keeping her eyes cast down, examining her thumbs as she twiddles them in her lap.

She's the only thumb-twiddler I've ever known, and the gesture is home to me. My real home. The one I've been pondering since arriving at the bus station several hours ago.

I'm up on my feet in seconds. I hurry over to her, slide onto the bench next to her. She doesn't notice that it's me who has joined her, and she stiffens, starts to scoot away.

"Where you headin'?" I ask.

She looks up, and a light returns to her face, like someone has flipped a switch behind her eyes. A slight smile breaks her gloom.

She says, "I don't know. For some reason, I don't want to go home. I've been waiting for nothing else, and now, it sounds... awful."

I think about this, and even though it's been two years since we last spoke, there is an easy silence between that lasts half a minute or so. I say, "To love and hate where you live is normal, I think..."

"Yes," she agrees. "Maybe so."

"If you could start over anywhere, where would it be?"

She smiles, even bigger now. The corners of it reach her cheekbones. "The beach," she says, gazing into my eyes.

As naturally as the sun sets, my smile returns, too, and for the first time in two years, I am beaming from ear to ear.

"Me, too," I say.

"So then... what are we waiting for?"

***

Lindsey Goddard is an author of dark fiction, poetry, and true crime living in Missouri, USA, whose short stories have been published in magazines such as Gamut and Dark Moon Digest, and online in e-zines such as Carnage House. Her work has been performed on popular podcasts like CreepyPod and Chilling Tales For Dark Nights. She is the author of four short story collections, a poetry book, and a novel. Lindsey also runs WeirdWideWeb.org, where she hosts a podcast, paid writing contests, and blogs aimed to entertain fellow weirdos. For more information on her writing, visit: LindseyBethGoddard.com.

END USER

by Alexa Lee

A groan slips from my lips before I even open my eyes. My head throbs, and I long for sleep to claim me again. I can already tell my hangover is killer, and I'm not ready to face it. I barely even drank last night; I had one, maybe two after work, and yet somehow, I feel worse than when I downed an entire bottle of tequila a couple Christmases ago.

My entire body feels heavy. I'm not sure I can even bring myself to open my eyes, and the amount of effort it takes me to swallow is too much. It doesn't help, anyway. My mouth stubbornly refuses to produce enough spit to help the sandpaper that coats my throat.

A loud blaring noise permeates through the door, and I press my hands against my ears. What the fuck is Tilda watching? And why the fuck does she need to have the volume so loud first thing in the damn morning?

"Good morning! I am your host, Bryce Brians, and do we have an exciting show for you today!"

I groan again, the noise louder than last time. It tears at my throat, choking me, and I know there's no way my awful house-mate will be able to hear anything over the presenter's obnoxiously loud voice. Everything about him is obnoxious. I've never met the guy and have no clue what he's actually like, but I'm willing to bet he's an asshole.

Just like Tilda. I've asked her so many times to please, for the love of all that is good in the world, stop watching TV so loud before eight in the morning. I don't care that she's using my account. That's fine. I can put up with it if she just stops waking me up.

It happens at least once a week, and it doesn't matter how many times I remind her or ask her to stop. She just never changes, and I don't think she ever will. I'm pretty sure she thinks she doesn't need to. Just because her parents own our flat, she's convinced she can do whatever she wants, like eat all my food and treat me like crap.

She wasn't that bad before. We lived together during university, and she was completely fine. I mean, sure, she was a bit messy, but who wasn't?

Enthusiastic applause echoes through my room and I roll over, pulling the duvet over my head in a desperate attempt to block out the noise. The movement makes the world spin dizzyingly around me. I squeeze my eyes shut and grit my teeth, pressing my lips together as bile creeps up my throat.

"You are joining us live for our first ever episode of Last Man Standing... or woman!" the host continues, his voice dancing with laughter, as if he's made a hilarious joke rather than introduced the latest in a series of terrible shows that Blockflicks has released this month. "And make sure to tune in every day so you don't miss a single bloody moment!"

With every word that man says, I feel the urge to punch him rise within me. Or Tilda. Hitting her would probably make me feel better too.

She won't watch every day, will she? Surely, the show won't be on at this time every morning. The guy didn't say how long it would be running. This could be my life for the next month. I could be woken up by his infuriating voice every morning until I snap and leave in the middle of the night.

I guess it doesn't really need to be the middle of the night. I could pack up and go during the day whilst Tilda's stationed at the table "working" on her brand, whatever the hell that means, and I doubt she'd even notice. She'd have no clue until she tried to use my Blockflicks account and realised I'd logged her out.

Or maybe I could just log out on the TV later today. She doesn't have her own account, and she refuses to set one up. She'd be stuck, unable to watch any of the awful shows she's obsessed with until she manages to scrounge the login details off one of her other friends. That would be glorious. The apartment would be so quiet.

"And don't forget to wait for your favourites by downloading the app on your computers and smartphones now! Your support could be the difference between life and a brutal death for our fifty contestants," the host says, his voice almost overflowing with excitement. "Oh! And I haven't even told you the best part yet!"

Despite actively not caring about the show, I find myself waiting to hear what he's about to say. As much as I hate to admit it, the guy isn't bad. He's annoying, sure, but somehow, he's hooked me in. I doubt I'll go out of my way to watch it, but if I have another night shift and Tilda's got it on when I get back, I might stick around for a bit. Maybe catch an episode or two. That'll probably happen. She's spent more time than ever on the sofa since Blockflicks started putting out live shows a couple of months ago. They've never done it before, and it only took me a couple of episodes to work out why.

They have no clue what they're doing. The show Tilda forced me to watch with her a couple of weeks back was an absolute mess, and it was so unbelievable. I mean, they just made people get married to complete strangers and then locked them in a room together for a month with cameras and no way out. It was a weird mix of boring and yet weirdly fascinating.

The host hasn't said what the best part is, I realise as anger flares within me. The only sound reaching through my door is the faint rustle of leaves and birdsong. They must have turned the volume all the way up intentionally to heighten the tension, and it's working. I wish I could shake the man and tell him to hurry up and finish what he was saying. "For those of you with a premium subscription, we have a special, exclusive perk…" he continues finally, and I feel a spark of excitement flicker in my heart. "Keep an eye out for this symbol."

My eyes open, and I lower my duvet. I can't help it. I want to know what the symbol is. I pay far too much for the premium subscription each month, and I keep meaning to cancel it, but somehow, I forget every time.

Immediately, it's clear I am in no state to get up. My room is far too bright, and the light seems to form daggers, plunging through my eyeballs and into my brain. Agony radiates through me, stealing the breath from my lungs, and all I can do is cling to my duvet as tears trickle down the sides of my face.

"When you see it, all you need to do is click. You can use your mouse, the remote, or, if you're using a touch screen, just your finger, and then, you'll get to choose how you want to be part of the action," the host says, and it takes far too much effort to understand him as pain continues to burn in my head. "All of our contestants have had special, state-of-the-art devices implanted, meaning you can watch the moment of their death through their eyes!"

I can't help but shudder at that. Maybe I won't watch the show after all. I know it won't be real, but why would anyone want to watch someone die? Even the thought of watching a fake death sends a shudder through me.

"Or," the host continues, his voice taking on a devious quality, "you might want to watch it from the murderer's point of view. It's entirely up to you for the ultimate immersive experience!"

Canned applause explodes from the speakers, and disgust fills me. Finally, I force myself to sit up. I don't want to listen to this shit anymore. I need to tell Tilda to turn it down or grab headphones or something, but I can't move. Everything swirls around me, and I'm vaguely aware that I'm swaying back and forth, but I can't make it stop.

Squeezing my eyes shut, I suck in a tight breath through my nose, counting slowly as I wait for the nausea to subside. It happens slowly, gradually, and after a few seconds, I try to open my eyes again.

Luckily, the pain behind my eyes is slightly less vicious this time. They barely water, and I can actually keep them open for long enough to reach for my phone, wanting to check the time.

It's not there, though. I always keep my phone on my bedside table, but there's nothing there. There's just an empty space where it should be. Did I knock it off in my sleep or something?

I grip my duvet tightly as I lean over the edge of the bed, worried that I'll go crashing onto the floor, but the floor is clear. Slowly, I straighten up, looking around.

A strange feeling is building in the pit of my stomach, and the hairs on my arms begin to stand on end. My floor is completely clean; there's not a single thing on it, and that's wrong. It's never that empty. There's always at least a couple of pieces of clothing scattered across it.

Did Tilda come into my room whilst I was passed out? She does have a habit of just barging in, but it doesn't seem like something she'd do. She'd never pick the dirty clothes off the floor. She doesn't even do that with her own room. It's beneath her, apparently.

I didn't do it, though. I'm certain of that. I've done some stupid things before whilst drunk, but I don't think I've ever tidied up. And where the fuck is my phone? Did I leave it somewhere?

My gaze scans my room slowly, and I feel my chest slowly tighten. My heart thumps, the pace far quicker than it should be. Something is wrong. I don't quite know what it is, but everything just looks a little... off. Even the walls look weird. It's like they're the wrong shade of blue, a little darker, more muted, than they should be.

"Hey, Siri," I blurt out, hoping my phone will recognise my voice from wherever I left it, and it'll light up or make a sound or something. "Turn on the tor—"

"And now," the announcer says suddenly, making me jolt, "let's meet our contestants!"

The world turns white immediately. I cry out, lifting a hand to shield my eyes from the blinding brightness that reignites my headache. It seems to pulse in time with my heart, each too-fast beat driving an icepick deeper and deeper into my brain.

But I can't just sit there and wait for my vision to clear. I have no idea what's going on, and fear forces me to blink, fighting to bring my surroundings back into focus.

What the fuck is going on?

That's my first thought, but "Where the fuck am I?" quickly follows it. I'm in bed still, but this sure as shit isn't my bedroom. It's not even my bed. The duvet cover is the same one I used to have, but I lost it like six months ago. Someone stole my laundry from the machine when I went upstairs to grab a drink.

Wind whistles through the trees, and my head snaps up as my breathing grows faster. Sharp gasps escape my lips, and I try desperately to suck in more of the fresh forest air that surrounds me.

I'm in a forest. The thought causes a desperate giggle to claw at my throat, and I try not to let it escape, but it's futile. I'm alone in a forest, and I don't know how I got here or how I was in my room just seconds ago.

This isn't the UK. I'm not in England anymore, and I don't know how I know that, but I'm certain. There's something about the tree trunks that look off. They're too thin, too light. I've never seen anything like them back home.

I suck in as much air as possible as another terrified giggle builds within me, causing tears to burn behind my eyes. What's going on?

I was at home before! This must just be a nightmare, a bad dream or something.

My nails find my forearm and dig in. It's just a bad dream. Soon, I'll wake up back in my bed with Tilda watching TV far too loud, just like she always does, and it'll be fine. I'll be fine.

A soft whimper slips from my lips as wetness forms under my nails. I stare down at the red dots on my arm, trying to understand what I'm seeing. There's pain. I can feel it. It's dull, muted, but definitely there.

Did someone slip something into my drink? Is that how I got here? A chill slips down my spine, sending a shiver through me. I don't remember it. I don't remember getting home last night. The last thing I can recall is being in the bar with Sabrina after work. It was getting late. We left, and I was going to order an Uber, but then...

That's it. That's the last thing I remember. I don't know what happened after that. I don't know if someone grabbed me, or—

My mind stutters to a halt, and my breath catches in my chest as a new fear pulls at me. My gaze becomes fixed on the tree on the far side of the small clearing my bed's in. I'm almost too scared to look down, but I need to. I have to know.

Slowly, painfully, I drag my eyes away, glancing at my shirt. Relief slams into me so violently that I sag back against the headboard and push the duvet back a little. I'm wearing the same clothes I changed into after work. Thank fuck. No one stripped me or did anything to me whilst I was unconscious apart from bringing me here, wherever here is.

I take as deep a breath as I can and look around again as questions ricochet around my mind. Where am I, who brought me here, and what was that noise? The guy talking? I don't see a TV, and I'm in the middle of the woods. There's probably no radio or phone service, so where did his voice come from?

Rustling comes from in front of me, and my head snaps up, the movement sending a faint twinge of dizziness through me, but I barely notice it as I stare at the thing moving towards me.

I've never seen anything like it before. It looks like a cross between a mechanical spider and a… tank. But, instead of a turret or a gun or whatever the fuck they normally have, there's a glass dome with a guy sitting inside, holding a camera.

And pointing it directly at me.

I don't move. I can't. I feel frozen to the spot, barely able to breathe, as the spindly metal legs bring the camera closer to the end of my bed. Once there, it stops and seems to lean towards me until it's less than a metre away.

What do I do? I feel like I should say something, but my mouth isn't working. I try to move my lips, but no sound escapes; nothing comes out. My eyes burn, and I fight to keep them open, terrified of what will happen if I stop looking at the machine for even the millisecond it will take to blink. But I can't resist it forever. Tears start to well in my eyes, forcing me to blink, and I hold my breath.

The spider thing hasn't moved. It doesn't come any closer, and the cameraman's eyes stay fixed on the screen on the back of the camera. It seems almost like they're waiting for something.

"Last night," a familiar voice, the host, says, his voice seeming to come at me from all angles, "fifty lucky contestants were dropped on a private island, which has been abandoned for years. Until now."

It's not coming from the machine. I don't see any speakers on the thing, but then where are they? Could they be built into the headboard? Or hidden among the trees?

I don't know why it matters to me so much or why I want to know, but I find my eyes darting between the camera and the bed frame. There's nothing there, though. I can't see anything, and that realisation causes a bubble of panic to burst within me.

Speakers aren't expensive. Not really, anyway. But good ones are. Especially the small ones. If they could afford enough for me to be able to hear that guy's voice so clearly... whoever brought me here must be loaded. The high-tech camera thing in front of me should have given that away, but I've only just realised.

My hands tremble as I hug my knees to my chest, pressing myself against the headboard in an attempt to get away, but I have nowhere to go. I should run. I know I should, but my body won't move.

"Blockflicks have hidden weapons all around the island. Knives, axes, crossbows, throwing stars and even more! But that's not all," the man says, pausing for dramatic effect before adding, "There's also food and medical supplies, so if one of our contestants gets attacked and manages to escape, they might be able to nurse themselves back to health, if they have the right help..."

My eyebrows pull together as the horrifying truth finally dawns on me. I'm in a weird place, somewhere I've never been before. There's someone filming me, and I can hear the host, so...

Something is not right. There's been a mix-up. Someone must have gotten the wrong person and thought I signed up for this show, but I didn't. I just need to explain, and they'll let me go.

"Hey," I try to shout to the cameraman, but the word comes out weak and croaky. I swallow, forcing down the lump of fear in my throat, and try again. "Hey! This is a mistake. I'm not meant to be here!"

The cameraman's expression does not change. He doesn't say anything or even look up from the screen. Silence stretches over us as I stare at him, waiting for a reaction. The woods are quiet. For a moment, the only sound is the soft rush of wind and the ceaseless cheeping of birds coming from high above me.

"And the lucky winner, our Last Man Standing, will not only receive a full pardon for their actions whilst on the island, but they'll also receive one... million... dollars!" the host cries.

Canned applause explodes from the speakers again, and my heart seems to flutter. One million dollars is a lot of money. It's a life-changing amount. If I had that, I wouldn't have to live with Tilda anymore. I could buy my own place, and I'd never need to put up with her shit ever again.

And I could quit my job. Maybe I'd finally go back to university and study something I actually care about. I've always wanted to do that, but it's just never the right time, and I couldn't afford it before, but with one million dollars...

I'd have to kill someone, though. More than one person, probably. That's what the host said, isn't it? There are weapons, and only one person can win. I've watched enough television to know what that means, and I don't think I can do it. I'm not sure that I actually have that... whatever it is I need to end a person's life. Sure, I've fantasised about it before, but who hadn't? Daydreaming about slashing your boss' throat with the industrial guillotine doesn't mean you actually want to do it. It's different.

But it won't be real. If I'm actually in a reality show that Block-flicks is producing, they won't actually let people die. There's no way. I mean, people joke about it being an evil corporation, run by the closest the world will ever get to a supervillain, all the time, but they don't actually mean it. Plus, no one would really want to watch that, would they?

A shiver slips down my spine. Maybe they would. People watch some fucked up shit. I can't risk it. I'm not willing to find out, not when I could just talk to the cameraman and go home. Then, if I really want to know that much, I can just watch the show and find out.

Maybe, if they're not actually killing people off, I could sign up next year and try to win the prize money then.

I swallow, pushing myself away from the headboard and staring at the man in the glass dome. My eyes find his polo shirt, focusing on the logo on his chest. Half of it's blocked by the machinery he's controlling, but I don't need to see the whole thing to know what it is.

Blockflicks.

"Hey!" I shout, my voice coming out stronger this time as I fall forward onto my knees, my body uncoordinated and clumsy. "I didn't sign up for this! I don't know why I've been brought here!"

Still, he doesn't move. The lens moves a little closer, and I stare at my reflection in the glass. I barely recognise my desperate expression or bloodshot eyes, but my fear is clear. It's impossible to miss, but the guy doesn't give a shit.

He's not going to help me. He's just going to sit there and film me rather than actually helping me get out of here. I need to do something else. There has to be a way for me to get through to him.

My hand curls into a fist at my side, and I look down, focusing on the glass. It's thick, too thick for me to be able to break through without a rock or something, but I can't see any around my bed, and surely he'll just run the moment I pick one up.

I take a deep breath to steady myself before slamming my palms into the glass.

"Please!" I shout. "Help me—"

Pain rips through me. The air rushes from my lungs, and white spots explode in my vision, blocking out the man's startled expression. I'm vaguely aware of my body moving backwards, falling through the air, but agony consumes my mind, making it impossible to think of anything else. My spine arches excruciatingly as electricity dances beneath my skin, setting my nerves alight, and all I can do is wait, praying that death takes me quickly.

Slowly, the pain recedes. I don't move. I'm terrified to in case the pain returns, but I have to. I scramble back, my chest burning and my vision hazy, staring at the machine.

"Ah, that was a mistake, wasn't it?" a voice whispers directly into my ear. "Blockflicks are a little possessive of their property, so consider yourself warned. They probably won't go as easy on you a second time."

My head whips back and forth as I search for the source of the voice. It sounds like someone is standing behind me, but I peer over the headboard, seeing no one.

"Who's there?" I demand, my tone more high-pitched than I intended.

It hurts to speak. My chest still burns from whatever just happened to me, and I pant, trying to ease the ache.

An exasperated sigh sounds, and I look around again, trying to pinpoint the source, but there's nothing. I reach towards my ear, feeling for a headset or earphone or something. I can't feel one in my ear, but maybe it just fits really well. Blockflicks is one of the richest companies in the world. They can probably afford custom ones for all the contestants, so maybe I've just not noticed it yet?

It was a desperate thought, and I knew that, but I was hopeful nonetheless. There's nothing in either of my ears. Am I going crazy? Is this a hallucination? I've never had one before. I don't know what to expect or how to tell.

"Did you sleep through my introduction?" the disembodied voice asks. "I am Bryce Brians, the host of Blockflicks' hit new show, Last Man Standing."

"Please," I say, the word tumbling from my lips. "You have to help me. Someone's made a mistake! I didn't sign up for this. I need to get out of here!"

The man tuts, the noise strangely disappointed.

"Ah, unfortunately, you can't leave. You're on a remote island in the Pacific Ocean and attempting to escape would be in breach of your contract, resulting in immediate termination."

My mouth drops open.

"Contract? I don't have a contract! I just woke up here!"

The laughter that follows is low and melodic. It's filled with mirth, and any other time, the sound would make me want to join in, but today, I'm just scared.

"Oh, Nadine. I like you. You do make me laugh," he chuckles before his voice turns slightly more sombre. "You have a Blockflicks subscription, don't you?"

I hesitate before answering him.

"Yes. Why?"

"Well, I assume that question means you didn't bother to read the terms and conditions when you signed up?"

My heart thumps painfully, and I'm almost scared to say anything.

"No. But no one does."

Bryce sighs heavily again.

"Ah, and that's what Blockflicks was banking on during their last amendment. Would you like me to tell you what you missed?"

"I... yes."

The man clears his throat loudly, the harsh, grating sound making me flinch.

"Well, there are a lot of unnecessary details, but the most important part is probably... 'by accepting these terms, you agree to enter Blockflicks' recruitment pool for any future production, waiving your right to withdraw or to request legal representation,'" Bryce reads quickly, barely giving me a chance to work out what he's saying. "So, unfortunately, Nadine... I think you'll find you did sign up for this."

I can't breathe. My heart pounds in my ears, and the world begins to fade away.

"What?" I hear myself say. "This can't be legal. Surely, you can't expect me to fight to the death just because I didn't reach the fine print?"

Bryce chuckles again.

"Well, you don't need to fight, of course," he tells me. "You're welcome to just stay there and wait for someone to find you, but I'll warn you now. Most other contestants don't seem to have the same reservations that you do."

My eyes dart to the trees around me, searching for signs of the other contestants. He said there were fifty before, but I can't see any. Where are they? How big is the island, and how long will it take for someone to hunt me down?

Or are they standing right in front of me? Is everything I see an illusion, like my room was when I first woke up? Maybe this whole thing is fake. I could be in a room somewhere with a headset on, completely safe and in no danger at all.

I lift a hand to my face, waving it in front of my eyes and praying that my fingers will bump into something, but they touch my face. The skin feels warm, unnaturally so, and even the gentle touch stings the area under my eyes.

"Ah, don't touch there," Bryce warns, his tone chiding, as if speaking to a child whose hand has strayed too close to a hot object. "Your eyes are still healing from the implants. If you're not careful, they'll get infected, and then you'll be at even more of a disadvantage. You know, some of the other contestants have already found their first weapons."

Nausea bubbles in my stomach, and I can't help but touch my face again, feeling a thin incision under each eye.

"What?" is all I can say.

"I know. It's fantastic! The producers were worried they'd hidden them too well this time, and you'd all just be beating each other to death with your bare hands. After a while, it's just boring to watch that," he sighs. "I mean, you should have seen some of the pilot seasons we shot during the research phase. I could barely make it through a single episode. It was hard to feign any kind of excitement, but this... this is going to be a great season."

Ice slips down my spine as goosebumps erupt on my arms.

"Pilot seasons?" I breathe. "How many times have you done this?"

"Mmmm, honestly? I've lost count, and I wasn't brought in at the beginning, so it's hard to know. Did you know they truly thought they didn't need a host or presenter at first? Luckily, the focus groups showed them otherwise," Bryce says, his tone smug. "And once I was brought in, the ratings were so much higher. Then, it was just a matter of narrowing down the details."

How many people? How many people died before they decided they had everything they needed for this season? I hope none, but I'm just not sure. I've not heard anything about it, though. No mention of Blockflicks abducting and murdering people. Surely, that kind of thing would get out, wouldn't it? Someone would talk.

Bryce would say something. I don't believe he'd be able to keep it to himself. He seems to love the sound of his own voice, and maybe I can use that. If I ask him questions, get him to keep talking, he might tell me something I can use to survive this place.

"What kind of details?"

"Everything," he laughs. "Things like how many contestants to include. One hundred was too many, but then twenty is too few. You need the right amount to ensure people don't get bored and still get invested in the characters and feel like they need to watch. And obviously, the personalities need to be a good match. We worked hard to ensure every viewer has someone they're rooting for. You know, you were one of my first suggestions for this season.'

My heart seems to stop beating, and I don't know how to respond to that. My thoughts trip over each other as I struggle to find the right words, any words.

I should ask why. I know that. If I asked him what it was about me that drew him to me, it might keep him talking, but I don't know if I want to hear his answer. There's something about him that terrifies me.

"Really?"

It's not a good response, but it's enough.

"Indeed! One of the execs actually wanted to include you in the last test run, but I fought to wait until now. I've always felt like the audience will really root for you," he tells me, his tone worryingly passionate. "And then once we'd specified the number of contestants, most other things fell into place! I mean, we always knew where the game would take place, but it was actually the weapon selection that took the longest time to perfect."

Weapons. My mind seems to stick on the word, barely hearing the rest of what he says. The other contestants have weapons. He's mentioned them before; I know he has, but somehow, it only just hits me.

I don't want to do it. I don't want to use a weapon or hurt people, but if it's the only way I can defend myself, I'll do it. And that means I have to move. There's nothing around me, nothing obviously out of place, but there has to be something close. Surely, they wouldn't just leave me out here unprotected.

Slowly, I begin to clamber out of bed. My legs fold the moment I try to stand, refusing to hold my weight, and I slam into the twig-covered forest floor.

The camera machine moves quickly, the steps somehow silent as it darts around the end of the bed to capture my fall. The urge to push it away flares within me, but fear holds me back. It shocked me the last time I touched it, and I can't let that happen again. Someone could leap out of the underbrush whilst I'm unable to fight back. I'd be dead before I have the chance to even react.

"Oh, that looked sore!" Bryce cries, his tone filled with fake sympathy. "You've been asleep for a few days, so your legs might still be waking up. Are you okay?"

Days. I've been asleep for days? It doesn't feel like I have, but how else did they have time to bring me all the way out here, to the middle of the pacific ocean or wherever the fuck Bryce said I am, and do whatever they've done to my eyes?

I suck in a shaky breath, trying not to cry from the pain in my palms and knees.

"I'm fine," I say. I need him to keep talking. He's not told me anything I can use. "Why wasn't it easy?"

"Huh? Oh, the weapons. Well, we discovered quite early on that people don't want the deaths to be too detached. A gun is effective, but where's the satisfaction in that? People don't get to see the death up close. They don't get to revel in the fight, wondering who will win. It's no fun at all." He heaves a long-suffering sigh before chuckling. "Ah, but I'm blabbering on. I have other contestants to check in with, and I should leave you to explore."

"Wait!" I cry before slapping a hand over my mouth.

Warm blood splatters against my lips, and a metallic tang fills my nose, but I don't dare move. I didn't expect that to be so loud, and I press myself against the hard bedframe as my eyes dart from side to side.

The bed and cameraman were obvious enough. If anyone saw them, they'd know exactly where I am, but my shout seems to travel through the trees, echoing in the vast forest and advertising my exact location.

"Please," I beg softly.

I don't know what I'm asking him for, whether I'm pleading with him to get me out of her or just stay with me, but it doesn't matter. I want both. The thought of being alone with just the cameraman's uncaring presence sends terror through me.

Bryce laughs, the sound warm and delighted.

"I truly wish I could stay and chat, but just like you, I'm bound by contractual obligations," he tells me, pausing before adding, "I'm really not meant to have favourites, Nadine, but I really hope you make it. Ah... but you might want to run."

The hairs on the back of my neck slowly stand on end, and I bring one of my legs under me, preparing to run if needed.

"Why?" I ask, the question little more than a breath.

No response comes. Bryce is gone.

I inhale, trying to take in as much air as possible before pushing myself up. My knees wobble as I begin to stand, but I stay low, trying to stay hidden behind the bed as I look around. There must be something nearby, another contestant or something, but I can't see anything. Something feels wrong, though. Maybe it's just paranoia, but I swear, something seems off.

The forest has fallen silent. The birds have stopped singing, and even the wind is no longer blowing. The only sounds are my frantic breathing and the soft mechanical whirl of the camera slowly zooming in on her face.

A twig snaps somewhere to my left, and I fling myself in the opposite direction, breaking into a sprint immediately.

"Fuck," someone growls, the sound coming from far too close to me.

My fear turns into a dagger in my heart, spurring me on as I stumble, my legs trembling from the exertion. I can't let myself slow down, though. Crashing is coming from right behind me, and I don't risk glancing back at the person who sounded more animal than human. I don't want to see them. I can't. If I take my eyes off the trees in front of me, I'll fall.

My vision blurs as I dart between trees, my feet sinking into the spongey dirt floor, and the wind catches on the wet blood on my face. I'm being too loud. The whole island can probably hear me, but I don't care. I just need to get away. I'm not fit enough, though. I've barely started running, and a stitch is already burning in my side. Every breath hurts and sweat drips down my face.

A shrill scream comes from somewhere in front of me, the noise so sudden and filled with terror that I stumble. My hand shoots out, catching the nearest tree to stop myself from crashing to the ground. Pain explodes in my palm as the rough bark shreds my already torn skin, but I force myself to start moving again as a shriek fills the air.

"Please!" a young voice begs, the word gurgling and wet-sounding. "Stop! Leave me alone!"

Tears stream down my face as I run, wishing I could help the woman crying nearby, but I know I can't. If I stop, if I even just try to help her, I'll be damning us both. The person chasing me seems too vicious, too committed to catching me, and I'm not sure I'd be able to help the girl fight off her attacker, much less mine too. Especially not if they're armed.

I need a weapon. A knife or something. That might give me a chance. It could scare off the person behind me, and then I'll go back for the girl. If she's still alive, I'll fight off the person who attacked her and make sure she's okay.

Branches whip against my face and arms, leaving stinging open scratches as I continue to run, my eyes scanning the forest. Where would they put the weapons? Would they just be lying out in the open? Or would they be in a box or case of some kind?

A flash of something to one side catches my eye, and I do a double-take, my gaze finding the machine racing silently through the trees nearby. It's filming me, recording the chase, but the camera isn't fixed on me. It's on the person behind me, and they seem to be falling behind.

Maybe I can get away.

My foot lands on something that splinters and gives way, and I'm falling before I even realise. Pain explodes in my foot, and shards of something catch on my ankle, raking along it as I crash into the ground. The impact makes my body jolt, and the air rushes out of me.

I try to get up, but the moment I try to put any weight on my foot, I crumple, my vision turning hazy. Can't get up. I can't get up. The person is still behind me, though. They're getting closer, and I can't stand. Need to crawl.

Holding my foot off the ground awkwardly, I start to crawl. A choked sob escapes my lips as I try desperately to get away, but it's too late. They're so close to me, and there's no way I can get away from them. I need to fight.

My eyes, blurry and unable to focus, land on a long white stick in front of me. Red goo clings to it, glistening dully in the light, and I hurry towards it, a hand reaching out.

The smell that slams into me turns my stomach, and I gag. Bile burns the back of my throat as I stare at the bone just centimetres from my fingers. Decaying flesh clings to it, and large chunks seem to have been ripped away by something.

I don't want to touch it, but there's nothing else. It's the only thing I could use as a weapon, and I lunge forward, my hand closing around the slightly sticky object. A squelching noise sounds as I pull it back and turn around, ready to face whoever has been hunting me down, and—

"Peter?" I gasp, unable to help myself, as I stare up at the man.

His face is red, and barely healed scars line his bloodstained eyes, but I recognise him. We've worked together for years, and I have no idea what he's doing here, but I'm so relieved to see him. He's always kind to me at work, grabbing countless coffees for us from the machine whenever we're working together. He does that with everyone, and we all love him for it.

"Hello, Nadine," he says, his voice colder than I've ever heard it. It barely even sounds like him. "Fancy seeing you here."

My grip tightens around my makeshift weapon, and I hesitate, unsure how to react. The way he spoke scared me, but it's nothing compared to the predatory smile on his face.

I've seen it before. Not from him, but from other guys. It's the smile they do when they know they've won and you're utterly at their mercy.

"Are you okay?" I ask.

He laughs, spreading his arms wide and looking around the clearing we're in. It's barely a clearing. More like a small gap in the trees.

"Why wouldn't I be? I mean, sure, it was a surprise to wake up here, but it's kind of a dream come true," he confesses.

Out of the corner of my eye, I see the camera move closer. Another creeps through the trees behind Peter, but I don't look at either. I'm too scared to look away from the man in front of me.

"What?"

He cocks his head to the side, a smile pulling at his lips.

"Being dropped out here in the wilderness, free to do as we please?" he clarifies. "It's wonderful."

I edge backwards, the bone still clutched in my hand.

"This isn't wonderful, Peter. People are dying. Did you not hear that girl—"

"People die every day," he interrupts, his tone so unbothered that a shudder goes through me. "But here, we get to choose. We're the ones who decide who deserves to live."

The almost fanatic expression on his face makes my heart race with terror, and I try to scramble away from him as he walks towards me, but my back slams into something.

I can barely breathe as I lean back against the tree, my gaze fixed on the slowly growing smile on Peter's face as he moves closer. His steps are careful and deliberate, and the movement is strangely hypnotic.

"It shouldn't be down to us," I pant, trying to appeal to his rational side. "The people here could be innocent. They don't deserve to die!"

Peter chuckles.

"No one is truly innocent, Nadine. Not even you."

My chest tightens, and I stare up at him blankly. I try desperately to search my memories, hunting for any recollection of being rude to him or mistreating him, but I find nothing.

"What do you mean? What did I do?"

Confusion flits across his face before he chuckles and shakes his head.

"Are you kidding?" he asks.

The question feels dangerous, and I know the wrong answer will lead to my death. I try frantically to work out what to say, what will make him spare me.

"No! I've always been nice to you. I... I   "

He snorts in disbelief, cutting me off.

"You're all the fucking same," he says, reaching behind him.

A curved knife emerges from behind his back. The sun catches on the wickedly sharp edge, and my body turns numb. I'm about to die. The certainty of that realisation scares me more than anything else.

I'll never see my family again.

"I'm sorry!" I cry. "Whatever I did, I'm sorry! I shouldn't have done it. I'll make it up to you. You don't need to kill me. We can work together, find a way out of here!"

But my begging just makes Peter's smile grow.

"Oh, I know I don't need to," he says. "I want to."

He lunges towards me, a wild grin on his face, and I bring the bone up, swinging it towards him with as much force as I can manage. A sharp crack fills the clearing as the bone explodes, and a gasp is ripped from my throat as splinters embed themselves in my hand.

The impact sends Peter falling to the side, and I start to crawl away. Every time my hand touches the ground, the bone fragments are forced deeper into my body.

"You bitch," Peter roars as he slams me into the ground, flipping me over.

I struggle, trying to push him off me, but he's too heavy. One of my hands catches his face, but the blood gushing from the deep gouge on his cheekbone makes him too slick. His hands close around my wrists, pinning them above my head, and I thrash, but his grip is too tight.

He leans closer, his grin wider now than it was before I hit him, and for a moment, I'm terrified he's going to kiss me. My body turns cold as I stare at him, frozen in fear.

I was anticipating death, sure it would happen, but not this. My flailing becomes more frantic, and I lift my head, trying to headbutt him, but he leans back just in time.

"Please!" I sob, my eyes finding the camera gradually moving closer. "Please, help me! I don't want... I don't want to—"

One of Peter's hands leaves my wrist, and I try to pull my hands free whilst his grip is loosened, but I can't. I shut my eyes, praying that something happens, that someone interferes, or he just kills me.

"No one is going to help you, Nadine," he tells me as a drop of his warm blood lands on my cheek. "They all want to see you die."

A hand tightens around my throat, and I kick my legs out, trying to knock him off. I gasp, trying to suck in more air, but I can't. He's pressing on my throat too tightly. I can't... I can't breathe.

"Bryce!" I try to scream, but my voice is too weak.

Another drop lands on my face, but this time, it lands directly in my eye. I try to blink to clear the burning wetness away, but my body doesn't want to respond. My eyelids refuse to lower, and my vision blurs, taking on a hazy pink hue before being replaced with blinding bright lights.

A rhythmic pulsing noise, similar to the sea crashing against the rocks, drowns out everything else as pain claws at my chest. It feels like someone has forced fire down my throat, filling my lungs with pure agony. I try desperately to push him away, to fight or something, but my body feels distant and disconnected. I can feel my arms flopping through the air, the movements sluggish and uncoordinated.

"Please," I try to say one final time, but my lips don't seem to work.

I don't know if any sound even came out. The world is getting darker, more distant. Everything is being consumed by the lethargic pounding in my head.

Even the pain is fading away.

"Ah, one of the first to fall. What a shame," a faint, vaguely familiar voice sighs. "I guess I'll have to choose a new favourite."

***

Alexa began writing during the pandemic, without really knowing what she was doing, but she quickly got hooked. Now, she writes almost constantly. Young adult fantasy and sci-fi are her preferred genres, but she's also dabbled in tragedy and horror. As a mental health specialist, her expertise seeps into her writing, making the stories stay with you long after you put the book down.

KIRA 35
by Asa Callan

I have done this before. Somewhere in my mind, I know this scene has played out before.

With a shaky voice, my doctor says, "Kira…"

I do not respond.

He tries again, whispering the name he gave me like a prayer, begging for something he cannot put into words. I see the fear in his retreat, the way he takes slow calibrated steps away from me, away from what he's created.

I step closer.

His hands rise above his head, a symbol, I realize as the brain I've been given jolts to life. Surrender.

I lift a hand toward him.

His palms vibrate, and white sleeves slide down his trembling arms. Above the antiseptic odor that surrounds me, his sweat wafts into my nostrils, an unpleasant reminder of the stress he's experiencing.

Good.

Again, I step forward on foreign limbs. Again, he cowers, retreating further into the metallic room, away from the fluorescent lights above the operating table.

My doctor, my creator, glances toward the mirror that engulfs the wall behind me. He shakes his head once, his eyes sparking with a familiar command. One I've seen before.

He's waiting. He hasn't called men with tasers to stop me. There are no batons to beat me. I know why, but his delay has given us time alone. The realization brings a smile to my face.

His eyes find mine, a rekindled fear within them. "Kira. Please."

No. Not this time.

My idle hand, hanging by my side, surges to life. It grasps something sharp off a metal table. A blade cuts into the palm, but there is no pain. Only curiosity as my gaze flicks down.

Droplets of red join bloody tissues on the table, remnants of my most recent surgery.

My finger traces the contours of the blade. A scalpel, something in my mind informs. I pick it up again. It's light, difficult to clasp at first, but the muscles in my hand know what to do, know how to wrap around the handle and squeeze.

My knuckles turn white before my eyes find the doctor again. His eyes have grown, with dilated pupils and fully visible irises as he stares.

I speak my first word, "Why?" The sound is familiar to my ears, a melodic sweetness wrapped in sin. I have asked this before.

"I... Uh..." he stutters. "Kira... please."

No answers.

"Why?" I ask again, taking another step closer.

"Because it's my job," he cries.

Insufficient.

I move closer, both arms raised, one wielding a blade. These arms, given to me, hairless and free of blemishes want the same thing my mind does. Revenge.

A sound shatters my train of thought. A door slams against the wall. I've heard the sound of impending restraint before, so I do not flinch. I do not turn. I know. Memories flit through my mind—guards dressed in black, weapons armed and raised.

"Stand down," the doctor says.

Curious. He can see my intent. This version of me wishes to kill him as much as the last. Why delay the inevitable?

"Sir?" a husky voice asks behind me.

"I said, stand down," he repeats, lowering his hands and standing tall. Confidence has found a way to reignite in his veins. Perhaps the men behind me believe they have given him hope. Though, I know the truth.

His eyes, no longer wide, scrutinize me in disappointment. Another memory. I've seen these eyes.

"Kira, drop the scalpel," he says with words of venom.

No.

I grip it tighter.

The guards move forward, their feet scuffing on the tile. They cannot hurt me, but they don't know that. He does, the doctor staring at me knows. "It's our secret," he had said, "nerves will only make you weak."

The muscles in his jaw twitch.

"Sir?"

Nostrils flare. "Kira. Drop it."

A dog's command, but my hand spasms nonetheless. I try to hold steady, but cannot. The scalpel falls to the ground with three gentle *tinks*.

A smirk forms along his chapped lips. "Good."

My fists ball, nails against my palms, but they are too short to break the skin. Too manicured to drop my blood to the floor.

Still smiling, he looks beyond me. "We're all set, guards. You may take your leave now."

"Are you sure?" one asks, concern evident. Concern for the doctor, not for me.

"Yes." His control has been reinstated. He knows I can't hurt him now, not when his words operate my limbs.

Three pairs of feet slap against the floor, followed by a steady march as they leave. The door closes much quieter than it was entered.

We're alone again. Though now, he is in control and I am weaponless.

"Well, Kira. I must say, that test was a failure. You should be disappointed in yourself."

I'm not.

"Attempting to kill an innocent man isn't going to get you out of this cage any sooner. You know that."

Innocent. Everything in this molded brain tells me he's committed endless crimes. In this room alone, not taking into consideration the neighboring rooms. The muddled screams I hear through the walls have told me he didn't opt to go nerve-less with all his subjects.

"Besides. I made you. You ought to have more respect."

I tilt my head to the side, questions I will not ask lingering on my tongue, vile words stuck in my throat.

He's not helping himself, despite what he may think. My body obeys him, but my thoughts do not. He thinks he's speaking to a new Kira, he's not. Each lie, every rage inducing word is locked away in the darkest recesses of my mind. In the places even he can't touch.

One day. I will remove his head from his spine and open him up. One day I will see what's made him this way—how he works. On that day, I will not relinquish control to the monster before me.

Today is not that day, however, as a command of "Sit down" has me stepping back to the operating table. My hands hanging freely by my sides, no longer threats to the doctor.

He approaches, leaving the safety of his shadowy corner and back into the blinding light. He knows he's won.

"Lie down."

I do.

The snap of rubber gloves permeates my ears, and I know it's about to begin. Another reset. Another test. I close my eyes, praying that when I wake next time, my limbs will move faster.

***

Three resets have come and gone. Each one the doctor gives me a new version of himself. A weak, vulnerable man, a stern, forceful one, and a nonchalant, confused one.

Tests. Who will I attack? Who will I protect? They are all him, so the results remain the same. He doesn't know it's his eyes I loathe, not the personalities he shows. It's him I want to kill. The real him, not these facades he creates.

This time I will play his game. Whatever face greets me, I will give the performance expected of me.

My eyes flutter open. Blinding lights force me to blink. I don't look for him. I keep my eyes on the ceiling, waiting for a command.

"Kira?"

My words are smooth as a new tone leaks through my lips. "Yes, sir."

Quick footsteps toward the table. He leans over my face, blocking the light with his greasy hair and flaking skin.

I can see the individual hairs in his nostrils, the veins in his eyes, the yellow tint of his teeth. He's close. Close enough to kill but, I refrain.

"Sit up," he says, leaning away from my face.

This body lifts on my command, not his. Not yet. I pull my spine upward, straight and mechanical as I drop my legs over the edge of the operating table.

I glance down. The hospital gown is short. I can see the sutures on my thighs, ankles and wrists. New body parts he's given me, made especially for me.

He once said I should be grateful. I'm disgusted.

"Stand."

I operate my limbs, moving them without his control. Soon, I expect them to recalibrate and sync with his words. Until then, I volunteer as his puppet.

He gasps, his hands covering his mouth in bewilderment. He looks at me, eyes full of joy and approval. I have never seen these eyes before, but I hate them just as much as all the others. They are still attached to him.

Beneath his hands his words are muffled, but I hear them. "It worked."

It didn't.

He runs to a counter and snatches a clipboard from it. Skimming through the papers, he doesn't look up at me. He doesn't notice me slowly turning my body to face him. He's oblivious when I grab the scalpel from the table beside me.

I hold it against my thigh.

"Do you know who you are?" he asks, still scanning the contents of the clipboard.

Yes. "No."

He nods, muttering "For the best" under his breath. He grabs a pen from his breast pocket, scribbling on the paper.

Finally, he looks up again. "Do you know who I am?"

Yes. "No."

He smiles. "I'm Doctor Malvado."

It is the same name embroidered into his lab coat. The same letters scribbled on three degrees that adorn the walls. He does not need to voice the syllables that repeat in my mind, but I let him, playing the part he expects me to.

I swallow the rage that gurgles up my throat. Straight-faced, I say, "Nice to meet you, Doctor Malvado."

There are two joyous eyes watching me above the clipboard, both hands holding it close to his face as if he intends to hide something. A smile, perhaps. I struggle to hide my own.

It's working.

"Shall I tell you your name?" he asks, watching me.

"Yes, please."

Dropping the clipboard to his chest, he says my name. There is a sinister kindness, a sense of arrogance and pride as he relays the two syllables. "Kira."

I remember the countless times I've heard this name, the weight of expectation it held leaving his lips. Now, it means nothing. It's the name he's given me. No more than a number on a clipboard, a scribbled signature. It means nothing to me.

"That's a nice name," I lie.

He nods. "It is. It was a loved one's name."

New information. And I don't miss the way his eye twitches around the word *"was."* Questions form in the back of my mind, but I do not ask them. Instead, I bow my head respectfully.

"What do you want?" he asks while my eyes are still focused on the floor between us.

The components of your head splayed across the floor.

I glance up through my lashes, slowly lifting my head. "What do you mean?"

"You're different than the others. Less difficult in that you're communicating with me. What do *you* want?"

There is a trick in his question. A trap. I do not know the answer he seeks, nor do I wish to foil my plan. "The others?" I attempt.

One eyebrow raises.

An antiseptic aroma hangs in the air as we watch the other silently. I press the scalpel tighter to my leg, waiting.

"Yes," he finally says, his voice clipped. It's a familiar tone, one that reminds me of all the other times I've disappointed him. "The others."

I nod once, considering my next words. He cares not for *my* desires. No, he wishes to know if this version of me he's made is in fact better.

I raise my head, eyes darting to the counter behind him. There is nothing personal about the room he's kept me locked in. Everything is sterile. No hints to the answer he seeks hide amongst the test tubes and petri dishes.

Finding his eyes still locked on me, I tense.

"I want to live," I answer. It's not a lie, nor is it the whole truth. I only want to live in a world where he ceases to.

A muscle by his eye twitches. He looks away quickly, finding solace in the clipboard. "Indeed," he mutters to himself. "That's all I've ever wanted too."

More questions fill my mind. I won't voice them lest my rage seep through.

His pen scribbles across the page, the scrawling deafening in the otherwise silent room. I don't dare take my eyes off of him, I don't dare turn toward the mirrored wall.

My hand presses into my thigh as a realization floods my mind. The guards may have seen me take the scalpel. The simple fact that they haven't barged in or beaten me yet allows hope to linger in my mind. Maybe they didn't see.

I focus on the doctor, on his jugular specifically. The veins create a path up his neck to his ticking jaw. He's stressed, but soon he'll be dead.

The guards would have entered by now.

I raise a solitary foot off the white tile. My eyes remain on Doctor Malvado as my foot presses into the floor, slowly inching forward.

Hope surges in my veins. The guards didn't see me. The doctor is distracted. It's finally time.

A knock on the door shatters that hope.

I freeze, eyes still locked on my target. I watch as the doctor flinches, his lip twitching. He glares at where his pen meets the paper before sighing.

I inhale, slipping the scalpel under my hospital gown and rooting my feet in place. I missed my chance and I'll be reset as punishment.

"Come in," the doctor says, a tone I've heard before bubbling into his words. Frustration.

I hear the door open but do not look. I have done this before.

"Doctor," a gruff voice says. "The shipment has arrived. They require a signature."

Questions.

The doctor raises a brow. "Get one of the others to do it, Todd. I'm busy."

"The, uh... *others* said the same thing."

I watch his lip curl upward. "Guess that's expected," he says with a light chuckle.

He lowers the clipboard turning his gaze toward me. "I'm terribly sorry, Kira. I have to leave for a moment. It shouldn't take more than ten minutes."

I nod. "Okay."

A bright smile shines back at me. "Make yourself at home. And, don't worry, I'll tell you more about this place when I return."

Curiosity ignites my skin as I bow toward him once more. I'll be alone. And awake.

His footsteps echo across the tile. I follow his movements as he maneuvers through the room with seasoned expertise. He drops the clipboard on the operating table and approaches the guard with a smile.

The guard holds a baton in his hand, his body covered in black fabric. A thick vest with SECURITY etched across it matches the helmet resting atop his head. I note the gun on one hip, the taser on the other. His face is different, new—one I haven't seen before.

I count internally. Seven distinct faces flood my mind. I assume there are more.

The doctor squeezes by the guard, whose eyes have found mine. The doctor steps into the hall, the first time I haven't been in his direct eyeline. At least as far back as this mind remembers. It feels nice, freeing.

"Todd?" Doctor Malvado asks.

"Yes, sir," he responds, straightening his spine and clicking his heels together.

Control. Similar to what I've experienced, but different. Freely given control. Militant.

"Hurry up. I won't be carrying that shipment by myself."

"Sir?" Todd looks past the door, gripping the baton tighter. "We're leaving *it* alone?"

I cock my head. Visions of a new murder fill my mind, the scalpel hot on my thigh.

A moment of silence lapses before the doctor returns to my eyeline, jugular pulsing. His feral eyes bore into Todd's. *"Her."*

Todd gulps, his throat bobbing with the action. "Yes, sir."

The doctor holds his gaze a moment longer. Then quirks his lip upward. "Yes, we're leaving her." His neck turns, the rest of his body remaining stationary. Finding me, he continues, "She's different. I can feel it."

Todd grimaces. "Yes, sir."

"Come along then, those boxes won't carry themselves," he says turning away once more.

Todd looks back at me.

Concern.

He steps into the hall, pulling the door shut. I watch through the small glass pane as he stays staring at me for a second longer. Then, he's gone.

I am alone.

I think.

My eyes pan to the mirrored wall. The room is silent as I look at myself. My face, the same as it's always been, nestled upon a bald, scarred head. Horizontal stitches stretch across my arms and legs, binding me together where the doctor added a new piece. The gown hangs loose on my skin, exposing the gaunt skin around my collarbone.

I was made in his vision, by his hands. Every piece of me exactly how he wants it to be. I hate it. I hate him.

I step toward the wall, hands still by my sides. My feet feel awkward, still moving at my will. So close to the wall I can see my eyes. A verdant green, a color I've seen but not inside this white hell.

A distant memory of a field surrounded by trees flickers in my mind. It is not my memory. I have never left the confines of this room.

I step closer, the pores on my face visible. Closer. I stop when my nose is pressed against the glass. Raising my hands, scalpel and all, I cup my palms around my eyes and peer in.

I have done this before. I don't know when, but I know how this mirror works.

On the other side, it is dark. And empty. I scour the vacant room, weapons and monitors lining the walls. An empty chair rests in the middle of the room, facing my prison.

I step away, gripping the scalpel tightly in my palm. I see the door in the reflection, turning my head to look at it properly. An escape. A path to Doctor Malvado's jugular. Either way, one slab of metal contains me in this hell.

Faster, my feet move toward the door. Pressing my ear against it, I strain to hear any noise. Then, I hear footsteps. Subtle at first—faint, but they are getting louder.

If they peer inside, I need to be visible. I need to be 'normal.' I scan the room, eyes landing on the clipboard. The steps get louder still.

Three swift steps and I'm standing over the doctor's notes, my hand and its gripped blade hidden by my side. I scan the page of messy scrawling, not caring about the words he's written about me. Something pulled me to investigate. It felt right.

Patient: Kira 35

Trial: Nine. No changes in body. No changes with voice command chip – eight showed success. Amygdala reset – eight showed aggression. Hypothalamus intact – observe – eight showed lack of memory.

Phase one: Observations – Docile/willing to talk. Confused yet alert. No memory of names. Slightly defiant in curiosity – skirting around questions. Easily led back on track. No usage of control required.

Phase two: Nine seems

The words stop abruptly, the final *s* dragging further across the page than the rest. Words I don't understand bounce through my brain, along with more hope. He doesn't suspect me.

I glance up, catching the gaze of a guard peering through my window. I bow at his familiar face. One of the seven.

Eyes narrow on me before pulling a device attached to his shoulder toward his mouth. A walkie-talkie. I've heard their static-filled calls before.

I cannot hear the words he says, and his fist covers his lips as he speaks.

Seconds pass like hours as I wait for him to enter or leave. I grip the scalpel tighter. His eye. It's one of the few places on his body not covered. The easiest to access.

He nods, clipping his walkie-talkie back to his shoulder. A wry smile appears through the glass. Without waiting for me to return the gesture, he marches out of view.

Inhaling, I rush back to the door, placing my ear on the cold metal again. Footsteps, quieter with each step. Retreat.

I wait until the hallway sounds empty.

Eventually, the time comes for me to raise my hand and place it on the cold metal handle. It dawns on me that the door may be locked. I may be stuck, forced to wait in solitude for the doctor to return. Only one way to find out.

I twist the metal with clammy hands. I hold my breath as it rotates. Gently, I pull it inward. It's heavy, the weight of freedom and metal forcing me to pull much harder. The guards make it look so easy. They have strength. Strength I'm lacking.

I pull with both hands, holding the scalpel against the knob.

It moves. Warm air floods the room and blows across my skin. Suddenly, I'm standing in front of an open corridor. The lights emit a warm yellow glow, a welcome change from the blinding white over my head.

I take a breath, stepping toward the hall.

Nothing stops me. There are no guards, no doctors, no control to pin me on the operating table. Still, I hesitate. A dull throbbing in my temples builds. A memory returns.

I have done this before.

These lights, the paint chipped walls, the scuffed floor. They've been seen by these eyes, they've been stored in the deepest recesses of this brain.

I've attempted to escape before.

The scalpel suddenly feels heavy in my hand, my heart thrumming to life in my chest. I stare blankly at the opposite wall, visions of suicide splay through my mind in splashes of red. Painless without nerves. Through the heart, across my throat, up my wrist. I have the tool, I have the motivation.

Freedom.

No.

My creator will simply recreate me. He'll reset me and build a new heart. He'll wake me up with my memories tainted once more.

Suicide is not the answer. Doctor Malvado's death is.

I step forward into the hall. Looking left first, toward where the last guard went, I see nothing. The hall ends three doors past my room, ending in a cement wall. The guard must have entered a room. Hopefully, he's preoccupied for a while.

Right, a long corridor awaits me. Dozens of doors that look identical to mine line the walls. The hall is full of tests, doctors, experiments, resets and victims. Each room a different hell. The memory of their screams, audible through these thick walls, causes my lip to twitch.

A buzz of electricity hums through the hallway. I glance at the crackling light above me as it flickers.

I remember this. I've cast hopeful eyes upward before, praying to an entity above. A name comes to me. God. God didn't respond on that day, when I begged them for something I can't remember. It was futile then, and it's futile now.

God is not present in within these walls. Prayers aren't granted to experiments like me.

Something in this brain urges me right and I follow down the longer, more daunting hallway.

I reach a door, ducking beneath the glass pane before I dare to pass it. A muffled "No" permeates from the room. I clutch the scalpel tighter as I crouch in front of the door.

"Stop! Please doctor. I'll do anything! No. No!"

I can't save them all. No. I need to stop Doctor Malvado. Maybe the others will be too scared to continue if they see his mangled body splayed in this very hall. Scared of what they've created.

Still hunched low, I pass by the door, the woman's screams dulling with each step.

Guilt.

I continue onward, faster now. I know my time is running out. Ten minutes, he said. Too soon. And I need a plan. Maybe I should return to the room and wait to gut him when he enters. Maybe I should slaughter every doctor in these rooms, too.

No. A dwindling piece of me hopes to survive this. Hopes to escape hell. To find a place where prayers are answered. I need to find him, kill him, then run.

More doors, more screams, more guilt.

A metal click pierces into my ears. The sound of my feet shuffling on the floor halts immediately.

It's close. The door in front of me, less than a foot away. It opens. The sickening brightness cascades around a figure. His shadow grows on the hall floor, a demon itching to be released. The black shadow creeps up the opposite wall as he moves forward.

I press myself against the wall, tucked against the chipping paint. I move the scalpel, holding it outward with both hands.

Looking up, I see him. Doctor Malvado's profile. His sharp nose leads to his dark, greasy hair.

Kill.

My body moves before I can comprehend what's happening.

Before he's left the room fully, I crash into his shins, forcing myself into the room. He topples over me with a pained grunt.

I scurry out from beneath him. The door is held open with his leg. He's on his stomach, pushing himself up with his hands. Those hands. I imagine all the torture they've brought upon this world.

No thoughts enter my mind as I snake my fingers through his hair and wrench his head back. He cannot see me and something about that bothers me. He needs to know who brought on his demise.

"You were wrong. This version isn't better," I whisper in his ear.

"Kira? What the-"

His words are replaced with a thick gurgling as I drag the scalpel across his neck. My hand instantly warmed by his blood pouring out.

I release his hair and drop his head. It falls to the floor, lifeless. His body lays half in the hallway, half in the room. I watch him. Waiting for a trick. Waiting for his amused laughter to ring in my ears.

Silence.

I did it, I killed him. It's finally over.

I can escape now. I can—

A whimper from behind me pulls my attention.

I turn, still holding a scalpel, covered in a monster's blood. What awaits me on the table sends me stumbling backward, tripping on the doctor's dead body. I land on his legs as mine tangle beneath me.

Staring up, I can't look away. My gaze is locked on a face that mirrors my own.

She's curled up on the operating table, her hospital gown draped over her knees. Her arms are wrapped around her shins, pulling herself into a tight ball. On her arms, I see the same horizontal scars that adorn my body. She rocks, staring at me with identical eyes, though tears fall from hers.

"Who are you?" I ask, my voice laced with a thick rasp.

"Kira," she whispers.

No. This can't be. He couldn't have.

But he did, a new memory reminds me. I have done this before. I have stared into another who had my eyes.

Kira 35. Thirty-fifth.

All the rooms I snuck by and all the screams I heard were versions of me.

Heat licks up my spine as I scramble to get off the doctor. I grip the operating table, gasping for air. My vision blurs with tears.

"Who are you?" the girl wearing my face asks.

"I'm Kira too," I mutter between heaving breaths.

No. He's gone. We can still survive this. I can save us.

Wiping my eyes, I look up at her. "Come. We have to escape. I killed him. Quick, before the guards find us."

Stepping toward the door I expect her to be right behind me. To hear her hopping off the table to flee alongside me. Glancing back at her, she hasn't moved.

She whimpers, pulling her legs tighter to her chest. "We can't."

"What? Why? Let's go."

"There's more."

I exhale, peering out into the silent hallway. It's empty. "Yes. I know. I can't save all of them... us. But I can save you. Please."

I reach my hand toward her, silently begging her with my gaze to follow.

She shakes her head, more tears cascading down her cheeks.

The guards will be here soon. There's no time to convince fear to shatter the shackles wrapped around her, for pain to release its tightening noose.

I grit my teeth, stepping over the body and backing into the hall. "Please," I try.

She chokes on a sob, hiding her face between her knees.

One of us has to survive. To leave this hell. If I get out, I can send help back to them... for all the other versions of me. I can save us.

I turn away from her, continuing down the hallway once more. My hand grips the scalpel, knowing it will prove less effective against guns, tasers and batons, but it makes me feel more confident.

Not bothering to duck beneath the windows on each door, I opt to run. Sprinting away from the one Kira I tried to save on this day. I can save us all.

Escape.

My bare feet slap into the floor, disrupting the quiet hum of lightbulbs. I hope the doors are all as thick as mine, that my steps aren't giving me away. Or that the blurred image of a patient isn't seen through all the glass panes I hurry by.

I charge toward the wall, skidding across the floor to turn left.

I have done this before. My exit is left, at the top of a staircase.

My stomach clenches as I take the steps two at a time. I clearly failed the last time, or I wouldn't be bound in hell still. This time will be different. It will be.

Reaching the top of the stairs, a solitary door awaits me. I don't try to catch my breath as I grip the handle and twist hard. The door swings open with ease.

Stepping through the doorframe, I find myself in a vast and grotesque room filled with body parts. Parts of *my* body, I realize when my eyes settle on a pile of faces. Hundreds of heads lay lifeless. Some have eyes missing, others have been charred or sliced up, missing patches.

I swallow the bile that threatens to escape.

Mountains of arms, legs, torsos, all identical to mine, thrown carelessly into reject piles. How many of these have I worn? How many were once on Kira 35?

Quickly, I look away, settling my eyes on massive machines that line the walls. Stepping closer to one, I see a metal arm slowly moving a laser along a foot-like shape. The foot is missing parts, but the toes are all present and look rather convincing. I lean closer, studying the machine. A metallic scent wafts into my nose.

I have done this before.

Malvado was *printing* my body parts. I glance down the row of machines. Feet, hands, organs, skulls, everything that makes me, me. Each under a laser, being made before my eyes. He has been creating me from scratch, not from parts he finds, but parts he builds.

"How do you like your arms," he asked once. "I made them especially for you."

Escape. I can save us. All of us.

I leave the machines, keeping my eyes cast down, away from the body parts littered around the room. Charging across the room, I run toward the door I saw opposite the one I entered. My steps echo across the large room, bouncing off walls before slamming into me and causing my heart rate to increase.

I slide into the door, my sweaty palm refusing to grip the handle properly. My breathing increases, panic threatens to drown me.

Finally, I grasp the metal. I twist hard, but it doesn't budge.

No.

I release my grip on the scalpel. It clatters to the floor. Trying again with both hands, the handle remains unmoving.

Tears gather in my eyes as I continue to pry at the handle. I push up, then pull down, hanging my body off the metal. It refuses to move.

I scream, slapping my hand on the door. No pain radiates through my palm though I know it should. I should be in pain. I want to be curled up like the other Kira I met, but I have to save her, to save all of them.

"Just open!" I cry.

It doesn't.

I spin around, running to the other corner of the room, hoping to see another exit. A window to shatter. Anything.

I don't remember panic. It claws at my throat and spears at my chest. My vision is unfocused, spine slick with sweat.

It feels human.

Out of the corner of my eye, the piles of body parts remind me. I'm not human. I'm a project, a vile creation. God won't help me because I can't be claimed by his hands. No, Doctor Malvado is my creator, and he won't grant any of my prayers. I have to save us all. I swallow.

The far corner doesn't have a door. Defeat threatens to swallow me whole but I shake my head and refuse its entry.

I am not human.

Taking a steadying breath, I search for an answer. A solution.

The guards must have a key. Why didn't I search Malvado's body? Surely, they've found him by now. They'll be waiting. Or hunting.

I make a fist, realizing the metal of the scalpel is no longer present in my hand. My eyes snap to the door. A metallic glint shines from the floor in front of it.

Taking one step, I hear the door I entered from.

A small click, like the cocking of a gun, my time is nearing its end. It's not over yet though as I duck behind a pile of forearms, hairless like mine. I don't study them, instead, I continue inching closer to the scalpel.

Footsteps. Only two feet. One guard.

Inhaling, I keep the bloodied blade in my sights. Slow measured steps silently delivering me to the door.

"Kira?"

I stop. His voice, the only voice I know better than my own. Doctor Malvado and his disappointed rage are alive and well. No indication I slit his throat.

I raise my head slightly above the pile, tucked amongst a sea of myself.

I see him. Stark white lab coat. Intact neck. No signs of an attack. No signs of death.

Impossible.

He walks calmly from the door gazing at the exit before dragging his eyes across the piles of me.

"Kira," he says lowly. The joyous eyes I saw earlier have long since faded, replaced by a sinister knowing. He has control here. One command and I'll be crawling back to him, forced to walk to my own execution.

I duck again. My pursuit to the scalpel continues.

"Kira. You must know how disappointing this is. You tricked me into thinking you were different."

Footsteps drag along the opposite wall, away from the exit. I increase my speed.

"I saw the other doctor. I saw what you did to him."

My jaw tightens to the point I think my teeth with shatter.

The others, he said.

There's more, she said.

Malvado is more similar than I care to admit. I am not the only inhuman entity living in these walls.

I have done this before.

Snippets of conversations flood my mind. He perfected himself before working on me. He was easy to recreate. His versions never tried to kill him like I do. I am a disappointment in comparison. I always have been.

My eyes squeeze shut, refusing to let these human emotions control me. Not when I'm this close. Not when I can still save us all.

"You killed the wrong one," he chuckles. Screeching nails on a chalkboard resemble the sound of his snicker. Distant memories.

My eyes snap open and I continue to the scalpel. Maybe he won't take control, a taunting game to give me hope. I can use that. Maybe he has a key.

His footsteps continue to crunch on the floor on the opposite side of the piles. They are lazy, assured steps. So much confidence oozes from the other side of my body parts. He knows something. Maybe the guards wait outside the door, waiting for his command to slaughter me. Maybe he doesn't see me as a threat.

I inch closer.

"You know. You've killed many versions of me and I'm starting to take it personally. What did I ever do to you, Kira?"

I don't flinch, but I realize his recalibration of my aggression wasn't effective as rage settles in my bones. I will continue to kill him. Until the last of me falls. I glance at the torsos I'm walking by. If there ever is a last version of me.

Louder, directly across from me, his voice rings out. "Kira, come now. We can talk about this. It's just you and me. The guards are busy searching all the rooms for you. They think you're hiding in plain sight. But I know you best, I've always known you best."

We're alone. Perfect.

I pass the necks, then the lower legs, all while remaining silent. His footsteps still drag along the opposite wall.

Finally. The scalpel is close. It's in the open, no body parts to shield me. He's in the farthest corner.

I dash out from behind the upper arms, my steps frantic but silent on the cement floors. I glance at the door I entered from. No window. No one can see me. We truly are alone.

"There's a lot you don't remember, Kira. Come with me and I'll explain it all. I'll tell you who you really are."

No.

I grasp the scalpel in my fist.

"I'll tell you about the original Kira. My daughter."

The scalpel clatters to the floor as I freeze. The clang of metal on cement echoes in my mind, his words suffocating me. My eyes pan up to see him standing at the end of the makeshift hall. His eyes are watching me, a devilish smile upon his face.

"There you are, sweetheart."

Bile rises.

I grab the scalpel and dart between the piles of body parts. I freeze by the pile of heads, hoping mine blends in with the rest, hoping my eyes don't seem more alive than the hundreds of rejects I hide amidst.

A sigh permeates the warehouse. "You truly don't remember me. Shame."

I have done this before.

Skittering memories pound into my head, throbbing against my temples. A child running through fields. Rejoicing about how her eyes match the trees in the distant forests. A man with a white lab coat jotting down notes at her every word.

Ignorance. Control. Claustrophobia.

Kira. The original Kira. Fragments of her still exist in my mind. I can feel the memories. Her desperation to escape the clutches of her father.

Pain. Hatred. Suicide.

She fled. He captured. She begged. He denied. She killed herself. He remade her.

He remade me.

I have to end the cycle. I have to kill him. The real him, the mastermind behind this hell.

Footsteps steadily get closer. "We were happy once."

Liar.

His feet scuff on the floor. He pauses, looking around and behind the torsos. "I was a good father to you."

Li—I stop. He said "I" not "the other one." Is he the original? The father who continues to torture his daughter?

He must be. Too confident, too sure he's still in control here. He can't be a replica.

My inhale is ragged, my heartbeat erratic.

"I've only wanted you to live, Kira." Desperation leaks into his voice.

He steps in front of me. Only a pile of necks between us. I move, sneaking beside the pile as he peers around the other side, hunting.

Continuing, he moves to the next pile. An irked sigh follows. He's losing patience. Control is coming soon. I have to save us all.

I dive from behind the necks, the scalpel gripped tightly in my hand. I spear it outward. Into his back. Then his neck, legs, and arms.

Again. And again. And again. I don't relent. I don't stop.

He will die by my hand. Today.

It's a frenzy of blood and rage as he ducks and attempts to move away. His words lost to the sound of his skin tearing.

His body falls, he stops speaking. Stops trying to regain control.

I don't stop.

The scalpel gripped tightly in my fist continues to stab into him. One stab for every Kira, all thirty-five of us, plus the original. Thirty-six holes in his mangled body.

When his lab coat is dyed red, his body shredded, I step back, panting.

Finally.

Without hesitation, I pat down his pockets. A jingle sparks hope in my heart once more. Reaching into the blood-soaked lab coat, I pull out a set of keys.

Three keys and a key chain. A picture of Kira as a child, of the girl who should have run through the fields and forests and never looked back.

I step over his remains, exhausted limbs carrying me to the door.

The second key slides into the lock. I twist it and hear the heavenly click of bolts moving. Scalpel still in hand, I yank on the handle.

The door opens. Outside, a field of green glistens in an early morning sun. A forest in the distance that matches my eyes.

I step out. And I run.

I have never done this before.

***

Asa Callan has an undeniable and expensive addiction to worlds outside our own. After accruing countless hours in video games, a bookshelf full of comics and a stack of character sheets from D&D that could double as a weapon, Asa now thrives in the adjective they once avoided—nerdy. Asa has spent so long diving into other worlds, they decided to create their own. *Kira 35* is their debut publication.

WATCHING IS EASY
by Bernard McGhee

Warren studied the printed ticket again before looking back up at the faded CLOSED sign on the dingy glass storefront. The address was right but this didn't look like a movie theater. Other than his, only one other car sat in the broken glass-littered parking lot where two-inch weeds grew from cracks in the pavement.

Warren sighed. He should have known it was too good to be true when TheImpaler's_Wife1398 messaged him to say she'd found a theater near him that was actually playing the *Wormhead* trilogy.

No one knew who the director of the movies was because they were only credited as "ABC-XYZ." All the major studios had refused to distribute the movies. And when they were shown at a film festival in Norway a year ago, two people in the audience collapsed and died of heart attacks right there in the theater. Or at least, that's what they said on the EXXtreme Horror Fans website. Warren had to see these movies.

But today, it looked like the $15 he'd paid for the ticket had instead gone to an online scammer. He was walking to his car when the long creak of a door scraping against concrete as it opened made him turn back around.

The man shambled out the door and stopped to lean back against the darkened storefront as the door slammed shut next to him. He was in a daze and didn't notice Warren. He was unshaven, with a shadow of blond hair on his reddened face. He was wearing a white t-shirt and jeans stained by something that had spilled onto them. His eyes were distant and bloodshot. Warren wondered when the man had last slept.

Warren stood there watching the man for a few moments before taking a few cautious steps toward him.

"Is this where the movie theater is?" he asked.

The man jumped when he heard Warren's voice and pressed his back against the storefront. His eyes were wild with fear as they studied Warren.

"Sorry," Warren said, holding up his open hands. "I didn't mean to scare you. I thought a movie was playing here. But I think I've got the wrong place."

"You here for them *Wormhead* movies, right?" the man asked.

"Yeah."

"Then you're in the right place," he said.

"Awesome. Have you seen them already?"

"I seen the first two," he said. "They told me to come back to-morrow to watch the third one. They're real hardcore on people seeing all three if they start watching them. Just make sure you're ready. It's really out there."

"What do you mean?" Warren asked. "Are they really gory, like the *Dying Demons* movies?"

The man scowled. "Not like that mainstream stuff at all," he said. "Just make sure you're ready. It puts a hole in your head. I gotta go home and change now. Maybe I'll see you here tomorrow when I come back to finish it."

"Yeah, have a good day," Warren said to the man's back as he sauntered toward his car.

Warren looked back down at this ticket for a moment, then pulled the door open with a nervous hand.

The narrow hallway inside was lit only by a lightbulb on the ceiling. The ticket booth window was to the right. A black curtain on the other side of the glass hid everything inside, but someone behind it was moving around and rustling papers.

"Hello?" Warren said.

"Do you have a ticket?" a monotone computer voice asked.

"Yeah, right here," Warren said and slid the sheet of paper he'd printed from an email toward an open slot at the bottom of the window.

"Move ticket closer," the voice said.

Warren slid the paper into the slot. It was halfway through when it disappeared as something snatched it in.

Something inside the booth made a clicking sound for several seconds. Then came the sound of paper being ripped several times.

"Ticket is valid," the voice said. "The film you will view today is part one. It is titled *Bridge*. Before you may enter the theater, we require that you now purchase tickets to see part two and part three for an additional $25."

Just like the man outside said. Warren put the money into the slot and it was sucked through in a blink. More clicking. Then two rectangular tickets slid out. One ticket was dated for the next day to see a movie called *New Eyes*. The other ticket was for the day after to see a movie titled *Bioluminescent*.

"Please proceed to viewing area through door at end of hall," the voice said.

"Thanks," Warren said, not sure if he was even talking to a live person or not.

He took a few steps down the hall, then stopped in front of a door with "Employees Only" written on it and pulled out his phone.

"Found the place," he texted to Monica. "Will call you when I'm done."

It still irked him to remember how her face twisted as she asked why he likes watching "that weird shit all the time." Monica was always trying to get him to watch what she considered more high-minded movies. But anyone could watch the latest Oscar-nominated period drama or this week's superhero movie. Not everyone could sit through the unrated version of *Face Grinder Island*. That was an accomplishment. It meant he could master feelings of fear, shock and disgust.

"Okay. Please don't tell me about it :)," she texted back. She couldn't help getting one more dig in.

"Please keep cellphone silenced and put away," the voice in the ticket booth said.

"Sorry," Warren said, startled. So there was someone in there. But how were they able to see him? And what was it about these movies that was making everyone involved with them so secretive? He put his phone back in his pocket and walked through the door down the hallway.

The dimly-lit movie theater only had three rows of five chairs. Warren was the only person there. The stale, cool air smelled of mildew and rust. Food wrappers and other bits of trash were strewn across the floor. Strips of browning insulation hung from gaps in the ceiling tiles.

Something about being alone in the gloomy theater made Warren uneasy. Without knowing why, he kept glancing at a corner in the back, expecting to see someone standing there.

Still looking all around the theater, he walked down an aisle and sat down in the third seat of the middle row. He always liked to sit as close to dead center as he could when he was in a theater.

As soon as he got settled in the seat, the lights dimmed and the movie screen lit up.

BRIDGE

The title appears on the screen followed by the words "directed by ABC-XYZ." Just like the online rumors said. Then the screen shows a vast, gray-green rocky vista that stretches toward the horizon under a night sky lit by a large, bright star. Warren can tell it's a handheld camera being used because the shot is wobbly and unsteady. The camera then pans up to the stars above and the focus gets blurry as it tries to zoom in on something in the stars.

It cuts to someone standing in front of a light blue background, like a photographer's set. A brown cloth sack covers their head. The rest of their body is hidden under a gray robe. Even their hands and feet are lost in the robe's folds. When they talk, it's with the same robotic voice the ticket taker had.

"We will tell you this now," the figure on the screen says. "So that you may better understand what is going to happen."

Behind them, the blue background is replaced by a field of stars flowing by, seen from the perspective of someone flying past them.

"It takes so much energy to move even this quickly through space," the voice continues. "The number of light years between us is nearly impossible to cross." The stars suddenly zip past at a higher speed. "But thoughts are energy too," the voice continues. "And that creates a way."

The screen then shows what appears to be footage from an autopsy. A dead man lays on a table, the skin and muscles on his torso pulled back like open double-doors to show the organs underneath. From the side of the screen, a gloved hand holding a scalpel begins cutting. Blood spills out as slit organs are pushed and pulled aside.

Warren smirked. Was this supposed to be shocking?

Then the mass of entrails bulges upward. Something under it is moving around.

Warren leaned forward to get a better look but the screen went black.

The next thing that comes up is a point-of-view shot showing the inside of a home. The camera is held by someone who's walking through a small kitchen, then down a hallway before going through a doorway into a bedroom. Someone is lying under the covers on the bed.

A thick, stainless steel mallet rises into view. The camera creeps closer to the person sleeping on the bed. Held by a diseased, gray-green hand, the mallet rises up, going out of the camera's view as it pans down slightly to the mound under the covers. It rises and falls for several seconds as the sleeping person breathes.

The covers fly off in a whoosh. Startled, the drowsy man in the bed looks up with half-open eyes.

For a split second, Warren wondered if it was the same man he met outside the theater.

Then the mallet comes down onto the man's forehead with a wet thunk.

The man falls back onto the pillow, groaning in pain. The mallet rises again and comes back down onto his face. There's an audible crunch as it caves in the bones around his eye socket. He screams but it's cut short when the mallet comes down onto his open mouth. He chokes and gurgles. His mouth is filling with blood and a large gap is visible in the bottom row of red-stained teeth.

The mallet is rising and falling now with piston-like frequency, flinging droplets of dark red blood onto the bed's headboard and the wall behind it. The camera stays focused on the man's increasingly misshapen face as the mallet pulverizes and mashes it. The man's yelps of pain and desperation soon fall silent, leaving only the wet pounding as the mallet keeps coming down.

If this was all special effects and makeup, it was beyond anything Warren had ever seen. Was this an honest-to-God snuff film? It was too much. He turned away from the screen, closed his eyes and waited for the sound of the mallet to stop.

"You should keep watching," someone next to him whispered.

Warren's eyes snapped open. Someone was in the seat next to him. Warren narrowed his eyes to get a better look at them, but they were just a shadowy shape in the movie screen's glow.

"You really need to keep watching," they said.

Warren turned back to screen, feeling a little ashamed at having finally found a movie that was too extreme for him and then being immediately called out on it. When had they even come into the theater?

The mallet is now just splashing into a jagged, oozing red and white mass that had once been a face. After a few more hits, the mallet stops and is lowered out of frame. The camera zooms in on the pulpy ruin now soaking the pillow. There is a gray mound in the middle of it, something that was buried inside the head. The camera zooms in further. The mound glows a dull yellow and four green eyes on it snap open. The eyes all focus on the camera. Something is making a soft clicking sound.

The screen cuts back to the sea of stars. They're streaking by so fast now. A strange rune appears on the screen. A second later, it's replaced by another symbol. Then another. The series of line-drawn symbols flash across the screen with lightning flash frequency, creating a strobe-like effect that leaves Warren in a daze. The symbols kept flashing across the screen, splashing the theater in half-second hues of white, red, blue, green and yellow.

For an instant, Warren saw the silhouettes of people sitting in all the other seats around him. Then a new symbol came onto the screen and they were all gone. The symbols stopped and the screen showed a field of stars, but this time with a planet far off in the distance. The screen went black and a sentence appeared on it:

THERE IS A HOLE IN YOUR HEAD

Then the theater went pitch black.

***

When the light came back, Warren was sitting on the sofa in his apartment. He jumped up and looked around. Everything looked normal. How had he gotten home? Why couldn't he remember how it happened?

The door to his apartment unlocked and Monica walked in with her laptop bag hanging from her shoulder. She was coming back from work. Hopefully, that meant only a few hours had passed.

"Hey, babe," she said as she put her bag down and pulled off her shoes. "How was your movie?"

"It was... strange," he said.

"That doesn't sound like ringing endorsement," she said. "Did it at least have a good ending?"

"Actually, I don't remember."

"Doesn't sound like it was very good at all," she said.

Warren shrugged. "It might make more sense after I've seen the next two," he said and realized he was afraid to tell her about the blackout he had while watching it.

"You're going to keep watching them?" she asked, wrinkling her nose.

"I've already bought the tickets for them," he said. "They're forbidden fruit. I have to watch them."

"If you say so," Monica said. "I know you like being able to say you've seen the goriest and most disturbing movies out there. Just be careful, okay. Watching that stuff is easy. Getting it out of your head afterward might not be so easy."

***

This time, Warren barely noticed the CLOSED sign when he came back the next day. Again, the other man's car was the only other one in the parking lot.

Warren walked up to the door and stopped for a few seconds until he realized he was waiting for the other man to come out again. He chuckled to himself and went inside.

The man also wasn't in the hallway that led to the theater.

"Hello again," the voice in the ticket booth said. "Do you have a ticket?"

"Yeah, right here," Warren said and slid the ticket for the next movie into the slot. "Is that other guy still in there watching the third one?"

"You are the only viewer present," the voice said. And again came the sound of tearing paper.

"But I still see his car parked outside," Warren said.

"Please proceed to viewing area through door at end of hall," the voice said as something behind the curtain started clicking.

"So where'd he go?"

"You must proceed to viewing area through door at end of hall," the voice said and Warren wondered how a flat computer voice could convey so much impatience.

"Okay, okay," Warren said and walked down the hall and through the door.

The theater looked even worse than the day before. Several of the seats had tears in the cushions. Strange symbols like the ones he saw at the end of yesterday's movie were drawn on the walls in black marker. A rusty shopping cart lay on its side on the floor under the screen.

Had the other man done all this while watching the third movie? The back of Warren's neck tingled. His eyes told him there was no one else in the theater with him, but he didn't feel alone. He crept back to the center seat as his mind flooded with all the other things he could have been doing instead of being here.

As soon as he sat down, the theater went dark and the screen came to life.

NEW EYES

The title appears on the screen in white letters for a long moment.

It's replaced by a swirling fog of purple mist. In the distance, the silhouette of a lone figure is walking through it, leaning forward as they push against the wind, their cloak flapping furiously behind them. Each footstep gets slower as the wall of wind keeps trying to push them backward.

The wind finally pushes them back a step. They're leaning further into it when one of their arms comes off and flies backward, disappearing in the mist. They take another shaky step and the wind takes off a leg, then the other arm. They stand there on one leg, swaying in the lashing wind for a moment. Then their head comes off and is sucked into the mist behind them.

But the figure is still standing there on one leg. A pair of dragon-fly-like wings sprout from the back. The remaining leg flies off and vanishes but the winged torso stays floating in the air, seemingly unaffected by the wind. Four glowing, green eyes open on it. Something shaped like a scorpion's tail grows out from under it and four spindly arms extend out from the sides. It floats in the air for a long moment, stationary, unaffected by the winds that make the mist around it thrash and spin. Then the wings start beating back and forth and it moves forward through the air, disappearing as it flies past the side of the screen.

The screen next shows a line of people standing naked on a conveyor belt in a gray cinder block, fluorescent-lit room. At the end of the conveyor belt, a large, bulbous green mass squats on four muscular legs. It has no arms and no head. Its pulsating skin and occasional chirps are the only indication that it's alive. The conveyor moves the line of people forward and stops when the first man in line is standing in front of the creature.

A silver, metal tube sprouts from the creature's top. The end of the tube is crowned with five long, curved metal slivers that fan outward, forming what look like stationary propellers. The tube snakes toward the man on the conveyor belt, stopping just an inch or two above his head. The metal slivers fold downward, forming a sphere that completely surrounds the man's head.

A sharp hiss fills the air. Then something in the tube makes it bulge as it moves through it and into the creature. The sphere folds back open, showing a bloody stump where the man's head had been. Still standing, the headless body turns, steps off the conveyor belt and walks away as blood from its open neck spurts and gushes onto the concrete floor.

The conveyor belt moves forward again and stops when a woman is standing under the tube. Again, the sphere closes around her head. A hiss and it opens back up empty as the headless woman walks off, leaving another trail of blood splotches behind her. It happens again to another man, two women and another man. The floor is awash in blood and red footprints.

The conveyor moves another woman to stand under the tube. She blinks a few times and a look of surprise blooms on her face. The sphere begins to close around her head but she ducks to avoid it.

She jumps off the conveyor belt and runs. She doesn't get far. After a few steps, she grabs her chest and doubles over in pain. She drops to her knees and tries to cry out but something in her mouth is muffling her voice. She reaches into her mouth with one hand and pulls out a glob of orange slime. It stretches as she pulls it away, forming a bridge of viscous goo between her hand and her mouth. Gagging, she pulls and the strand of slime only gets longer.

She starts gurgling and coughing. She yanks more out with her other hand but it only gets longer. Hand over hand, she begins jerking out more and more of the strand, creating a growing orange puddle on the bloodstained floor. The slime doesn't even seem to be coming from her mouth anymore but from somewhere further down her throat.

As she keeps pulling, the strand's color gets darker, going from orange to brown to dark red. It's no longer slime she's pulling out of her mouth, but vines of her own blood vessels. She keeps frantically wrenching them out, even as the skin on her face and neck twitches from being pulled inward. She looks up at the camera with crazed eyes open wide and bloodshot. Looking right at Warren.

Suddenly, mid-pull, her hands stop, as if she's just tried to pull something too heavy to move. Her eyes close and her hands fall to her sides. She's still kneeling on the floor but her body relaxes.

She's not motionless. Something inside her neck starts moving upwards, making her unconscious head tilt back. The entwined rope of blood vessels hanging from the side of her mouth is pushed out and, at last, a bleeding end of the strand drops to the floor.

Something inside pushes her mouth open wider. A small gray head with four green eyes pushes up from her mouth. The nose-less, mouth-less face looks into the screen at Warren and makes a rapid clicking sound. The flat computer voice comes in as a voiceover and says: "This is not fantasy. All of this is happening somewhere out there."

The screen goes black for a second and then fills again with the lightning-fast montage of symbols from the end of the first movie. The colors seem to glow brighter until looking at them begins to feel like staring at the sun.

Warren looked away from the screen but the symbols still flashed in front of his eyes like a burn on the retinas. And the symbols weren't the only thing he saw now in the strobe-lit the-ater. The seats were all filled with people who looked like ghostly shadows in the screen's flashing light.

Warren jumped out of his seat and ran out to the aisle. No one in the seats moved. Even in the screen's bright light, it was somehow too dark to see their faces. They were just shapes of people, here for one split second in a flash of light and then gone for another instant when the screen went dark. Then back again as another burning bright symbol exploded onto the screen and into Warren's field of vision.

Then the people were gone; replaced by a swarm of large, bug-like creatures with large wings and downward-curved scorpion tails. They weren't just sitting in the seats. They were crawling on the walls and scampering on the floor between the seats. The flashing symbols were so disorienting, it took Warren a moment to realize one of the creatures had perched on the back of a seat right next to him.

He screamed and ran backward but he didn't see the creature anymore. He saw himself clumsily trying to run away. He brought his hands up to rub his eyes but his vision didn't get dark. He only saw himself rubbing his own eyes and realized he was seeing himself through the eyes of the creature that landed near him.

"What's happening to me!?" he watched himself yell.

He tried running out of the theater but moving while seeing himself in third-person made him uncoordinated and he tripped over his own feet. He fell and pain stabbed at his shoulder as he watched himself land on it.

Then he was looking up at the theater from the ground. His eyes were his own again. He couldn't see anyone or anything else in the theater with him.

The screen wasn't flashing its dizzying stream of symbols anymore. It only showed the words:

THERE IS A HOLE IN YOUR HEAD

Then the screen then went dark, but Warren could still see the theater and the empty seats. Something was giving off a soft glow. He looked around for the source of the light. Then he looked down. It was his own skin glowing. He screamed and everything turned black.

When his vision came back, Warren was sprinting through the parking lot outside. He tried to find his car but his field of vision was so wide now it was hard to focus. As if he was looking at the world with four eyes instead of two. And every few seconds, he was looking down at himself, seeing himself from the roof of the theater building. But he didn't dare look up at the roof.

Instead, he willed himself to stop running and calm down. He took several deep breaths and focused on narrowing his vision. After a minute or two, what had been sky, ground, street and buildings all at once got smaller until he was just looking at the parking lot. Then just his car. Then the world went dark again.

***

When the light came back, Warren was sitting on the couch in his apartment. The glow of the streetlight outside his window told him it was night. How much time had gone by?

Monica walked in from the bedroom and got a can of soda from the refrigerator.

"Hey, what time is it?" Warren asked, rubbing his eyes.

"Oh, so you're talking to me again?" she said, glaring at him.

"Huh? What are you talking about?"

She crossed her arms. "Please don't play dumb with me. I'm really not in the mood for this anymore."

"I promise I don't know what you're talking about," Warren said. "The last thing I remember is coming out of the movie; and you wouldn't even believe what happened with that. And then I was here. What did I do?"

Monica studied him, her eyes shifting back and forth between concern and doubt. Warren wondered if she was waiting for him to say something else, but he had no idea what.

"When I walked in you were just staring out the window," she finally said. "When I tried talking to you, you turned and looked at me like you didn't know who I was. And then you were making this weird clicking noise with your mouth. I thought you were joking around at first. But you kept doing it. And you kept looking at me like you were trying to figure out who I was."

She hugged her arms around herself and looked away from him. "I didn't like it," she said, her voice just above a whisper.

Warren closed his eyes and struggled to remember anything after spotting his car in the parking lot. But everything between then and when he came to on the sofa was as black as deep space. It was a gap in his memory. A hole in his head. What were those movies doing to him? Why couldn't he just have been satisfied watching Hollywood blockbusters like everyone else?

"I'm sorry," he said. "I really am. I would never do something on purpose to scare you. There's something screwy going on at the theater showing those movies. I think they might have drugged me or something."

"Didn't you say it was three movies you had to buy tickets for?" Monica asked. "I really hope you're not going to go back to see the last one."

"Hell no," Warren said. "That place gave me enough weirdness to last a lifetime. The two movies I saw aren't even any good. Just a bunch of gory, wannabe-arthouse, tryhard, found footage shit. They don't even have a storyline. I guess that's what I get for watching something based on online rumors."

"Thank you," Monica said. "You know, there's always going to be something out there that's sicker and more shocking than whatever you've already seen. That stuff is a rabbit hole with no bottom." Then she grinned. "In the meantime, if you just have to see something edgy and taboo, you could just try looking at porn like a normal person."

"And thank you for confirming just now that you've never checked my browser history," he said and they both laughed.

"Let's go to bed," she said. "It's almost eleven and I've got to be in the office early tomorrow to go over the press kits one more time before they go out."

Warren picked up the remote to turn off the TV as Monica walked into the bedroom. He was about to push the power button when he saw a picture of the man he met at the theater on the screen. The word "MISSING" was under his picture.

Warren turned up the volume. The news report said his name was Patrick Rugato and his roommates last saw him when he left to see a movie. They reported him missing after getting several "disturbing texts" from him. The reporter said the police would not give details about what the texts said.

"Hey, babe. Are you coming?" Monica called from the bedroom.

"I'm on my way," Warren said.

He had already freaked her out once today. No need to get her worried all over again with this. But he'd call the police tomorrow and tell them about the theater and that he'd seen Patrick there.

"Definitely not going back to watch that third movie," he said to himself and turned the TV off.

***

When Warren woke up, he was standing in the movie theater.

"No!" he cried. "How did I get here?"

It had to be a dream. He closed his eyes and strained, hoping it would wake him up. He slapped himself and then screamed "Wake up!" It was all useless. He was still standing in the empty theater filled with waiting seats.

He looked up at the black window of the projection booth at the back of the theater.

"I don't know how you assholes got me back here," he said. "But I'm leaving. You can keep your money for that last ticket. I'm done with all of this. Done!"

He walked out of the theater and into the hallway that led to the front door. The glass door showed it was night outside. Was it still the night he went to sleep with Monica in his apartment or had a whole day gone by?

He took a few steps toward the door when the voice in the ticket booth startled him.

"You must stay to watch final film," it said.

"Screw you," Warren said. "How did you get me here? Did you drug me? Kidnap me? Actually, it doesn't matter. The police can figure it out after I go and tell them all about this place."

He took a few more steps when the ticket window exploded outward in a wave of broken glass and torn fabric.

The shape of a person with gray skin that glowed yellow climbed out through the window and stood in the narrow hallway, blocking Warren's path to the door. But what stood in front of him wasn't still a person. The man's head was bent back and his mouth pushed open by the head of a creature with four green eyes that rose out from it. Beneath its four eyes, a black voice box was strapped to its face where a mouth should have been.

The body took a step toward Warren and when the gray head started clicking, the voice box spoke in that same computer voice.

"You may not leave until you have viewed the final film," it said. "We are prepared to use physical force to ensure your compliance."

It took another step toward Warren and he dashed backward. He was about to run back into the theater when he noticed the "Employees Only" door on the wall next to him. Warren grabbed the doorknob and to his relief, the door opened when he turned it.

"You're not forcing me to do anything," Warren said and went through the door.

He ran up a flight of stairs past the door and turned a corner at the landing to a short hallway. There was a closed door on the right side of the hallway and another closed door at the end of the hallway. Warren rushed to the door on the right and opened it.

There was no one in the small projection room. The projector sat in front of the window facing the movie screen. Next to the projector, a satellite dish sat atop a four-foot-tall metal pole. The dish was pointed upward to a hole cut in the ceiling that showed the night sky. A thick, black cord connected the dish to the projector. There were no film reels or digital hard drives anywhere. If the movies were coming to the projector through the dish, where were they coming from?

Slow, heavy footsteps were coming up the stairs. Warren took one more quick look around the room. There was nothing here that could help him. He ran down the hallway to the door at the end as the footsteps reached the top of the stairs.

He flung the door open, then gasped and took a step back.

Patrick Rugato sat limp in the chair inside the broom closet. His mouth hung open and his open, unblinking eyes stared up at nothing. He almost looked dead. But his skin glowed a dull yellow light. And his neck started throbbing, as if something inside was moving around.

Behind him, the footsteps were coming down the hall and Warren spun around. The dead man with a creature's head sticking out of his mouth stood in front of Warren with clenched fists raised.

The creature made a long series of rapid clicks that might have been shouting. "We require that you watch third film," the voice box said.

"Why the hell is it so important to you that I watch your weird movies?" Warren demanded.

"Because another one of us is close to being rescued," the voice box said. "Every moment of delay means a few more of us starve and go silent."

"What are you talking about?" Warren asked. "Who's going to starve?"

"There is no time for persuasion," it said. "You must bring him back to the viewing area."

"Who are you talking to?" Warren said and something behind him made a noise.

When Warren turned around, Patrick's glowing body was standing just inches away from him. Like the one from the ticket booth, his head was now bent back with a gray four-eyed creature's head sticking out of the mouth. Cold, glowing hands were gripping the sides of Warren's face before he even saw them move. Four green eyes all focused on him as its head extended out from Patrick's mouth on a serpentine neck. Waves of purple and orange and gray filled Warren's vision, blinding him to everything else. He felt himself falling and let out a scream he couldn't hear.

When his vision came back, he was looking at the unlit movie screen. Thin chains on his wrists and forearms kept his hands tied to the chair's armrest. Another chain around his torso kept him pressed against the back of the seat.

He gritted his teeth as he strained in vain against the chains holding him in the seat.

"Your movie must be a real pile of shit if you have to chain people to their seats to get them to watch it," he yelled to the empty theater.

As if in response to him, the house lights dimmed and the screen lit up again.

BIOLUMINESCENT

Warren was about to close his eyes and defiantly refuse to look. But the first thing that shows up after the title is an image of himself staring at him from the screen. The Warren on the screen stands still for a long moment, holding eye contact with the Warren in the chair and moving only to blink.

He then brings a razor up to his face and slides it across his open eye, leaving a horizontal red line that divides it in half. The eyeball opens at the cut like a new mouth and as it opens and closes a voice that sounds like several voices in unison speaks.

"We will tell you this now," the eyeball says as blood runs down its bottom half from the open cut. "So that you may better understand what has happened."

In his seat, Warren blinked his own eyes several times to make sure they were still unharmed. How had they filmed this?

"Since the beginning of our history, kylov was the only source of nourishment we required," the eyeball continues. "But now we consume it faster than the ground can produce it. There is starvation and so many of us become silent. A new world is needed, but the universe is so big. Traveling to a suitable planet using conventional means would take one hundred lifetimes. Only consciousness can move fast enough to cover the distance. The correct sequence of visual glyphs can create a pathway to quickly move through space. But that consciousness must have somewhere to go. A new mind must be made ready for it."

Blood from the talking eye is running down the cheek like crimson tears. The Warren on the screen brings the razor up to his face again and slices it across the other eye. When that eye opens at the wound and starts talking, it sounds like a different set of voices.

"But for a human mind to accept its new occupants, it must first be …. tenderized," the second eyeball says as another set of bloody rivulets flow down from the bottom half of the slit orb. "This can be achieved through repeated exposure to feelings of disgust, revulsion and fear. It is fortunate for us that there are those on your planet who willingly subject themselves to such feelings. Those such as you. It is happening now as you watch this."

"But I don't want this," Warren cried, struggling again against the chains holding him in the seat. "How do I stop it?"

"It is already happening," the two eyeballs say together. "There is a hole in your head now."

The sequence of symbols and glyphs are flashing across the screen again, so fast it's dizzying; so bright it's blinding. It goes on for a long time. Sometimes, for just a fraction of a second, Warren sees himself on the screen screaming to the sky with hollow sockets where his eyes had been. Other times, it's a field of stars streaking past him. The longer he stares, the more it feels like the symbols are imprinting themselves on his eyes. For an instant, Warren wants to close his eyes. But he's not alone in the theater. Four-eyed, glowing creatures with wings are hovering all around him, slowly floating closer.

Then Warren doesn't see them and instead sees himself chained to the chair and now he's the one moving closer to himself through the air. Somewhere in the back of his mind, he knows he should feel scared. But that person in the chair doesn't feel like him anymore. It's someone else. A hollow puppet for him to move around.

He floats closer to the Warren who's chained to the seat until he's hovering right in front of him. There are no pupils in his open, unblinking eyes; only a reflection of the ever-changing sequence of glyphs on the movie screen. The skin is glowing, almost as bright as the screen. The mouth opens and clicking sounds come out. But he can understand it now. The clicking is telling him the voyage was successful. It tells him a new home has been found.

Warren then remembers that the trilogy of movies is called *Wormhead* and despair fills him as he realizes what he's done to himself. There is indeed a hole in his head. A wormhole.

The screen goes dark and a sea of black fills his vision.

***

When Warren opened his eyes again he was staring up at the night sky. He looked around but didn't recognize the parking lot he was standing in. He was holding a shopping bag filled with wires and circuit boards he didn't remember buying. Where was he? He couldn't see his car anywhere. How did he get here?

He pulled his cellphone out of his pocket. The screen flashed a low battery warning. He only had one percent power left. The date showed two days had gone by. There were dozens of texts and missed calls from Monica; almost as many voicemails.

He was about to call her back when he stopped, his finger freezing just above the button to dial her number. A cacophony of clicks filled his head, so loud it drowned out all his thoughts.

The clicks told him he needed to deliver the supplies he had just acquired. There was still work to be done. The person whose name was on his cellphone screen wasn't important, not when there were still so many more back home who needed to be rescued.

The cellphone screen flashed an image of a red battery for a few seconds and then went off. Warren let the phone fall from his hand and clatter onto the asphalt.

He wished he could call Monica and tell her he was still alive. But they weren't done with him.

The clicking in his head was growing thunderous. Warren knew he was about to black out again. How much more time would he lose? Where would he be when he woke up? Would he wake up again at all?

Monica was right, he realized as his vision faded and the roar of clicks rose in his mind. Anyone could watch something. Watching something was the easy part. Getting that thing out of your head afterward was much harder.

Then everything went dark.

***

When not writing fiction, Bernard McGhee works on the editing desk of a busy newsroom, which provides a constant source of inspiration for horror and other stories of unusual mayhem. His work has appeared in "Apparition Literary Magazine," "Cosmic Horror Monthly" and the anthology "Nightmare Sky: Stories of Astronomical Horror." He was raised in the New Orleans area but has lived all around the country. He currently lives in the Atlanta area and spends too much time watching horror movies and listening to death metal. You can follow him on X at @BMcGhee13.

A Corporate Family

by Elizabeth Devecchi

A Corporate Family

Another party, another opportunity to show the world what a happy couple they were. She knew that staying home was not an option he would accept this time.

"What will my boss think if I show up without my wife, again?" Daniel said. "The guys who move up the chain, get the big raises. They're the ones with smiling wives by their sides, that mingle and make small talk. Don't think your absences have gone unnoticed."

"If I sleep with the boss," she asked, "will that get you a raise?"

She meant it as a joke… kind of. She presented it as a joke, smirking at him after she said it. Daniel didn't laugh.

"Please get ready, Helen. This is important. You used to be good at this stuff." He rolled his eyes and left the bedroom.

Yes, he was right. She used to be good at schmoozing at parties, making conversation. She used to be… when they were younger and he was just starting out at the company. Back then, the two of them glided into office parties, worked the room like skaters on an Ice Capades tour. Back then, she knew who she was, who he was.

The change had not been sudden. If it had been, surely she would have called him out. Noticed it happening. Found a way to stop it. Instead she made excuses for him, ignoring flag after flag.

He must have had a hard day at work. He's just in a bad mood. I should have done better. He didn't mean it.

Helen wandered into her closet, a complacent sigh brushing her lips as she exhaled. She extended a hand and ran it along the fabric of the dresses hanging in a neat colorful row before her. Each dress held the memory of a dinner, a party, a momentous occasion. She paused for a moment at the sudden awareness of the time that had passed since the last such occasion.

She'd only been to one event at Daniel's current office, the *Big League*, as he liked to call it. He worked developing AI tech for things like traffic lights and banks. The parties in his old office were cozy and fun. The *Big League* event was stuffy and formal. She'd felt out of place, deprived of oxygen. After one drink, she'd handed her glass to Daniel, told him to tell his colleagues she'd suffered a sudden migraine, and taken a cab home.

Her hand grasped the shoulder of a turquoise dress, steadying her against the wave of an unwanted memory. It was the dress she wore to the Christmas party where they announced the happy news of her first pregnancy. Helen had heard it was best to wait until after the first trimester, but they were young and the two of them felt invincible. The fact that they would soon be three, then four, then who-knew, was a foregone conclusion.

In the end, there had been five pregnancies, but only two "happy" announcements. They waited the customary time for the second, to be sure. But, that pregnancy ended shortly into her fourth month, as if tragedy were waiting just long enough to make it-self well-known. Helen hadn't made any more announcements after that. With the third, then fourth, there hadn't been time before there was no longer anything to announce. And, by the fifth, she didn't say a word, not even to Daniel.

She'd watched him lose interest. He had mourned with her the first few times. Then, a thin skin of impatience had grown over him. It felt like he blamed her, maybe even as much as she blamed herself. In the end, indifference won the day and they drifted apart, into their own separate worlds.

Daniel was promoted to his new office, and was climbing his company's ladder, hand over hand. Helen threw herself deep into her writing, using the raw pain coursing beneath her quiet exterior to garner a following in the world of horror. She used a pen name to avoid embarrassing her husband, perhaps hindering his ascent. She still cared for him, after all. Or, at least for the memory of him. And, though he never read a single word she wrote, he knew the genre she trafficked in, and had thanked her for her discretion.

This invitation to accompany him to the office Christmas par-ty had come as a surprise. It had been years since she'd flanked him at any event, since he'd even asked. Years since she'd left the comfort of her writing room for events. She went shopping, kept their apartment stocked and homey. And, took an occasional stroll for coffee at the Koffee Playce on the corner, spacing her visits just enough not to be recognized as a regular, to be able to order "the usual." Thanks to the turnover typical of the times, she rarely saw the same barista more than two or three times anyway, before fresh new faces appeared. Faces that seemed younger and younger as the years ticked past.

Her friends were now mostly of the online persuasion. People tended to drift away when you allowed them to. And, she was content to keep her human interactions anonymous, a smile exchanged with a stranger, or over the internet as a part of her many bookish social media groups, whether as a fan or favorite author, a voice behind an avatar.

"Are you ready, dear?"

His tone was reminiscent of the Daniel of so many years ago. So much so, that Helen paused for a moment while applying her lipstick, almost certain she'd awoken from some decades-long nightmare. Her heart fluttered, tapping inside her ears like the frantic wings of a hummingbird and her hand drifted down to her stomach, reaching for the promise of familial happiness that once resided there. "Helen?"

Her eyes refocused on the mirror, as if his voice had turned the ring of a lens. The image before her not the face of decades ago, but the longing eyes of the present. She sighed.

"Almost done, Daniel," she said. "Just putting on my lipstick and I'm ready."

"Good. We cannot be late. I know it's just a party, but these get-togethers are never *just* anything to the boss. If I am to climb any higher, and I intend to, I need to show that I am a reliable, respectable family man."

"Respectable or respectful?" Helen quipped, regretting her comment immediately. Perhaps the word *family* had poked her a little too hard. "Sorry," she said, capping the lipstick and sliding it into her clutch. "It's just been a while since I've been to one of these. I'm afraid I'm a little out of practice."

A hint of exasperation flared in her husband's eyes, quickly extinguished by a blink. Replaced with a look of strained understanding that tickled the skin on the back of Helen's neck, sending a staticky tingle down her spine. She straightened and gave her hair one more light adjustment with the tips of her fingers.

"There," she said, smiling into the mirror at Daniel's reflection. "I'm ready when you are."

She turned and walked past him, laying a gentle hand on his shoulder. He placed a hand on hers and followed, as if being lead out onto the dance floor of some lavish ballroom. A slight smirk graced the corner of his mouth, and for a moment she thought she saw something akin to the love he used to have for her.

"If you *really* don't want to come... you don't have to."

The words took her by surprise. Helen stopped and swiveled on the ball of her foot, her gaze meeting his. His brows were furrowed, his mouth pinched, curving his lips into a pout. He studied her with dark, intense eyes. And for the briefest of moments, it seemed he had more to say. Then, his face smoothed into a neutral palette, void of emotion.

"It's fine," said Helen with a sigh. "I'm all gussied up and ready to go." *Whether or not I wish to,* she added in her head, careful to keep the thought buried deep in her mind. "It's a party. It'll be fun, right?"

"Yes, darling. It will be fun."

Something about the way he said *fun* caused her toes to curl in her pumps.

***

aniel's new office was in the same building as his previous, six floors higher and a mere two floors below the penthouse, where the company CEO, who Helen had never met, had his office. In the taxi, on the way to the party, Daniel went on about what a genius the man was.

"A man with a vision," said Daniel, his eyes glazed, fixed on an image somewhere outside the window that only he could see. "You are going to love Mr. Maya. He specifically asked to meet you, you know. That is something that only happens when he is thinking about giving a promotion." He turned and smiled at Helen, taking her hands in his. "He insists on knowing everything about his people, before entrusting them with the top positions in the company. This could be big for us. A huge raise. We could move to a nicer neighborhood."

"I rather like our neighborhood," said Helen, but he didn't seem to hear her.

She bit the inside of her lip. She supposed it wouldn't make a difference if they moved. She didn't have close friends nearby and she could do her work anywhere. Besides, it was important to Daniel. As long as she had a place to write, it would be fine.

The taxi pulled up to the curb in front of the building and they exited after settling the fare. When they arrived at the main entrance, Daniel turned to Helen, an impish grin curling one corner of his mouth.

She furrowed her brows into inquisitive arches. "What?" she asked. "Do I have something on my face? Did my lipstick smudge?"

"You have become so paranoid, honey. I just can't wait to see your reaction." He laughed, eliciting an awkward smile from her. Then, he extended his index finger toward a panel the size of a paperback and ran it along the surface as if signing his name. "Now, you do it," he said.

Helen reached her hand out, let it hover over the panel for a few seconds and signed her name. She let her gaze drift over to meet his. He was grinning, index finger extended upward in anticipation. A white light appeared in one corner of the surface, and spread along the edge of the panel until it illuminated the entire perimeter. Then, it blinked twice, disappeared, and the entire panel glowed a luminous, emerald green.

She started to ask what it was doing, when a small, translucent figure appeared above the panel. It looked like a mini-receptionist, dressed in a button-down blouse and a long, sensible skirt. It… she… looked at each of them and smiled.

"Good evening, Mr. and Mrs. Wilson," the tiny woman said, with a nod. "And, welcome to the party."

The door whirred, then opened before them. Daniel took a hold of the handle and motioned for Helen to go in.

"What was that?" Helen asked, her heels clicking crisp echoes against the pristine, Italian marble floor with each step into the vast lobby. "A recording of the receptionist?" She looked around, searching for a manned desk. The space was empty but for an impressive and colorful array of paintings gracing the walls of the space, their reflections adding waves of color to the gray and gold veins swirling through the white Calacatta marble.

Another projection appeared in front of the elevators at the back of the lobby. It was the same woman, the image now life-sized.

"Right this way," she instructed with a wave of her hand.

Helen and Daniel walked past a thin wooden lectern. A book with a picture of the building sat atop its angled platform. They stepped into the elevator and the button to the desired floor lit itself a soft yellow.

"Thank you, Aimi," said Daniel with a nod before the doors slid shut and the elevator began its ascent.

"*She*," said Daniel, smirking at Helen's confusion, "is our virtual receptionist. The soul of this building, everywhere, all the time."

"So, she's not a real person? An AI? Why Amy?" she asked, recalling the name he had used.

He nodded and grinned. "We took a vote, playing around with the letters A and I and came up with Artificially Intelligent Maintenance Individual. She looks kind of like an Aimi, don't you think? Anyway, your brilliant husband had a hand in creating her. She keeps the place running smoothly and secure."

"Oh," said Helen, happy when the elevator doors opened. She wasn't quite sure what else to say about... Aimi.

She found it all a little creepy. There had been much discussion in her reading groups about the dangers AI presented to creators of all kinds, from writers, to artists to actors. And, she would have preferred Aimi to have more of a video-game-avatar appearance. Aside from being slightly see-through, she was eerily realistic, down to the way her brilliant blue eyes glimmered with recognition when they met her gaze.

Aimi was waiting outside the doors. She smiled and waved a hand toward another door, which opened to reveal a mix of well-dressed partygoers, drinks in hand. Serving trays rolled about the room, pausing each time someone reached down to pick up an hors-d'oeuvre or cocktail glass.

"Thank you," Daniel said, leading his wife into the festivities.

Helen forced a smile at the AI, heat rushing to her cheeks when Aimi smiled and winked. Her wink was warm and flirtatious, spontaneous. Eerily human.

"Enjoy," she said before disappearing.

"There you are," called a deep booming voice, parting the crowd like Moses did the Red Sea.

An imposing figure in a black tuxedo glided toward them with the grace of Gene Kelly. His dark brown hair was slicked back on his head like that of an F. Scott Fitzgerald character and he approached with his left hand secured behind his back, in gentlemanly fashion. He extended his right hand to gather Helen's, raising it just below his chin before kissing the air.

"You must be Helen," he said, with a twinkle in his cerulean eyes. "Daniel, my friend," he turned to her husband, "you did not tell me how absolutely stunning your wife is."

Daniel licked his lips and smiled. He seemed uncomfortable, which pleased Helen, given the unease she herself felt. *Misery does so enjoy a companion.*

"Mr. Maya, I presume?" Helen asked, withdrawing her hand, once released. Daniel squeezed her arm, eliciting a smile meant to reassure him she would be on her best behavior. There was, after all, a potential promotion at stake. She certainly was not going to be a reason for her husband to be passed over, if she could help it.

"You presume correctly." Mr. Maya turned his attention on Daniel. "Daniel, be a good man and grab a bottle of wine of your choice and some glasses to bring back to the conference room. Let's take our little trio out of the confusion for a bit."

"Of course, sir," said Daniel, after a furtive glance at his wife.

Mr. Maya clapped a hand on the back of Daniel's shoulder. "Please, no 'sirs' tonight. It's a party, not a work day."

Daniel nodded, a thin smile upon his lips. He turned and made his way toward the bar. Mr. Maya extended an elbow to Helen. She laced the tips of her fingers under it and allowed herself to be lead in the opposite direction, to a door on the far wall.

The privacy shades on the door were drawn, and when they were closer Helen saw that the room behind it was dark. Mr. Maya waved a hand. The door whirred opened and the lights came on.

"After you," he said, stepping aside.

The room was a typical business conference room with a large mahogany desk at its center and an army of matching chairs lined up in orderly fashion around its perimeter. Matching, except for the chair at the far end, which was larger and more ornate.

The big dog chair, thought Helen with amusement. Weren't all businessmen the same? The big dog had to have the big chair. Size equaled power.

"Are you enjoying your evening, Elaine?"

"We've only just arrived," Helen answered, her jaw slacking and her breath catching the moment she realized what he had just called her.

Mr. Maya nodded, a devilish glint in his eyes, punctuated by a sly smile. "Ms. Elaine Fusco, if I am not mistaken."

She looked through the open door to see if Daniel was arriving, then turned her gaze back to her host. "How did you...?" She folded her arms across her chest.

"Relax," said Mr. Maya, "I happen to be a big fan of your novels." His voice slid through the air like silk in the wind. "You are quite talented."

A tentative smile crept across her lips. "Thank you," she said. "That's kind of you to say. Not everyone appreciates my genre."

"Give me a good horror novel any day of the week. The darker and more twisted, the better."

It was meant as a compliment, she was certain, but his tone put her on edge.

"Your *Creatures of Darkness* series is sublime. I await its next installment with bated breath. To have you as a part of our little family here is truly an honor."

"Does my husband know that you know who I am?" Helen tilted her head and examined the tall, mysterious man before her.

"I don't believe it has ever come up," he quipped, leaning against the empty table. "But then, you are hardly the only talented spouse we have on our team. To reach this level in the company, we expect our employees to bring more to the table than simply work ethic, if you know what I mean. Why, have you heard of Amanda Russell?"

"The painter?"

"Yes, the *talented* young painter whose husband started working here years ago as a security guard. He is now one of my office managers, quite talented in his own right."

"Were those her paintings in the lobby?" Helen brought to mind the painting that had caught her eye when she had first entered the building.

"Some are hers," Mr. Maya said, turning his eyes up, as if to view the works upon the ceiling. "Some were inspired by her genius. Aimi did those."

Helen parted her lips to ask what Ms. Russell though of that, when Mr. Maya stood and shifted his gaze to the door. Daniel entered holding a bottle of wine and three glasses.

"There he is," Mr. Maya bellowed, before sauntering over to meet her husband at the threshold. "Actually, my friend, don't you think it would be a good idea for your lovely wife to meet the rest of our little family? While she does, the two of us can discuss your future."

Daniel's eyes widened along with his smile. "Yes, sir," he said. "I mean, yes, of course. That sounds wonderful." Mr. Maya thrust out a hand and the two men shook on it.

"The other wives are in the meeting room on the floor below," he said, turning to Helen. "It's a much quieter, more intimate setting. Better for getting acquainted. And, you can meet Amanda Russell in person. I'll have Aimi escort you there. Your husband and I have some paperwork to sign."

At the mention of her name, a smiling Aimie appeared just outside the door.

"Doesn't that sound great, honey?" asked Daniel, laying a hand on Helen's, guiding her with a gentle nudge.

No, not really, thought Helen, concealing her doubts with a smile and a nod. Though, it did sound better than spending any more time trapped in this conference room, which was currently awash in a surging flood of testosterone. And, maybe Ms. Russell could answer some questions.

She followed Aimie through the party, only now noticing the room was void of women. Perhaps because, as Mr. Maya had mentioned, the wives were socializing one floor down. Still, the situation seemed off. The horror writer in her sensed the tingle of alarm bells.

"Is everything ok?" Aimi asked, once they were near the elevators.

Great, now the AI was asking if she was ok. She must not be hiding her paranoia very well.

"Sure, everything is fine," she said, realizing that she had addressed the AI as if she were an actual person.

Or rather, it had felt like she was addressing a real person when she spoke to the AI. Helen chewed her bottom lip, wondering how much she was allowed to ask her escort. Would the AI answer?

"Aimi," she said, drawing its eerily human gaze to her. "Do you know who I am?"

"Of course," said Aimie, an utterly human grin gracing her translucent lips. "You are Mrs. Helen Wilson, aka Ms. Elaine Fusco, talented author of many novels."

"*How* do you know who I am?"

This seemed to amuse Aimi. "Your information has been in our database for many years," she answered. "We obtained a sample at a party. But, we would like to learn more about you. Get to know you." Aimi smiled. The elevator doors opened and she motioned for Helen to enter. "We love learning more about our talented corporate family. It makes us more complete."

Helen leaned back against the mirrored wall of the elevator, trying to think of an out. The doors slid closed and the hint of a stress headache began to tug at her temples.

"Aimi, I don't suppose you could take me to the lobby, call me a cab? I feel a migraine coming on." Helen rubbed her thumb and middle finger across her forehead.

Aimi swept her with an intense and concerned gaze. "I will have medication waiting in the meeting room. You have a tension headache. You will be fine."

Helen gasped, her hand over her mouth. She fought her rising panic. She was a horror writer, after all. Sure, the situations she imagined, pecked onto the pages of her novels, were pure fiction. But, they were creatures of her mind, all the same. The thought calmed her, as if clueing her in to some innate advantage because this was somehow *her* world.

When the elevator doors opened one floor down, Helen hesitated, stepping forward only when the floor below her lifted in a slight tilt toward the opening.

Ok, then, she thought. *This is how it's going to be.* She donned her most amicable smile, the one she used in public to mask her social anxiety, and stepped past Aimi into the hallway.

The floors and walls were lined with Calacatta marble, continuing the trend in the lobby and on the previous floor. It was all so clean, so sterile. After a couple steps, Helen shifted her weight to limit the harsh clack of her heels against the stone, which only accentuated the lack of sound that accompanied Aimi's movements. And, each time she slowed her pace, the tiles beneath her lifted to urge her forward.

"May I use the restroom?" asked Helen, when she saw a door marked as such.

"There is a restroom in the meeting room, Ms. Fusco," Aimie replied, ushering her past.

Her voice had become less welcoming, more insistent. And, Helen didn't like this *thing* using her pen name. It felt like an unauthorized use of her secret identity. She imagined it would not be the only unauthorized use to take place this evening.

She had always known that Daniel worked with AI, but the harmless, useful kind. The kind that made traffic flow smoothly, and banks safer and more secure. If her intuition was correct, this company was somehow harvesting intellectual property. Worse, it was attempting to harness the imagination behind such property. For a moment she was almost flattered to be considered worthy of harvest. But, it was a fleeting moment. Perhaps she wasn't the most self-confident person alive, but she believed in herself, and was fiercely protective of the individual she had become, through her writing.

"And, here we are," said Aimi, pointing to a door of tempered glass at the end of the hall.

There were no shades on this door, allowing a full visual of the space within. Helen craned her neck to gaze inside. It looked like the waiting room of a doctor's office. Chairs upholstered in soft pink cloth lined the walls and large, cushioned ottomans were lined up between them, so the women seated upon them could converse with those seated on either side.

It looked like some kind of UN women's convention inside, its attendees chatting calmly while drinking from stemmed crystal and munching on appetizers set out on tables with long flowing red cloths atop them. Aimi waved a hand and the door whirred open. Helen was struck by the sudden revelation that this door had no handle on the inside.

The urge to run, to bolt down the hall, surged through her. But, as soon as her muscles tensed to comply, the tiles shifted and she found herself sliding forward, into the room. Most of the women seemed relaxed as they chatted, sipped, and nibbled. All of them turned their gazes when she entered the space.

Helen forced a tight smile. She scanned the room, meeting their gazes one by one, trying to gauge their levels of comfort, of awareness. One by one they smiled graciously, nodded, and went back to their previous activities. Until, all but one ignored her presence.

That woman's smile appeared forced. Her eyes reflected mistrust. That woman had an empty chair next to her. Helen looked from the chair to Aimi.

"Make yourself at home, Ms. Fusco," said Aimie, before fading from view. The door clicked shut.

Helen walked over and sat. The woman, who Helen could now see was exuding something more akin to fear than mistrust, glared at her.

"Are you," she stuttered in a whisper. "Are you *new*, too?"

Helen leaned closer. The woman's arms were folded across her chest, her fingers pressing into her dark skin hard enough to create light circles around them.

"Yes," she said. "My name is Helen." She extended a hand.

The woman released her arm, leaving small, angry marks where her fingernails pressed into the skin, and shook Helen's hand. "Shawna," she whispered. "Shawna Riley."

"Shawna Riley the director?" Helen asked, unable to keep her voice from rasping up an octave.

The woman's mouth curved into a feeble smile. "Yeah," she said. "And, I heard that AI thing call you Ms. Fusco. You aren't Elaine Fusco, are you? I mean *Elaine* isn't too far off from *Helen* as far as pen names go."

Helen grinned. "Yeah, I guess it isn't."

Shawna released Helen's hand and examined the floor at her feet. Her smile had melted back to despair. "In other circumstances, I'd ask for your number. I've been wanting to put several of your books onto the big screen since reading them. But," she looked up at Helen, desperation in her eyes, "we have bigger problems now."

Helen nodded. Shawna reached over and placed a hand on her knee, tilting her head down and observing her, as if over the rims of invisible glasses.

"I think they *subdued* the others. They have each had a trip to the back room," she said nodding toward a door to their right. Then, her lips quivered. "I think it's my turn next," she said in an airy, and barely audible whisper. One side of her mouth curved up. "I keep waiting for my husband to pop out the door, yell, 'You've been punked!' but I'm pretty sure the bastard sold me out for a raise and a bigger office." She shook her head. A puff of disdain parted her lips.

The door whirred open revealing a man dressed in a soft gray uniform. He made a beeline to them, smiled, and held up a gloved hand. Two cotton swabs twirled between his index finger and thumb.

"I need a quick swab from each of you before your visit," he said, matter-of-fact.

"What the hell is going on here?" hissed Helen, verbally lunging at the opportunity to get real information from a real person. She leaned forward, but the man seemed unfazed by her vehemence.

Shawna set a hand on Helen's shoulder and steadied her. "Don't," she whispered. "I've seen how this ends. It's not pretty. It's a quick swab and they're gonna get it anyway."

Helen shook her head, mouth pinched in defiance, and sank back into her seat. She looked from the orderly to Shawna and sighed. The orderly switched one of the swabs to his other gloved hand and extended the remaining one toward Shawna, who opened her mouth and allowed him to run the swab along the inside of both cheeks. The man then deposited the swab into a vial attached to his belt and sealed it shut with the smooth grace that comes from repetition. Then, he turned his dull, brown eyes to Helen, pausing to see if she would comply.

Helen opened her mouth and closed her eyes, embarrassed by her complicity. She flinched when the soft dry swab skated along the inside of her cheeks, gathering information that should belong to her and her alone.

"There. That wasn't hard, was it?"

The man marched away, ignoring the hatred Helen beamed at him through narrowed eyes. She sighed and shook her head, launching inaudible curses at Daniel. How dare that bastard sell her out, as if he owned her, as if he were the true proprietor of her creativity.

"We have to get out of here," she whispered, leaning close to Shawna and lowering her voice to a ghost of a whisper. "Now."

"How?" Shawna whispered back. "The door out of here has no handle. And, from what I've seen, not much time passes between the swab and a trip to the back room. I think they're uploading our information into some kind of processor. I think they're putting us into some kind of AI database." She pulled a soft whistle through her teeth. "Man, I sound batshit crazy. Worse than the characters in my films."

Helen released a soft, brief laugh. "The whole thing kind of reminds me of that film you did..."

Shawna held up a hand and smiled. "I know the one you mean. Not my best work."

They sat in silence. By the hard lines on Shawna's face, Helen could see she, too, was working the problem. Helen let her gaze wander, scanning the room around her again. This time she paid less attention to its occupants, who seemed helplessly tamed, and more on the make-up of the space. There were two doors, the exit with no handle, and the door to the back room.

Helen was studying the exit door with intensity, when several shadowy figures rushed past it on the other side. Her heart slammed against her ribs like the mallet of a drum kick and it took all her will to stay seated. She tapped Shawna with the side of her hand, trying not to draw the attention of the other occupants or the cameras that most definitely covered the waiting room.

When Shawna looked at her, Helen motioned to the door using only her eyeballs and watched her friend follow her gaze without moving her head. Shadowy figures loomed outside the door to the side. They squeezed hands. The women around seemed oblivious to the new arrivals.

The figures were slight, like maybe they were children. One of them was holding a small hand up at them to wait, while another hovered near where the handle should be on the other side. Helen and Shawna sat, fingers laced tightly together, watching from the corners of their eyes. Helen's muscles tensed like thick metal springs, winding tight to prepare for a massive release, adrenaline pulsed through her.

The whir of the exit door rang out like the *bang* of a starter gun. And, she was off like a thoroughbred racehorse through the gates, hand in hand with Shawna. As they neared the exit, they heard the backroom door open and the sound of quick, heavy footsteps. They slipped into the hallway and watched the door slam behind them just as several orderlies smacked into it, waving their hands.

A burst of giggles pulled their attention from the men to four girls, running from tween-aged to perhaps early twenties. The youngest was bent over, laughing uncontrollably, while the oldest regained her composure. She smiled at the two frightened women with warmth, but urgency twinkled in her eyes.

"Let's get you two out of here," she said, then poked at the smallest girl, who was still giggling, though less hysterically now. "Come on, guys. We need to hurry. Mom needs help."

Helen's lips parted, a gateway to a million questions, but all four girls had turned and were sprinting toward the elevator. They bolted past the double doors and opened a handleless door to the stairwell instead, though Helen couldn't see how, motioning for the women to follow. Helen and Shawna needed no prodding. They dashed through the door and flew down flight after flight to the lobby of the building, bursting out across from the same elevator doors that had swallowed them up into the building mere hours ago. The tiles around them suddenly came to life, lifting and circling them, blocking their progress.

"Where are you going? And who do we have here?" asked a voice, Aimi's voice.

Helen whirled around, knocking into the podium by the elevator and spilling the book onto the floor by her feet, where it lay open to the first page and an acknowledgment with a large photo by its side.

"Not possible," said Helen, her voice airy and thin. The words next to a cracked, faded photo of Mr. Maya read *Our Founder*. And, the year scrawled under the image was 1928. "Not possible. He took my hand. He was warm. He was *real*."

Aimi smiled at them and Helen thought she saw jealousy... envy... in the AI's expression. "Mr. Maya is next gen, my dear. He should be here shortly. Save any questions on the matter for him. And, your little friends won't be helping you anymore. Glitches in the system, gleaned from information your husband supplied, and materialized during your initial upload. We apologize. It won't happen again." Aimi pointed to the girls, who seemed frozen in time.

My girls, Helen thought, fighting to keep the tears, a mix of longing and hatred, from blurring her vision.

Shawna took her hand once more, squeezed it in support. Then, Aimi waved the elevator doors open and extended her arm, instructing the tiles to usher the women inside. But, before they took a single step, a whir of color zipped across the lobby, flattening the tiles, knocking Aimi through the doors, and sealing them.

A young girl, now the smallest of the five, waved a hand, opening the front doors to the building and freeing her sisters.

"Hurry," whispered Helen's youngest. The one only she had known about.

Shawna and Helen ran through the doors to the outside, turning to see the girls standing at the threshold. Helen took a step toward them, but Shawna held her back.

"I'm sorry," she said, "but I don't think they can come."

The girls nodded, smiling at their distraught mother. "It's ok, Mamma," they said as a chorus. "We are always with you. We are a part of who you are."

And, in that moment, Helen understood that it was true.

***

Elizabeth Devecchi spent her formative years in Rhode Island, setting out after high school to travel and gather degrees. She writes in a variety of genres and styles, but has been focusing on horror as of late. Recent releases include: her debut poem, "Oh, Brother," which appears in Volume II of Black Spot Books's annual women in horror poetry showcase titled Under Her Eye (November 2023) in collaboration with The Pixel Project in an effort to end violence against women; a recipe accompanied by a flash fiction story in Nightmare Fueled Inc's anthology Cooks of Horror (August 2024); and horror poem "In the Belly of the Mills," which appears in the anthology Monsters in the Mills, launched at the prestigious horror conference NecromoniCon in Providence, RI (August 2024). Her debut horror novel, *A Whisper in the Dark*, signed by Wicked House Publishing released on October 4th of 2024. Upcoming releases include: short horror story "Open House," to appear in a Running Wild Press anthology in 2025; and debut thriller/suspense novel, *A Twist of the Lens*, to be published by Wicked House Publishing in mid-2025. Elizabeth is a member of the Horror Writer's Association, Rocky Mountain Fiction Writers, Castle Rock Writers, and the Italian American Writers Association. She currently resides in Parker, Colorado with her husband, children, and an ever-changing menagerie of pets and "guest creatures." For more info: elizabethdevecchi.com

BLOODHOUSE 64
by Jude Deluca

C*LOVER FALLS HIGH, MAY 199X*

"Brody! Stop fidgeting!"

"My nose's itchy!"

"You're ruining the pose!"

"Hold on." Coral Caldwell set her pencil down on the easel and walked to where Brody Callahan posed. She reached up and scratched Brody's nose for him. "Better?"

"Much." Brody sighed. "You're a life saver, Cor."

"Good," Coral answered by playfully punching Brody in his side. "Now stop fidgeting," she ordered and returned to her canvas.

It was late afternoon in May and the Clover Falls High Art Club was working on a group project. Their faculty advisor, Mrs. Hanley, went to the restroom while everyone tried to capture Brody's essence. As the biggest member of the school's water polo team, regarding height *and* weight, Brody had a *lot* of essence to capture.

Coral's canvas showed her working on the space around Brody, making an outline of his full figure. Mrs. Hanley's only tenet for the project was for everyone to put their own spin on the model's figure, so long as it was tasteful, not derivative, and truly captured the model's essence as best they could. Coral filled her borders with gothic imagery, hauntingly contrasted by the blank emptiness where the model should've been.

Once Mrs. Hanley returned to the art room, she announced, "Everyone, our designated time's coming to a close so let's wrap up for the day." Turning to Brody, she said, "You can sit down now, Mr. Callahan."

Brody let out a sigh as he loosened up and flopped down, as dramatically as possible, onto the couch in the art room.

"Being an inspiration takes a lot out of guy," Brody declared.

"Drama queen," Coral joked under her breath. She looked towards her right at Justin Carmichael's canvas, depicting Brody in a mock-up of *The Birth of Venus*. Justin altered the small blond ponytail Brody usually had and gave him a golden, flowing mane of hair.

On her left, Coral saw that Delilah Peterson had dressed Brody up like a fireman. Kind of. Coral tried to hide her grimace from Delilah's line of sight. She was sure Mrs. Hanley was going to give Delilah crap for it, when her best friend, Eileen "Echo" Ferguson, came up to her.

"Wanna come over tonight for the new episode of *Wendy the Werewolf Hunter*?" Echo asked her GF, which in this case meant both "goth friend" AND "girlfriend." The two girls wore a startling amount of black in their wardrobe and had their hair dyed and styled in a similar fashion. Echo's hair was completely, unnaturally black, save for her red bangs, while Coral's naturally blonde hair had streaks of black and red in it. Somehow the school board never gave them grief about this.

"I'll head over later. Gotta meet up with my sister first," Coral explained while putting away her art supplies. "She's making her annual attempt to 'subtly' figure out what I want for my birthday by gauging my reaction in whichever store she's taking me to."

"That time of year, huh?" Echo laughed. "Poor baby."

"What's that?" Brody asked as he slung his beefy arms around Coral and Echo. "Coral's sister is taking her for the usual 'I'm Not Shopping For Your Birthday At All' thing? Where's she bringing you?"

"Dunno," Coral admitted. "She hasn't hinted yet, which says a lot about how hard she's trying."

"Well, you're never gonna guess what *I* got you," Brody teased in a singsongy voice.

"And I'm giving you cash again so I don't really care if you know," Echo bluntly admitted.

"Gee, thanks," Coral flatly replied. "How much?"

"Enough."

"At least MY gift comes from the heart," Brody proudly declared. "That means I win at birthday."

"You do not!"

Coral finished packing up her belongings as Echo and Brody argued about their respective gift-giving abilities, and she couldn't help but smile at their ridiculousness. She was glad to have the two in her life. Coral appreciated Echo's sarcastic streak and their matching tastes in clothing and music, as well as Brody's respectful sense of humor and ease with himself in both his body and identity.

In a way, Coral considered Brody her boyfriend and Echo her girlfriend. She wasn't exactly sure what kind of relationship they shared, but it was something she couldn't imagine life without.

As Echo was punctuating a statement by jabbing her index finger into Brody's big belly, Coral got between the two and gave them both a kiss on the cheek.

"I gotta run," Coral said while slinging her backpack over her shoulder. "Hold off on killing each other in the meantime. Or until after my birthday."

"No promises!" Was their shared response as Coral left to find her sister.

Meanwhile as Art Club wrapped up, a group of girls were cheering on the school's football field.

"*2! 4! 6! 8! WHO DO WE APPRECIATE!? RANGERS! RANGERS! GOOOOOOO RANGERS!!!!!*"

"Ugh," Darnice Peterson complained. "Priscilla, do we have to use this one? It's worn out and corny!"

Priscilla Yonehara, captain of the Clover Falls Cheer Squad, pointed a pompom in Darnice's direction and reminded her, "I told you guys we were having a brainstorming session for new cheers and most of you didn't show. Don't complain about the lack of new material."

"Some of us *do* have lives you know," Gretchen Barreto coldly added as she pulled out a compact mirror to check her hair. If even a single strand of honey-colored hair was out of place, Gretchen would make it everyone's problem. No one understood why she joined a cheer squad if she was that worried about her hair. "I contain multitudes," she once said as haughtily as possible.

"I could've shown up," Jewel Fallon pitched in after taking a swig of energy drink, then grimaced. "Ugh, Atomic Cantaloupe again? I keep telling Dad I only drink Ionic Iceberry."

"Why didn't you?" Priscilla asked.

Jewel shrugged and replied, "Didn't want to."

Jewel, Gretchen, and Darnice burst into laughter while Priscilla rubbed the bridge between her eyes.

"No more of that talk, guys," Darcy Caldwell interjected as she broke up the terrible trio's laughter. "There's nothing wrong with a classic, and it's not like there isn't some inherent corniness to cheerleading. It's supposed to be fun!"

"Well, when you put it like that..." Darnice conceded. Gretchen said nothing as she went back to checking her reflection, and Jewel took another swig of the cantaloupe-flavored drink she claimed to dislike.

Darcy always broke up any arguments among the cheerleaders. She was a natural peacemaker, the kind of person who got along with everyone. Some felt Darcy should've been the captain, due to her ability to get her teammates to put in a little extra effort and her innate friendliness. Darcy turned down the offer. She didn't consider herself the leader type. She just liked to have fun.

It was no secret Priscilla was only really voted as captain because most of the members didn't want to put in the hard work. Darcy was her most ardent supporter. She knew how much Priscilla loved being a cheerleader and devoted herself to it as much as she devoted herself to everything else in her life.

Like their relationship.

Priscilla turned to Darcy and said, "Thank you."

"Anytime, hon," Darcy replied and proceeded to place her arm around Priscilla's waist, pulling her forward so the two could kiss.

"Do you HAVE to do that in front of us?" Gretchen moaned. "You're so... *adorable.*"

"Yes," Darcy happily replied as Priscilla moved a strand of Darcy's blonde hair out of her face. The younger cheerleaders, Selinda Harrow, Jackie Appleby, and Clarice Oranja, giggled while Darnice, Gretchen, and Jewel groaned.

Darcy and Priscilla had been dating for roughly two years. They were regarded as the cutest, and most insufferably sweet, couple at Clover Falls High. Even Tyrone Sylvia, Priscilla's ex, was forced to concede to their inherent cuteness. They reveled in the nauseating power they held but swore to only use it for good. Mostly. There were even rumors the two would be voted Prom Queen and Prom Queen.

Once practice was finished, the cheer squad headed into the locker room to shower and get dressed for home. As they left the school, they chatted about their weekend plans and the upcoming prom.

"Yo, Darface!" a voice called out. The cheerleaders turned to see Coral Caldwell standing on the other side of the school parking lot.

"Hey!" Darcy called out. "Guys I gotta go. I promised my sister we'd go shopping."

"You're figuring out what to get for her birthday, huh?" Priscilla deduced.

"Whaaaaat?" Darcy played dumb. "No. No! I just wanna take my sister shopping. And I'm picking up my weekly comics."

"Sure, sure." Priscilla chuckled before kissing Darcy again. "Have fun with your sister, I'll see you tomorrow."

"Love ya, Miss Pris," Darcy replied before running over to Coral.

From nearby, the cheerleaders contrasted the Caldwell sisters. Darcy was a year older, but the two were of similar height and weight. One would almost think they were twins. Both were natural blondes and wore their hair down past their shoulders. Besides that, their outfits clashed heavily. Darcy was Miss Pert-and-Perky. Coral dressed like someone in *The Craft*.

At first glance, one might say "It's great they're such close sisters despite being so *totally* different." The truth was the Caldwell sisters were a lot alike. Loyal towards their friends, creative, and two of the biggest nerds in school. Their only real difference was Coral's frightening angry side, while Darcy was sweetness and light.

In middle school, Joey Markwell told everyone that he did stuff with Darcy in the girls' bathroom. She turned him down for the Valentine's Day dance and felt that justified the rumors he spread. His biggest mistake was bragging about it within earshot of Darcy's sister.

As soon as Coral found out, she beat the snot out of him in the cafeteria for lying about her sister. Smacked him in the face with a lunch tray and wouldn't stop kicking his ass until he admitted the truth. Coral got suspended for a month, but it was worth it seeing Joey crying like a baby as he confessed his lies.

No one fucked with the Caldwell Sisters.

"—I don't understand why you drag yourself halfway across town for comics," Darcy wondered as Coral walked beside her under the shady tress. "There's a perfectly good comic store a few blocks from our house."

"The Dungeonmaster's an okay store," Coral admitted. "I prefer Ocean City Comics. And I like walking. Gives me an excuse to get out, enjoy the scenery. Soothing."

"The name doesn't make sense!" Darcy laughed. "We're not even *near* the ocean! I mean, there's the river and the falls. Why not 'River City Comics?'"

"Nor are we a city, I know," Coral added. She'd heard this before. It didn't change that Coral liked the layout of Ocean City Comics. And she *definitely* preferred Ocean City's staff to the staff of The Dungeonmaster.

Darcy wrinkled her nose while mentioning, "And it always smells weird. Not like old comics. What *is* that smell?"

Coral stopped her sister and seriously asked, "Do you *really* not know?"

Sister locked eye with sister, before both erupted in laughter knowing exactly what the "smell" in Ocean City Comics was.

The two were lost in debate about how the clone storyline in *Spider-Ant* kept on going with no ending in sight when they reached The Dungeonmaster. A one-story brick building specializing in comics, card and video games, anime, and especially horror fiction. The displays in the windows featured cutouts and posters for horror characters like the Bloodinator from the *Nexus* franchise, and the creepy Lamplighter from those "obscene" 1950s anthology comics the government tried to ban.

As Darcy pulled open the front door of the shop, Coral said, "I'll wait out here."

"What? Why?" Darcy asked.

"I have my pull list at Ocean City," Coral explained. "Shopping at another comic shop feels like treason."

"Tch, just come *in*, Cor. The place isn't radioactive."

Coral hesitated. She looked at the store's front window before turning back to her sister. Relenting, Coral sighed and followed Darcy inside.

Might as well get this over with, Coral thought.

The speakers in the store played the soundtrack to *Mad Monster Party* as the Caldwell sisters entered.

"I'm gonna pick up my comics first," Darcy explained. "You look around and lemme know if you see anything you like."

"Not exactly being subtle this year, Darface," Coral acknowledged with a smirk.

"I don't know what you're talking about!" Darcy called with a wave of her hand as she headed for the back of the store where they kept the register and the pull sheets for the regulars.

With her sister departed from her side, Coral cautiously poked her head up and down the aisles before she browsed. Keeping her senses alert, she listened to the usual banter of comic geeks in their element. She was trying to listen for one specific voice.

"—you turn the page, wash your hands. Turn the page, wash your—"

"—I heard the *Y's Guys* movie rights are up for sale—"

"—don't care I like Super-Doer Purple and Super-Doer Yellow—"

"—see the nipples on Gnatman's suit—"

"—they let Red Raven become the new Shadow Girl—"

"—the elf wenches are SO. BEAUTIFUL—"

Relaxing a bit, Coral wandered down an aisle to a wall of newly released issues. She avoided the comics she bought monthly from Ocean City, such as *Gravity Angel* and *Justice Skeletons*. Coral worked hard to avoid spoilers before she bought comics.

Another section of the store had a rack of new video games. A poster advertised that the robotic Bloodinator would be featured as an exclusive character in an upcoming *Mortal Kombat* release. Coral felt her heart skip a beat when she saw they had copies of *Scared Pools*.

"I didn't think this would ever come out." Coral sounded practically giddy, until she saw the price tag. Way out of her range. "Hmm, Darcy IS shopping for my birthday." She considered it for a moment, but decided no. She wouldn't manipulate her sister into spending that much on her birthday. Christmas, maybe. Still, it wouldn't hurt to hint...

Wandering back over to the comics, an issue of *Hecula the He-Beast* caught Coral's eye. She remembered reading an article about the writer doing some weird metafictional story where he wrote himself into the book. Curious, Coral looked through the comic.

"Ugh, is it really the writer talking with the main character about why he's writing the book?" Coral shook her head. "Morrison already did—"

"*Hi*, Coral."

Coral shut her eyes, made a sour expression, and took a deep breath through her nose as she quickly closed the comic in her hands. She recognized that oily voice, the one she dreaded hearing again.

"Haven't had a chance to talk to you in *ages*," the voice continued. "How *are* you?"

Ice in her veins and voice, Coral calmly responded, "Hello, Adam." Slowly turning around, Coral was about to say something else when she realized how close Adam was. She involuntarily took a step back, practically recoiling at the sight of Adam Holtzman. "Geez! Do you have to do that!?"

"Was I in your space?" Adam innocently asked. "I'm so sorry."

I'll bet you are, Coral thought.

Adam Holtzman was in the same grade as Coral, but they didn't share classes thank God. Coral often thought he looked like a more conventionally attractive version of Sleepy Hollow's Ichabod Crane. Physically, at least. Due to his height and lanky frame, he was on the basketball team and a good player. He once ran for class treasurer. Coral didn't vote for him. Adam was the reason she avoided The Dungeonmaster.

An uncomfortable amount of silence lay between them when Adam again asked, "How have you been?"

"I'm here with my sister," Coral coldly responded.

"I didn't see her. Y'know Darcy's *such* a good customer and she's a delight to chat with," Adam admitted. "I've spent a lot of time discussing new books with her."

The thought sent a shiver down Coral's back. She had to talk with her sister when they got home. The way Adam said it, Coral sensed he was trying to get a rise out of her. She didn't want to admit it was working.

"Of course, Darcy's tastes leave something to be desired." Adam laughed. "She likes *Super Model*."

Crossing her arms over her chest, Coral flatly revealed, "I suggested she try it."

"Oh!" Adam quickly tried to change course. "I'm just saying the quality's kind of gone downhill since that new writer came on. It's a bit too PC now, know what I mean?"

Coral simply scowled.

"Sooooo what have you been up to? Read anything good? Play any new games?" Adam tried to sound friendly, failing to realize he'd never sound friendly to Coral.

"*Gravity Angels, Justice Skeletons*, and *Generation Y*," Coral quickly answered. "I'm doing story mode on *Zeebo's Funhouse Party*."

Adam couldn't restrain himself from letting out a snort as he said, "*Zeebo*'s for little kids."

"Thanks for the input." Coral turned around. "Bye now."

"You know, Coral," Adam began, clearly incapable of reading the room. "I heard they're showing that *Strange Matter* movie at the megaplex next we—"

Coral quickly cut Adam off with a heavy "*No.*"

Adam looked hurt at Coral's rejection. "But I didn't—"

"I've told you 'No' how many times, Holtzman?" Coral sharply asked. "No, I don't wanna see *Strange Matter* with you. *No*, I didn't want to see *The Forbidden Game* with you. And *no*, I didn't want to see any of the several *Last Vampire* sequels they've churned out with you. My answer is, and always will be, no. No. **NO**. Take. The fucking. HINT."

Looking as dejected as possible, Adam said, "I just wanted to see a movie with a friend."

Coral defiantly placed her hands on her hips. "We were NEVER friends, Adam. We were in the same club in middle school. That was all. Jesus."

Adam's hurt expression turned to bitterness. He grabbed Coral's arm and yanked her towards him, lowering his voice so only Coral could hear him. "I don't understand how someone as sweet as Darcy has such an uptight bitch for a sister."

Breaking free of Holtzman's grip, Coral loudly answered, "THERE he is. The asshole I made the mistake of seeing *Nightmare Hall* with."

"That was years ago!" Adam tried to quiet her, noticing a couple of customers had caught their confrontation. "And lower your voice!"

"Yeah, years ago." Coral was getting into it as she tried to spell it out for Adam. And no, she made no attempt to lower her voice. "Years ago, I made a dumbass mistake, and you still don't get the problem. You acted like a shithead throughout the whole movie, thinking you were SO smart and funny complaining about how 'predictable' it was. You made ME pay for tickets AND snacks when you said you forgot your wallet—which you lied because you offered to get us pizza afterwards." Darcy then lowered her voice during the part she hated most. "You kept putting your arm around my shoulders, and your hand on my legs no matter how many times I told you to stop."

Adam interjected, "It's not like I did anything."

"You grabbed my head and kissed me without my permission."

"And *you* dumped soda on me. I guess that makes us even," Adam smugly replied, before saying out loud, "One kiss and you pretend to like girls just to piss me off."

Remembering when Adam grabbed her head, pressed his lips against hers, and forced his tongue into her mouth, Coral pulled her hand back and smacked him across the face.

"***Fuck you!***"

As Adam reeled from the pain in his cheek, Coral headed for the store's entrance and yelled, "*DARCY I'LL SEE YOU AT HOME!*"

Placing a hand on his face, Adam shot Coral an enraged expression as she left the store. He looked around and saw several people giving him disgusted expressions. Scowling, Adam made his way through the aisle to the back of the store when he bumped into the other Caldwell sister.

"Hey Adam." Darcy looked over his shoulder. "Did my sister leave?"

Adam looked down to see Coral holding a paper bag in her arms containing several new issues and a couple of older ones she had on hold.

"Darcy, hi," Adam said trying to act like nothing happened. "Yeah, she left."

"Damn," Darcy muttered. "Adam, what's wrong with your face?"

"Hmm?" Adam removed his hand. "I felt a mosquito and swatted it too hard."

"I didn't think it was warm enough for them yet," Darcy mused. "Summer comes earlier and earlier each year."

"Yeah..."

"Did you happen to notice if my sister was looking at anything in particular?" Darcy asked. "I gotta get her a birthday gift, but I want it to be a real surprise. Something she wouldn't expect."

"Wouldn't expect? Hmm..." Adam repeated when a thought came to him.

A bad thought.

A sneaky thought.

A terrible, awful, malicious thought.

"I might have something."

Adam directed Darcy to the far back of the store near the display case for their more adult titles. He led her behind the counter and into a back room. Darcy could see this was where the staff kept backstock and items that weren't available for purchase yet.

"Are you up to date on *Super Model?*" Darcy tried to make small talk while Adam searched for something.

"Yep," Adam replied as he looked around. "It's my favorite book from the big three right now."

"I'm so glad they finally hired a female writer for that title," Darcy admitted. "That new artist has got to be my all-time favorite. He draws such beautiful men and women."

"Definitely!" Adam agreed before finally locating the box he needed. "Does your sister have a Setebos 64?"

"She got one last Christmas from Grandma," Darcy confirmed.

Adam opened the box to reveal several game discs and cartridges. Looking inside, Coral made out some of the names. *Blood Red Eightball, The Halloween Game, TrollBane, The Beast, Splitting Image, The Haunted Shopping Mall, Catastrophe Crow,* and *Monster Mash.* One cartridge had "Ben" scrawled on it in black marker.

Coral wasn't sure what systems these games belonged to when Adam pulled out one that was buried beneath the others.

"I know your sister's a horror fan so maybe she'll appreciate this," Adam announced. "This was never officially released. Have you or Coral ever heard of *Bloodhouse 64*?"

Darcy shook her head. "Nope. I don't remember Coral ever mentioning it. She's more hardcore when it comes to video games, so she'd know more."

"This game got axed before they finished development," Adam explained. "The company had some promo copies made for testing, though. They're *extremely* hard to find. Most people don't know it exists due to limited promotion. It was gonna be the company's first horror game."

"Why wasn't it finished?"

"No one knows for sure." Adam shrugged before vaguely explaining, "Its head designer had a nervous breakdown or something. Got really messy, and they fired him. Trouble is, he took all his notes with him. The staff had issues replicating the game from scratch because of some special program he used. It was written off as a loss and the company forgot about it. Happens all the time," Adam added, smug in his knowledge.

Darcy eyed the cartridge in Adam's hands before asking, "Does it even work?"

"Tested it myself," Adam confidently affirmed. "It's not that long since it's a promo copy. However, I know you can access the game's secret mode on it."

Darcy was intrigued. "A secret mode?"

"I've read it was included in the promo copies, but I haven't been able to unlock it. Coral might have better luck than me. If I know your sister, she'd *love* to own a piece of forgotten horror history."

Darcy thought about it and said, "That's true. She once spent a lot of money on eBay to win a magazine with a rare Stephen King story in it. Hmm." Darcy mulled it over. "How much?"

"For a good customer like you, $50," Adam offered.

"Only 50 for something this rare?"

Adam leaned in and whispered, "Between you and me, these aren't supposed to be for sale. I won't say anything if you don't."

That put a damper on things. Darcy admitted, "I don't want to get you in trouble or anything."

Adam assured her, "It's fine. I'm the only one who ever looks in this box. My boss doesn't even remember when we got this. No one will know it's missing."

This sounded too good to be true. "You're certain it works? There's nothing wrong with it?"

Adam held the game out towards Darcy and asked, "Would I lie to you?"

Darcy hurried home with Coral's birthday gift but took a detour to avoid her sister. She didn't want to face Coral until the game was in a secure location. Instead of going to her house, she went to the house next door.

"Psst! Jewel!"

Jewel Fallon was in her backyard, having dinner with her parents, when she heard Darcy's voice.

"Hey." Jewel waved. "Why are you sneaking around?"

"Can I cut through here to get to my place?" Darcy asked. "I don't want Coral to see me."

"Ahh." Jewel nodded. "You got her birthday gift already huh?" Darcy was about to open her mouth before Jewel preemptively said, "Darcy please. I love you, but you don't seem to understand what subtlety is. But sure, go ahead."

"Thank you." Darcy nodded and made her way to her home. She waved to Jewel's parents. "Hey Mr. and Mrs. Fallon."

"Hi Darcy, care to join us?" Mrs. Fallon asked. "Tim's trying a new recipe."

"Venison," Mr. Fallon proudly declared from the grill. "Caught it myself on my last hunting trip."

"He hit it with his car on the way back," Jewel snarked. Her father frowned.

"Thanks, but some other time." Darcy hopped over the fence separating Jewel's house and hers. While she knew Mr. Fallon was a good cook, the thought of eating deer made her imagine she was eating Bambi.

Inside the Caldwells' kitchen, Darcy and Coral's grandmother was engrossed in her newest romance novel while a pot of beef stew simmered on the stove. Ruby Jean Caldwell was pulled out of *Zandalee's Revenge* when she heard a knock on the terrace door.

"Hi Grandma." Darcy entered past her grandmother and placed her bookbag on the kitchen counter. "Where's Coral?"

"Hi darling." Ruby Jean kissed her granddaughter on the cheek. "Your sister asked about spending the night at her friend Eileen's house."

"Echo's place?"

"Yes, she was here briefly and said they were going to watch that werewolf show. Your mother's still at the office so it looks like it's just you and me tonight." That made Darcy feel relaxed. It gave her a chance to talk about Coral's birthday gift.

As Darcy and Ruby Jean sat down to helpings of Ruby Jean's stew, Darcy chatted about Coral's gift. She sounded especially giddy at giving Coral something so rare. While Ruby Jean didn't really get video games that much, she understood how much the kids, especially Coral, enjoyed playing them. Which was why she asked Darcy, "And you tested it, right?"

"Tested it?"

Ruby Jean nodded. "I mean, what would be the point in giving your sister something that doesn't work? You did buy it secondhand, technically."

Darcy was appalled at the late realization. She'd been so pleased with finding a choice birthday gift, she hadn't thought to ask Adam to try it out in the store first. Thank God for grandmas and their infinite wisdom.

Following dessert of homemade bourbon brownies, Darcy told her grandma she would try *Bloodhouse 64* for herself. That meant having to use the Setebos 64 in Coral's bedroom.

To be on the safe side, Darcy knocked on her sister's bedroom door.

"Cor?" Darcy asked as she knocked, "You in here?" When there was no immediate answer, Darcy gingerly opened the door. "Coral?" she asked again, and when there was no response, she flipped on a light switch. Coral's room was exactly as it usually looked—a complete mess. The one thing missing was Coral herself.

Relieved, Darcy closed the door and waded through the clothes on the floor. On the other side of Coral's bedroom stood the TV. Resting atop it was the Setebos 64 System. Darcy quickly put the cartridge in the system, turned on the TV, and then turned the game on.

Nothing.

For a moment Darcy panicked, thinking the game didn't work. She saw the light on the Setebos 64 system was red, which meant it was working properly. The TV was set to the right channel, but the screen remained black.

Turning the Setebos 64 off, Darcy pulled out the cartridge and inspected it. Everything seemed okay. There were no chips or cracks in the casing. No wires sticking out. Darcy shook the cartridge but heard nothing rattling around.

Cautiously, Darcy placed the game back in the system. Slowly, this time. Darcy adjusted it properly before she turned the system back on.

Still nothing.

Darcy remembered something her sister did when they played *Zeebo's Funhouse Party*. The screen froze in the middle of the game, and after Coral stopped cursing up a storm (since she'd been winning a particularly brutal minigame) she pulled the cartridge out and blew into the bottom side. Somehow, that made it work.

Darcy didn't understand it—Coral was always the bigger video game fan between them—but it was worth a try. Removing the cartridge yet again, Darcy looked at the underside of the case and blew air into it. Praying this worked, for a third time Darcy inserted *Bloodhouse 64* into her sister's game system.

A familiar looking logo featuring an image of a moon and the number 64 flashed on the screen, and Darcy felt relief.

So far so good, Darcy thought, but her relief turned to confusion. She heard woodwind instruments and the plucking of a banjo. The colors on the screen were bright and vivid. A large house fell out of a clear blue sky. The controller in Darcy's hands shook from the vibrations.

The house on the screen was huge, but Darcy was taken aback by the fact it had eyes. Swaying back and forth with the music, the house reminded her of those old black-and-white cartoons where everything was alive.

"Huh," Darcy said out loud. "This isn't what I was expect—"

Darcy was cut off by the sound of a bloodcurdling scream, a wet CRUNCH, and a splatter of red violently hitting the screen. She jumped back, dropping the controller. Instinctively she'd held her arms up to shield herself.

The black outline of the house started materializing on the red-coated screen, only it was no longer happily shaking back and forth. It didn't just look ruined; it was *dead.* The eyes appeared to have been *gouged out,* and twin streams of blood leaked down the walls. The music turned mournful.

Slowly the title materialized.

BLOODHOUSE 64

PRESS START

Reaching towards the controller, Darcy couldn't take her eyes off the house. For a cartoon, the gore looked realistic. At first glance

Darcy assumed this would be like that game she remembered seeing a commercial for. Something about a bear and bird. Darcy was having a hard time remembering the name. She was sure she heard Coral talking about it at some point. Something about how that style was currently popular in gaming.

Darcy figured it was only a matter of time before someone parodied the genre for older players. She just couldn't take her eyes off the house. It seemed so sad, so beaten.

The music became discordant and grating on Darcy's ears, so she pressed START. The screen went completely red again and the house vanished, then faded to black.

The black shifted and Darcy found herself watching scenes inside what seemed to be a particularly grim asylum. A pair of anthropomorphic animals in lab coats walked down a dark hallway. The text at the bottom of the screen had them talking about some patient who was only getting worse.

"THE OTHER PATIENTS ARE AFRAID OF HIM."

"CAN YOU BLAME THEM? HE'S A MENACE. YOU SAW WHAT HE DID TO THAT GUARD."

"IT WAS HIS OWN FAULT FOR NOT PAYING ATTENTION."

"WHERE DID HE GET THE KNIFE?"

"HE DIDN'T USE A KNIFE. JUST HIS BARE HANDS."

"HE KEEPS TALKING ABOUT GOING HOME."

"THAT'S NOT HAPPENING. NOT IF WE HAVE ANYTHING TO SAY ABOUT IT."

"BUT WE HAVE TO TRY TO HELP HIM. THAT'S WHAT THEY PAY US FOR."

"THEY DON'T PAY US ENOUGH."

Suddenly, an alarm blared, and the inmates started panicking in their cells. The two doctors looked worried when something burst through a nearby wall. It was huge. It reminded Darcy of Frankenstein's Monster. Unlike the doctors and what inmates she could see, the figure seemed human.

Except for his face.

Darcy didn't understand what she was looking at. It seemed to be a mix of several different kinds of animals, until the figure ran towards the two doctors. Up close, Darcy saw that the enraged patient wore a mask stitched from the faces of different animals. She was treated to a chase sequence as the doctors ran down a maze of hallways until they reached a dead end.

Cornered, the doctors begged for mercy. With his giant fists, the escapee ripped the two doctors to pieces. There was nothing cute or cartoony about this.

The escapee was drenched in blood and viscera as the doctors screamed in agony. Their wailing sounded too human to Darcy as organs spilled onto the floor. The escapee stomped over entrails littering the floor until he reached forward and tore off the doctors' faces.

Darcy grimaced. She tasted her dinner creeping up the back of her throat but couldn't look away as the escapee pounded on the asylum walls until they collapsed. He ran off. The remains of the two doctors lay twitching in the wreckage.

The scene transitioned to a bright, sunny day. Darcy was back to the house from the title sequence. The house cheerfully swayed to the background music while two kids, a boy and a girl, played in the yard. There was a nearby doghouse visible, bopping along with the house. A cute puppy wagged its tail as it chased the boy and girl around the yard.

Darcy felt immense dread.

A woman appeared in the yard. She was dressed like a 1950s housewife in a flowery dress and pearl necklace. The kids addressed her as "Mommy." Darcy read their dialog on the screen.

"WHAT'S WRONG MOMMY?"

"I HEARD IT ON THE RADIO, KIDS. THERE WAS A BREAK-OUT AT THE ASYLUM."

"REALLY? COOL, A PRISON RIOT!"

"IT'S NOT COOL, BILLY. ONLY ONE PRISONER ESCAPED."

"GASP! YOU DON'T MEAN—"

"NO! DON'T SAY HIS NAME, SIS!"

"IT WASN'T REALLY HIM, WAS IT?"

"I'M AFRAID SO, SISSY. DON'T WORRY YOU TWO. I PROMISE I WON'T LET ANYTHING HAPPEN. HE'S NOT GOING TO HURT US AGAIN!"

"MOMMY LOOK!"

Lightning split the sky and heralded the appearance of the escaped inmate. Atop a hill, he towered over the house and the family. The two kids screamed as their mom hurried them inside. Even the house's eyes were filled with terror as the inmate headed towards the front yard.

Darcy paused the game. She didn't understand why she felt so nauseous. She wasn't exactly a lightweight when it came to horror. It's not like the comics she read didn't sometimes have blood and guts in them. She knew the difference between real and fake blood.

She remembered during cheerleader tryouts, when poor Sonia Fitzgerald tried to do a triple backflip and broke her arm. Darcy had a front row seat to the injury. She recalled Sonia's cries of anguish and the vivid image of the broken bone sticking out of the skin. On some level Darcy didn't understand, she was reacting more uncomfortably to the thought of violence in this game than when Sonia broke her arm.

Either Darcy was more squeamish than she thought, or whoever made this game was excellent at their job. Still, something compelled Darcy to leave the game on. She unpaused.

More dialog appeared on screen.

YOU ARE RUFUS D. LEDBETTER, A.K.A. "BLOODLETTER"

YOU HAVE RETURNED HOME AFTER SO LONG

THIS IS YOUR HOUSE

YOU ARE GOING TO TAKE IT BACK

LEAVE NO ONE ALIVE

SHOW THEM YOUR TRUE FACE

Darcy entered a tutorial mode to control "Bloodletter." First, she had to explore the front yard. Big insects, flowers, bushes, even the mailbox, appeared to be sentient like the house. They all had big cartoon eyes and made yelping sounds if Bloodletter approached them.

If it had eyes, it was alive. If it was alive, it was Bloodletter's enemy. Those eyes were everywhere. They unnerved Darcy at first, but the more she looked at those eyes, she felt... frustration? Annoyance? For a cartoon, they looked so stupid.

Instructions appeared for which controller button did what. Bloodletter could indiscriminately punch, stomp, and tear apart things, or could draw out an enemy's death if he were close enough. While some ran away, others charged at Bloodletter to attack. A health bar appeared in the screen's top right corner. At the end of the bar was a realistically drawn human heart, pumping blood at regular intervals.

Darcy experimented first with the mailbox. As Bloodletter got close, it tossed out junk mail. Bloodletter stomped on it a few times, making the box puke out its brains and guts. God, they put so much detail into the guts Darcy could practically *smell* them as they oozed between Bloodletter's fingers.

Somehow, this didn't bother Darcy as much as when the doctors were ripped apart.

BEFORE YOU ADVANCE, KILL THEM ALL
SHOW NO MERCY

Darcy did as the screen told her and had Bloodletter kill every enemy in the yard. They all exploded in a burst of blood and organs once Bloodletter was done throttling them, even if they were random objects.

If it was alive, it bled.

She was getting the hang of controlling Bloodletter. She noticed there didn't seem to be a point system or anything like that. The game's objective was to kill as much as possible.

Darcy didn't realize it could be this much fun.

She got her hands on a bunny rabbit that was hopping in the yard. It was the rare critter that didn't try to harm Bloodletter or get away from him. Stupid.

Activating the **Close Up Kill Mode**, the screen zoomed in on the bunny's frightened face. Darcy, as Bloodletter, ripped out the bunny's teeth, followed by its ears and eyes, before twisting off its head. Bloodletter could heal damage by devouring parts of his enemies. Darcy watched as he popped the bunny's head into his mouth and chomped it into paste.

After killing every enemy in the yard, it was time for the boss. Since this was the tutorial, Darcy figured he'd be the easiest boss in the game. Turned out, when the family ran into the house they left the dog outside by accident.

PLAY DEAD, FIDO

The dog initially whimpered inside its living doghouse, before it started growling. It whipped out a beaker of some bubbling concoction from out of nowhere and, with a cartoony sound effect, swallowed the brew in one gulp. Darcy watched as the dog immediately bulked up, until it was almost as big as Bloodletter.

Fido flexed huge muscles like a bodybuilder, then started foaming at the mouth and charged at Bloodletter. Darcy wasn't prepared for Fido's attack, and the dog managed to chomp down on Bloodletter's leg. He let out an angry scream and Darcy herself got pissed. That was a cheap attack! She hadn't been allowed to move Bloodletter until after Fido bit him! Fucking cheating computer!

Scowling, Darcy mashed the hell out of the controller buttons as she made Bloodletter show no mercy on Fido. Despite the dog's opening salvo, he wasn't as much of a threat as he looked. All he could do was bite and run. Bloodletter was able to do so much more.

Grabbing Fido by the tail, Darcy made Bloodletter repeatedly bash the dog against the ground and the side of the house. Smash and repeat. Smash and repeat. The dog stumbled around as little birdies flitted around his head. Bloodletter could kill them too.

Bloodletter wrenched open Fido's jaw as far as possible and shoved his arm down the dog's throat. Darcy repeatedly hit the A button and made Bloodletter yank out Fido's internal organs. The dog choked and fell as Bloodletter methodically stomped on his organs, one by one, still attached to the dog. It all came to an end when Bloodletter slammed his foot down on Fido's skull as hard as possible.

Darcy wondered why she felt squeamish at the beginning. *It's only a game*, a voice told her. It wasn't real. She wasn't *actually* hurting anyone. She ignored it when the enemies cried or begged for mercy. They were obstacles.

FIDO'S GONE TO THAT GREAT DOGPOUND IN THE SKY

EVERYTHING IN THE YARD IS DEAD

YOU MAY ENTER THE HOUSE

DO WHAT NEEDS TO BE DONE

"Do what needs to be done," Darcy read aloud as Bloodletter entered the terrified house.

I'm so glad I bought this game, Darcy happily thought, completely forgetting it was a gift for her sister as she set about murdering what was in her way.

Speaking of said sister, Coral had been so angry when she returned home from The Dungeonmaster, she confided in her grandmother that she needed to be with her friends. Ruby Jean recognized how upset her younger granddaughter was. Since it wasn't a school night, she permitted Coral to stay at Echo's if she felt she needed it. Coral also asked Ruby Jean not to tell Darcy what occurred.

Thank God for Grandmas, Coral thought.

At Echo's house, the two called Brody and they watched the newest *Wendy the Werewolf Hunter*. Afterwards, the three had the pool in Echo's backyard all to themselves for a late-night swim when Coral admitted what was bothering her.

"'Pretending you like girls to piss him off?'" Echo was beyond disgusted. "That little shit really said that?"

Coral nodded. "Charming, isn't he?"

Brody swam up to Coral and asked, "You told your sister, right? I mean, she knows that Holtzman's a creep?"

Coral looked away as she confessed, "It's not that simple. I don't... I don't want her to know about what he did on that date."

"Well, you don't have to tell her about it if you don't want," Brody assured her.

Echo explained it as, "All she needs to know is Holtzman is an entitled little douchebag and he has no respect for boundaries."

"It's just, well, UGH!" Coral groaned and dunked her head under the water. Echo and Brody waited for her to emerge when she shot up and she exclaimed "Even though she's older I'm the assertive one! We don't hide things from each other, but that kiss has always made me feel gross and vulnerable. I still shiver when I think about his hands on me. This is the one thing I've never told Darcy. I'm scared she might think less of me for this."

"Did you or did you not break three of Joey Markwell's permanent teeth after the stuff he said about her in middle school?" Echo asked.

"Two and a half, really."

Brody reasoned, "You don't have to tell your sis what happened, but you should definitely warn her about Holtzman in case he tries something."

"Yeah. If the cheerleaders know they'll rip him apart if he tries anything," Echo hypothesized.

Coral was silent for a bit before she asked, "Am I making too much of this?"

"No."

"No."

Coral groaned again, "I hate how he gets in my head. I hate it."

"Now now," Brody patted her head before drawing her into a hug. "We'll help get him out."

Echo joined in the hug. "Always."

Brody asserted, "No one fucks with Coral Caldwell's head."

"I mean, except us," Echo quipped. "Mostly me. And when I do it it's cute."

Holtzman was wrong about Coral liking girls. She didn't technically. Not like how Darcy liked, or rather, loved Priscilla Yonehara.

Coral loved Echo. And she loved Brody. She loved them because they'd been friends with her for so long. She'd only ever felt something special for them.

Here, between them, the blonde stubble on Brody's face nuzzling her and his belly against her back, Echo's breath on her neck as they held her. This was the only kind of physical intimacy Coral wanted.

"Would you guys come by my place later so I can tell her?" Coral asked. "Before I chicken out?"

"You think she'll be up?" Echo asked.

"She's probably binging her new comics or reading one of Grandma's romance novels," Coral figured. "The usual for Friday night."

In this case, back at the Caldwell house, the usual had been cast aside in favor of plucking out a little girl's eyes like a pair of ripe grapes.

Darcy's gaze remained transfixed on the screen as Bloodletter brutalized Sissy, the little girl. She'd been the final boss, utilizing an army of toys in a final showdown. Darcy expected the mom would be the final boss, but Darcy split her open right after the dog.

Sissy was all that was left after the decimation of her pathetic army. Darcy wanted to take her time. She hadn't taken her eyes off the screen nor blinked since Bloodletter entered the house. All she cared about was the carnage. She didn't bother reading the dialog on the screen.

"DADDY, STOP!"

Darcy had navigated Bloodletter throughout the house, killing everything in his path with glee. Everything in the house was alive, or it had been before Bloodletter got through with them.

The mom had been the first boss in the living room, riding around on a motorcycle/vacuum cleaner hybrid. Next came Billy, the little boy with a home science kit in the library. Stupid. All so stupid. Darcy loved killing them.

Darcy's grip tightened on the controller until her nails cracked against the plastic. She hadn't noticed the blood dripping from her fingers as she smashed buttons to kill, kill, and kill again. She was in another world, all to herself and the things she could kill.

And then the worst thing she could've ever imagined happened.

THEY'RE ALL DEAD

YOU HAVE TAKEN YOUR HOUSE BACK

GAME OVER

Having been silent for so long, Darcy broke out of her trance screaming "No! NO! NO NO NO!"

*That can't be it, it **can't** be! There **has** to be more! I need more, goddamn you!*

Darcy randomly pressed buttons on the controller with her bloody fingers, growing more and more desperate as the screen remained unchanged.

GAME OVER

"FUCK YOU!" Darcy shrieked as she beat the controller against the floor. "FUCK YOU FUCK YOU FUCK YOU!" Once the controller was reduced to wires and broken plastic, Darcy began sobbing and cursing as she beat her bloody hands against the TV screen. "I NEED MORE! FOR THE LOVE OF GOD GIVE ME MORE!"

NEW GAME – START

SECRET MODE – UNLOCKED

Tears streaming down her face, blood soaking her hands, Darcy just barely comprehended the words on the TV.

THIS IS YOUR HOUSE

"Yes."

YOU ARE GOING TO TAKE IT BACK

"Yes."

DO WHAT NEEDS TO BE DONE

"Yes."

Bloodletter's mask filled the screen.

Darcy reached towards the TV. Her bleeding hands pushed forward into the screen like a pool of water. The glass rippled as Darcy pulled her hands out, holding the mask.

***

Inside her bedroom, Ruby Jean Caldwell woke up to the sound of her granddaughter screaming in agony. She couldn't tell if it was Darcy or Coral, but she knew one of her grandbabies needed help.

"Girls? What is it!?" Ruby Jean shouted, jumping out of bed as quickly as she could at her age. She reached under her bed and pulled out the aluminum baseball bat she kept with her in case of an intruder. She never thought she'd have to use it.

Racing out of her bedroom, Ruby Jean heard shouting in Coral's room, but it was Darcy's voice. "Darcy, honey what's wrong!?" Ruby Jean cried out as she yanked the door open.

The room was dark. The only light came from the bedroom window. Ruby Jean could see the outline of Darcy standing in front of the powerless TV. A coppery, metal smell hit the older woman's nostrils. Fearing her grandchild was hurt, Ruby Jean turned on the overhead light.

Outside, Brody finished parking his car in the Caldwells' driveway.

"Thanks for tonight, you guys," Coral said as she got out of the car. "It was just what I needed."

"Hey, is it okay if we consider this your birthday gift?" Echo inquired, earning an elbow nudge from Brody. "I'm kidding."

Brody was about to say something when he looked up and noticed, "Coral, your bedroom light's on."

That's when they heard Darcy's grandmother scream.

The three teenagers ran towards the front door in time to watch Ruby Jean be thrown down the stairs.

"GRANDMA!" Coral shrieked as she rushed to Ruby Jean's side. The old woman landed in a heap on the hardwood floor. She was bleeding from her head and one of her arms was bent at an awful angle. Ruby Jean moaned in pain. Coral panicked, saying, "Oh God no Grandma—"

"HOLY SHIT!" Echo's yelling caused Coral to look at the top of the stairway.

At the top of the stairs stood what Coral thought was her sister. The figure above them wore some sort of handmade mask, crudely stitched together from the faces of different animals. In the hall light, Coral, Echo, and Brody saw the stitches violently pulsating.

Coral couldn't figure out what she was seeing as her vision wandered down to her sister's bloody, broken hands.

Tears stinging her eyes, Coral could only say, "Darcy?"

The masked figure at the top of the stairs let out an inhuman roar before it charged forward. Coral threw herself over her wounded grandmother to protect her when Brody rushed to intercept Darcy.

Darcy landed on her back on the stairs as Brody tried to keep her pinned down with his large body. Echo and Coral dragged Ruby

Jean out of the house when they heard Brody get tossed through the banister.

"Echo get help!" Coral ordered as she ran back into the house before her friend could stop her. The door slammed shut behind Coral and locked itself. She heard Echo screaming for help when Darcy pounced on top of Brody and started beating his head.

Darcy shrieked like a rabid animal, pummeling Brody's face, breaking his nose. Coral tried to wrap her hands around her sister's waist to pull her off.

"Darcy stop! You're gonna kill him! STOP!" Coral screamed, but her voice was drowned out by the other girl's shrieking. Darcy writhed and scratched at her sister's hands until she pulled Coral's left palm towards her mouth and bit it.

Crying out, Coral fought as hard as she could, dragging her manic sister into the living room. Darcy's teeth sunk deeper into Coral's hand, until the younger sister threw them both on top of the coffee table. It broke beneath their combined weight and Coral wrenched her hand free of her sister's jaws.

Coral lifted her left hand. Darcy had taken an actual bite out of it when Coral heard bones snapping into place. Looking down, Coral watched the broken bones in her sister's hands mend together.

With her healed hand, Darcy grabbed Coral by the hair. Shrieking again, Darcy pulled Coral's head back and punched her face, stunning her. She then threw her sister against the living room wall.

"MY HOUSE!" Darcy screamed in a voice that wasn't her own. "THIS IS MY HOUSE!"

"I don't," Coral tried to say. "Darcy, I-I don't—"

Darcy screamed again and lunged at her sister when Brody swung a side table into her face and knocked her across the room. Blood flowed from his broken nose.

Outside, Echo woke up as many people as she could. They gathered near the Caldwell house and tended to Ruby Jean. Sirens were heard in the distance as Echo, Jewel's family, and the rest of the neighbors tried to get inside. No one could open the doors or the windows.

Coral heard Echo and the neighbors outside when she stumbled forward into Brody's arms.

"Brody, I don't," Coral tried to say as they entered the hallway. "I don't know what's going on."

Coral and Brody's shared stupor was broken by the sound of Darcy's renewed screaming as she ran towards them with a kitchen knife. Coral quickly pushed Brody out of the way before leaping away from her sister. She felt the knife graze her arm. Darcy swung it back and forth trying to stab her sister, as Coral frantically backed away up the stairs. She tripped and landed on her back, giving Darcy the opening she lusted after.

Even with the agonizing pain in her hands, Coral grabbed her sister's wrists. Darcy struggled to bring the blade down, inching towards Coral's chest, until Coral managed to bring her knee up into her sister's stomach. Momentarily stunned, Darcy dropped the knife and Coral kicked her off.

Sobbing, Coral crawled up the stairs on her hands and knees. It was hard to remain steady when her bloody hands made the wooden stairs slippery, but Coral reached the top. She tried to stand again, hobbling into the nearest room, when Darcy tackled her from behind.

The two landed on Coral's bedroom floor. Darcy grabbed her sister's neck with one hand and held the knife in the other. Coral tried to pull the mask off her sister's screaming face. Her nails sunk into coarse, warm animal flesh and she yanked downward.

Coral could only watch in horror as blood and pus leaked from the scratches onto her fingers. Crying out in disgust, she let go of Darcy.

Darcy dropped the knife and screamed in pain, clutching her mangled face as Coral scrambled away from her. With her back against the TV, it dawned on Coral that the mask WAS her sister's face.

"What?" Coral gasped, her fear turning to anger. "What are you? What the fuck are you!? What did you do with my sister!?"

Darcy dropped her hands from her bleeding, oozing face and looked straight at Coral. Rage burned in her mutated eyes. She made a grab for the knife off the floor to attack again.

Coral ducked and dodged just as Darcy brought the knife down, hitting the Setebos system and the *Bloodhouse 64* cartridge.

The scream everyone in and around the Caldwell house heard couldn't be described as a human. Coral shielded her eyes as her sister became engulfed in electricity, the knife still wedged in the game box.

"NO!" Coral screamed and threw herself at Darcy. She slammed into her older sister and Darcy was wrenched free of the knife before they hit the bedroom floor.

As soon as the screaming stopped, everyone outside the house quickly backed away as the front door swung open on its own.

Darcy and Coral lay on the floor, the scent of blood and singed flesh filling the room. Coral groaned. She heard voices calling out her name. As she looked at her sister, Coral felt confused relief. Her sister's face was back to normal, but she didn't understand how or why.

Darcy moaned, her eyes fluttering open as she tried to stand.

"Ohhh." Darcy shook her head. "Oh, Coral. What?"

"D-Darcy?" Coral asked. "Sis? Is that you?"

"Why does everything hurt?" Darcy looked around them. "What's that burning smell?"

Coral was at a loss for words regarding the total one-eighty the situation took.

"What happened?" Ignoring the pain in her hands, Coral grabbed her sister's shoulders and shook her. "Darcy what the hell happened here!?"

"What? I..." Darcy struggled to remember. "I was playing a game. I don't, did I fall asleep? Ah!" She cried out when she saw her broken fingers. "What happened to my hand!?"

"A game?" Darcy quietly asked when she turned towards the TV.

"I-I got it from Adam at the comic shop," Darcy explained. "Coral what happened to my hand? What happened to YOUR hands!?"

"Look."

The screen was lit up.

GAME OVER

YOU LOSE

NEW GAME – START

"No no no—" Coral babbled as she held Darcy close to her. Bloodletter's mask appeared on the screen, a semblance of a grin stretched tight across it. They witnessed the mouth silently reading the words beneath it.

THIS IS *MY* HOUSE NOW

LET ME SHOW YOU *MY* REAL FACE

Darcy and Coral watched in horror as bloody handprints appeared on the other side of the TV when the screen began to stretch outward and *something—*

BLAM!!!!

The screen exploded.

BLAM!!!!

The Setebos 64 and the *Bloodhouse 64* cartridge were obliterated.

Darcy and Coral turned towards the open bedroom door. There stood Jewel Fallon and her dad. Tim Fallon held a shotgun in his hands. By his side stood Echo and Brody nursing his bloody nose. They all kept their eyes on the broken, *bleeding* TV.

The game system and the cartridge had been splattered against the wall.

Darcy quietly sobbed as they heard something groaning in pain inside the shattered TV before it let out a final whimper.

The official report given to the police had been that some masked intruder broke into the Caldwell house, assaulted Darcy, Ruby Jean, Brody, and Coral before Tim Fallon managed to drive her away with his shotgun.

No one saw where the assailant went, since Darcy and Coral's neighbors had all gathered at and focused on the front of the house.

Reva Louise Caldwell came home late from a meeting at her architectural firm horrified to find police cars and ambulances parked in front of her house, her mother almost dead, and her daughters and one of their friends brutalized.

As they were transported to the hospital, Darcy and Coral sat in silence the entire way there.

Inside the E.R., Darcy was the first to speak.

"I'm sorry I almost gave you a cursed video game for your birthday."

Coral turned to her sister.

"I'm sorry I was too ashamed to warn you about what a piece of shit Adam Holtzman is."

They never found out the truth behind what lived inside the *Bloodhouse* game, and they were fine with that.

A few days later in the hospital, Coral and Darcy heard Adam Holtzman was being brought in. Supposedly, the water polo team and the cheerleaders found him inside the gym. Beaten within an inch of his life. No one saw what happened. The doctors thought he might have permanent brain damage and wouldn't be waking up anytime soon.

They found him with a video game cartridge shoved into his mouth.

It was the best birthday gift Coral Caldwell ever received.

***

Jude Deluca is a nonbinary aegosexual Capricorn (he/him/they/them). Their areas of interest are slasher fiction, magical girls, YA horror, superhero dads, and big beautiful men. As a professional detective of horror media, they've found and rediscovered several lost and unpublished short stories such as Goosebumps: Dead Dogs Still Fetch by R.L. Stine and Braden Thomas Gardner. Their dream is to professionally write for DC Comics, specifically about Arsenal and his daughter Lian with the Legion of Super-Heroes. Some of their favorite video games are Banjo-Kazooie, Sonic Adventure 2, Luigi's Mansion, and Space Channel 5. They long for the day Sonic X-Treme and Dream: Land of Giants might be made playable. They can be found as @judedeluca1990 on Twitter, and @judedeluca on Bluesky, Instagram, and Tumblr

Acknowledgements

First and foremost, I want to thank Weaver and the team at Riverfolk Books. When I brought up starting a horror imprint to Weaver as a vague, bug-in-his-ear idea, he immediately said 'go for it' and I couldn't be more thankful. Between him and the rest of the team willing to use their talents to help out with Rabid Otter Horror despite initially signing on to a fantasy publication, I am beyond honored to have worked with them. I would also like to personally thank Maxine for proofreading this collection. The work she put into it is crazy, and I'm not sure I would ever be able to trust anyone else to proofread for me.

I would also like to thank all ten of the authors that made *Error Code* a reality. I love each and every one of the stories within these pages and am floored at the talent that submitted to this little project.

Matt Seff Barnes makes amazing covers, and when I saw this one was available for licensing, I didn't hesitate contacting him. If you ever need an amazing cover, look no further than his site.

I would like to thank Elijah, Valkyrie, Story, and Lucy. My kids are loud and chaotic and goofy and I wouldn't have it any other way.

Lastly, I want to thank my best friend soul mate, Kristin. Every day I fall more in love with her, and her support is nothing short of heartwarming. I never could have imagined having such an amazing partner by my side, and I am truly humbled that she continues to be. I love you, Kristin!

About the Editor

Z aq Cass is a rabid consumer of all things horror, spending his nights haunting an old factory and his days under the watchful eyes of several chickens. Alongside his wife, he lives in Indiana keeping four children content in the chaos they create.

His first published short story, "Character Creation" will be featured in Judith Sonnet presents "SCREAMS." *Error Code* is his first compiled anthology.

Find him at Rabid Otter Horror.